The Narrow Gate

A Novel By

Julianne B. McCullagh

The Narrow Gate
A Novel By Julianne B. McCullagh

Copyright © 2012 Julianne B. McCullagh

All rights reserved. No part of this publication may be reproduced, distributed, or transmitted in any form or by any means, including photocopying, recording, or other electronic or mechanical methods, without the prior written permission of the publisher, except in the case of brief quotations embodied in critical reviews and certain other noncommercial uses permitted by copyright law. For permission requests, email the author at julimcc@gmail. com.

This is a work of fiction. Names, characters, businesses, places, events and incidents are either the products of the author's imagination or used in a fictitious manner. Any resemblance to actual persons, living or dead, or actual events is purely coincidental.

First Edition [v2014.07]

To Gene, for all the love.

About the Author

Julianne McCullagh is a Mayborn Literary Conference First Place winner, has been published in Rose and Thorn Literary Journal, Ten Spurs Journal, is a Writer's Digest Literary Fiction winner, wrote a series for Loyola Press, and has been a writing instructor at The Writers Garret, Dallas. You can read more of her work at www.gracenoteslive. com .

Acknowledgements

Where do I begin?

My parents, who taught me to read and love language, thank you.

All the Sisters of St. Joseph and all the lay teachers in St. Clare's and Mary Louis.

To Professor Arthur Davis, a gentleman and a scholar and Dr. Angela Belli, mentor, St. John's University.

Peggy and Gene McCullagh, Sr. for watching Katie while I was in grad school and giving me my own desk.

George Getschow, The Mayborn Writers Conference, for boosting me to the next level.

The Writers Garrett, Dallas, Texas, a marvelous writing community.

Salon Quartre, the best literary group ever, who've read this book in its countless iterations: Bill Marvel, Drema Berkheimer, Judith Greene, Robin Underdahl. What would I do without you guys?

Frankie, always a puppy, who sits on my lap, keyboard on his back, while I write.

A big thank you hug to Myrna "Sissy" Meredith and my cousin, Tom Fucigna, Jr. for line editing.

To my husband, Gene, for everything; for holding it all together since we were kids with a baby, and then three more babies. All the editing, proof-reading, layout, design, teaching and patient help in the many tech emergencies and frustrations. How can I be so blessed as to have you as my husband?

Foreword

Seven years ago I was asked to help judge a competition for writers of nonfiction as part of what has now become one of the brightest gatherings of its kind anywhere, the annual Mayborn Literary Nonfiction Conference in North Texas.

There were seven of us. For weeks we had been reading the dozens of entries that had flooded in. Now we sat around a table passing manuscripts back and forth, reading and re-reading, gradually winnowing the excellent from the merely good. Towards evening of what had become by now a very long day we began our final deliberations–a polite word for discussion and maybe an argument or two.

But to my mind one entry already stood above argument, and my fellow judges agreed. And so the Mayborn Conference awarded Julianne McCullagh first prize for her essay/memoir "Sláinte."

I knew by the second or third page I was reading something extraordinary. The essay told of an Irish family, New York circa 1960, and the grief caused by that family's black sheep, both brother and son, who rebels against family and Church to go his own lonely, eccentric, and ultimately self-destructive way.

In the years since, I have come to know Julianne McCullagh as both a fellow-writer and a friend. We've lunched together, talked books, culture, politics, religion. What it's like to be the grandchild of immigrants–Juli was raised in one of those expansive Irish Catholic families that are woven into the American fabric, and I came from Polish-Americans. We spoke the same language, and still do, though with different accents. We read each other's work, frequently trading manuscripts, hoping for unstinting approval, of course, ("Oh, Bill. This is just marvelous!") but really needing something deeper and more critical and useful. ("The second chapter's not working. Could you change the point of view?")

I have watched as the seed planted in Juli's Mayborn-winning essay slowly germinated and began putting out branches, buds, flowers until it was something far more ambitious, and better: a work of the imagination, a novel. No longer the story of a young lad gone astray, now it was populated by an entire family, three generations of women, really, and their husbands, lovers and children, all making the stumbling transition from the Old Country and the old ways to the possibilities and pitfalls of a New Land. I've seen The Narrow Gate open up, as it were, to a broad vision of wisdom and folly. And with every reading, I've encountered fresh surprises and new pleasures.

To be Irish and Catholic in America is to be born into a culture in which family and Church and politics hang over your life like great towering clouds, sometimes gloriously sunlit and sheltering, sometimes dark and menacing. But always inescapable. This is literary territory visited by some of our greatest writers: Frank McCourt, Alice McDermott to name just two. And yet that landscape goes on, inexhaustible, as you'll discover in these pages. You don't even have to be Irish or Catholic to feel at home. Italian will do fine. Greek, Jewish, Hispanic, good old white-bread American melting pot. Even Polish. Anywhere human emotions get tangled up in the demands of kinship, of individuality versus loyalty, the demands of gender versus the allure of sex. The push and pull of our whole postmodern life.

Whether you are reading this in New York or New Mexico, Orange County or Orono, Maine, you'll feel at home here. We all come from such families in which the women are strong or not, the children cling to mother's apron strings or break free to go their own way, the men are faithful or something else.

If the generations of Banfrys seem familiar, it's because we're looking in the mirror.

Bill Marvel, a veteran newspaper writer, is co-author, with R.V. Burgin, of Islands of the Damned, a Marine's narrative of the Pacific War, and author of A Mighty Fine Road, a history of the Rock Island Railroad to be published in 2013 by Indiana University Press. His work has also appeared in Smithsonian, American Heritage Invention & Technology, American Way, D magazine, and other publications. He is currently at work on a narrative of the 1913-4 Colorado coal strike, the most violent labor conflict in U.S. history.

I kept myself so busy digging graves
Now I'm losing all the ground
That I was standing on

On my way down I managed to forget
Everything but this address
Trouble from the start

TROUBLE FROM THE START
Copyright © Mike McCullagh

Part One

2004

Chapter One

Rose was warned.

She felt the slow rise of light and peace. Her hearing keened, tuned to a higher frequency. A subtle shift, from here to there. A correction on the dial.

She'd had these feelings before. At first it feels like a gift, a consolation. The light, like the rising of the dawn. Peace spreading out from the center. Her center, the center, it was the same.

Years ago she had learned that the peace and light were a warning as much as a consolation. Still, she welcomed the translucent moments; they were a reminder that she was not alone, that the promise was still in effect.

So when the recent consolation wrapped itself around her she thought it was a gift against the coming death of her father. He'd been dying for months since his stroke last August. He made it through Christmas, a sad little affair in the common room of the nursing home. Patients like her father were wheeled in, some with IV bags attached to a pole, some on beds cranked to a sort of sitting position. The lucky ones made it in on their own legs, with only a cane or a walker to keep them from falling.

An artificial tree was decked out in tinsel and bright hanging things weighing down the branches. A CD player blasted carols, both devotional and juvenile. Staff in their multi-colored scrubs clapped their hands and smiled as they sang the lyrics. Some wore Santa caps with mistletoe or jingle bells dangling near an ear.

Rose was a little afraid that he would boil over at this childishness. That he would pull himself up straight and object, defending the residents, the captives, against the infantilizing of the old and dying.

But he didn't. Or couldn't.

They wheeled him back to his room because the next phase of the celebration was Christmas dinner and he was on a feeding tube. Rose thought the smells of turkey and cranberry and pies would be a torment to him. He would never taste these things again. The little pleasures in life. The little bits that make life, life.

A few weeks after the New Year is when the gift opened in Rose.

On a Sunday morning, after she wheeled her father back from Mass in the chapel to his room, she noticed he had a little more pep, a little energy and almost, almost, a touch of happiness.

"Dad, you're looking good. Do they have a pretty new nurse on the floor?"

His answer came slowly, garbled in the saliva he could not swallow.

She had to put an ear near his mouth to get the words.

"Jenny came. She brought Paul. A son to be proud of."

That's when it came. A power. A protection. Light filling her from the inside, bringing her to the thin place.

~ ~ ~ ~

His wake went well, pretty much. A good sendoff. He would have liked it. A respectable showing of mourners and well-wishers. Enough funny stories from old cronies from his school and work days. Neighbors, friends and colleagues of Rose and of her husband Dennis talked in near whispers, introducing themselves, threading thin connections in this ancient ritual of common fate.

For generations people have held themselves in the same posture, dropping smiles or laughter at the front door, resuming them only when some time has passed and the visitors have viewed the body and said a quick prayer in front of the paint daubed corpse. Then there are pockets of laughter when an old friend tells a story of boyhood pranks, shared remembrances, and then, inevitably, that shaking of the head in the acknowledgment that life goes by too quickly, silently wondering who will be the next one laid out in a box with a rosary twined through rubber like hands.

Rose and her brother Jimmy were the hosts of this event, the official mourners. Jimmy managed to act sober throughout the proceedings. Pockets come in handy for the shakes, and moving from person to person, just a little chat here and there, and an excuse, "I'll be right back, never did kick the habit, you know," as he pats the rectangle in his jacket pocket while heading for the door to light up.

He showered and shaved and his shoes weren't too badly scuffed. No one would have to actually know that he's spent the last twenty something years lost in a bottle. They can exchange glances and raised eyebrows, but they don't have to know.

Rose found one of their father's suits to fit him, enough. Jimmy tells the well wishers that his son Kevin lives out of state, in Kansas, working for a big firm. He fumbles for a name. He recalls John Deere as the sort of middle of the country company that people might believe, so that's what he says.

"Recently accepted a job at John Deere—big company out West, ya know, that's why he couldn't make it to his grand-dad's funeral."

"If anyone would understand the importance of work, it was your father, Jimmy. Isn't that the truth? Yep, that Philip Banfry knew about the value of work, he did. And could he work a room. Never met a stranger. Made everyone feel like his best friend." The hearty man with a beef red face pats Jimmy on the back as he says this.

"And, of course, after such a long illness, such a long time in the nursing home, hooked up, neck too weak to hold his head, it was a blessing, wasn't it? Now he can be with your mother, with his Maureen. Together after, what, five years?"

Betty Lawrence, founding member of the Rosary Society, shakes her head, just a little, and pats at the corner of her mouth with a delicate, embroidered handkerchief.

"And don't forget their little angel Priscilla waiting for her mom and dad. What's it been now? More than thirty years. My, where does the time go?"

This other woman, grey-haired, knuckles enlarged with purple veins riding the top, chimed in. Jimmy thinks he should know her name, but the only thought that comes is that her dress and her veins match.

Jimmy and Rose smile their way through the inanities of the well-wishers, playing their parts in this scripted ceremony.

Then Rose saw Jenny.

Jenny, the pretty secretary from Philip Banfry's practice. Smart, pretty, *young* Jenny.

What, she was about ten years older than me, right? Yeah, that would make her about twenty-three when Cilla died. Twenty-three when my mother retreated from life once the casket was lowered holding her youngest child, my baby sister. Twenty-three with her whole life ahead of her.

She married someone from Dad's office and had a child, a son. And here he is at my father's funeral. Handsome young man. Shake his hand.

"Paul Cellio. Sorry about your loss."

"Do I know you, Paul?"

"I don't think we've ever met, Mrs. McGuire."

"Oh, call me Rose, please."

"Jimmy, come here and meet Jenny's son Paul. You remember Jenny."

Jimmy turned to Jenny. A smile lightened his face. "Of course, how could I forget? I had a crush on you once. So funny, after all these years. Your son, Paul? Nice to meet you."

The two men shake hands.

Jimmy, gray around the eyes, skin soft on his jaw and this young man Paul, who looks so familiar. So familiar. Shaking everyone's hand like a pro. Like a star. A natural, like he was born to it.

The hushed, convivial chatter fills Rose's ears, shakes her brain. As the two men extend their right hands to meet, Rose cannot look away. The hands are nearly identical, the dark hairs on the knuckles, the square, neat nails, the same. She uses every ounce of will she has to not cry out, to not object. She pulls the question that contorts her face back in, back down. Unclench the brow, relax the eyes. Her hand closes over the back of a folding chair, her balance is off.

She looks to see if she can catch Dennis' eye, but he's absorbed in his own little conference with a woman from his office.

She excuses herself, goes outside. The frigid air with the promise of snow in those dark gray clouds whips her face, drives the water from her eyes. She wipes her cheek with the back of her hand. She has to move, has to run, but no, what would that look like?

Would they think she is running because her father, her dear daddy, is gone? That's what they would think, and no, she cannot give him that, not now.

No, her father, her daddy, left her alone years ago and had this other life while Rose stayed home with her mother who fell deeper and deeper into her own silent world.

Two pictures flash in her mind:

Jimmy and Paul shaking hands. Jimmy, the cuckold, if that word can apply to a father's betrayal of a son, shaking hands with his rival.

And Good Friday, the temple curtain ripping from top to bottom. What she thought was their covenant, her family, her story, has been a lie. Her life, a lie.

Chapter Two

Rose pushes against cold wind through the canyons of lower Manhattan. She wipes her gloved hands against tears. Down the hole she goes. And waits.

It's been a week since her father's funeral. She returned to work the next day. She didn't want to take the time she was allowed for a family funeral. But spending the last few days trying to work has been useless. It's a little before noon and she's headed home.

Subways in the middle of the day are strange and ugly places. The smell of garbage and urine, the sound of rats scurrying under the platform, and the fine black soot that covers the rails and hovers in the air coating nostrils and lungs seem less personal in the crush of rush hour. She inhales, and is abruptly aware of the dust of commuters that have made this descent for years.

Straddling her foot over the faded yellow line, a touch of vertigo warns her that she is close, too close, to falling into the dark ugliness.

She is almost alone. A man with his head submerged in the collar of a large stained parka sits on a bench across from tiles proclaiming this destination: Broad Street. *Enter by the narrow gate, for the road to perdition is broad.* These words startle her. He is muttering to himself. Did he just speak out clearly? A transit cop comes down the stairs, nods at her as he walks slowly by.

She stands far enough from the man to be able to run up the stairs if he stirs, but not so far as to be rude. He draws his head from the turtle's collar fashioned from the top of his coat, muttering as he turns toward Rose.

His face is cast in a pale charcoal against the shadow of a dark beard. His blue eyes are surprisingly bright. If he has asked something of her, she doesn't know what it is. She doesn't want to know.

The J train screeches to a halt, the doors open. Her companion stays put on the platform. She can have any seat on the empty train. She chooses the one directly across from him.

They look at each other through the scratched and filthy window, safe, she hopes, in this metal cocoon. When the train pulls out, she is relieved to be away from him. And slightly ashamed.

She left him on the bench at Broad Street. But he is there in the *whoo, whoo, whoo* flash of tunnel lights behind the speeding train.

She doesn't want to think about him. She wants to simmer in her agony; pound her fists at the lies she was pulled into, the blinders forced on her while she tried to balance it all, keep them happy so their lives would not dissolve like sugar in water, like snow in sun, like black slush under tires in dirty puddles.

But no, Rose sees that man in the dirty coat, probably crazy, probably drunk, probably stupid. Just because he looks like he stumbled out of the tunnels doesn't make him John the Baptist. He didn't look at her with vision that could read her heart and know her deepest fears, did he? He was probably just condemning her for her bourgeois ways and the crime of possessing a clean coat.

As the J train chugs its way under the East River and up the scaffolding of the elevated rails through Brooklyn, she stares out the window at the barren trees and wrecked schoolyards.

Her eyes are open; the familiar landscape a backdrop. She is arguing. With God. Well, not arguing, because she doesn't give God a chance to answer or defend himself.

You promised me!! Were you lying to me? Just laughing at me? All the times I defended you, and you leave me here by myself. You promised me grace and protection!

A fat tear forms in the corner of her eye. Oh no you don't, she orders herself. Not here. Not now.

~~~~

Dennis and the kids are gone to work and school. She says nothing about her plans for the day.

Rose climbs back into bed, wraps herself in the big quilt. Dappled streams of light come in through the blinds.

The naked limbs of the big oak outside the window are silhouettes on the wall; the weak sun lights on the Miraculous Medal hanging around her bedpost.

It was Cilla's, then her mother's. Her mother took it from Cilla's neck before the casket was closed, then fastened it around her own neck. Rose took it from her mother the day she died. For a long time Rose wore it, then retired it to her bedpost.

She reaches for it now. She holds this small oval in her hand, finger tips going over the familiar Mother figure like a blind person reading a face.

She presses the gold into the soft tissue below her collar bone, willing it to leave a blessing on her heart.

Mary conceived without sin pray for us who have recourse to thee. Over and over she says the prayer she has memorized since infancy.

This is her mantra, her charm, her shield against pain. She does not care if this is sentimental or superstitious or childish. She wants her miracle.

She wants a *Touched by an Angel* miracle, glowing and white and unmistakable, writ large so she cannot dismiss it as mere coincidence.

At 10:42 a rumble of thunder pokes her out of her stolen nap. The room is darker than when she went to hide this morning and her fingers are stiff from holding the medal tight while she slept, still murmuring the prayer as she falls out of sleep.

Rain is beating against the windows and the branches of the oak are scratching the house. She rolls over and tries to go back to sleep, but cannot. She needs to get up.

So down the back stairway to the kitchen to put the kettle on. Her favorite china cup for Blackberry Sage tea is just inside the cabinet.

It's delicate china, left over from her grandmother's set, with red roses around the rim and one inside the lip, with accents of royal blue and gold. Taking it into the living room she pulls her knees up to her chin in the stuffed rocker.

Not once in high school or college did she play hooky. Of course in those days, she didn't have her own home to hide in.

My own home. Hmm. It is my grandparent's house with the whispers of the years there under that fresh layer of paint, in the old tile floor, or the boxes in the cellar.

The steam in the pipes kicks and spurts, sending heat into the chilly room. The aromatic tea warms her face. The storm has quieted; sunlight falls on her from the side window.

She could be hiding in a cave, in a cabin in the woods in a fairy tale, waiting, waiting. For what, she doesn't know. Right now she doesn't care. She just knows she's waiting.

I want the light and warmth of the thin place back. I want it back with no strings attached, just a comfort, not a warning.

I want it to wash over me, over the pain, to loosen the knot in my gut that has been my companion for days beyond counting.

From somewhere deep—words of pain, of anger red hot glaring—*Was it all a lie? Was I so stupid* as *to believe that?* Her cup of tea rests on the wide arm of the chair. As she pulls her knees up closer to her chest, her left arm slips. Sunlight breaks through a moment's opening between masses of clouds. The cup falls, shattering on the old oak floor, bits of china dust sprinkle like snow. The red and blue and gold shards of delicate porcelain catch the sunlight in their pool of blackberry tea.

Part Two

1954 through 1967

Chapter Three

Meg
March 1954

MEG RUNS HER HAND over the bristles of the green mohair couch, back and forth, back and forth. How many years had they sat here, reading the paper, curled up with a book, her head on his chest, his arm around her shoulder? Stiffer than velvet, yet soft and inviting. Quite a remarkable fabric, she thinks.

She sits in the curve where back turns into arm, draped in Gerald's sweater. His scent is in the wool, his shaving cream, his aftershave, him. She knows this will dissipate, but she doesn't want to preserve it in a bureau drawer.

Mass cards and late arriving funeral bouquets clutter the house. Just two days ago he was laid out here, where the couch has been returned, under the bay window, drapes pulled closed behind the bier and the casket covered in a blanket of flowers.

His head, mostly bald, with silver hair that ran from ear to ear in a partial tonsure flattened and lacquered by the beautician's craft, lips daubed a pasty pink, wrinkles dusted with heavy powder, and glasses over his closed eyes.

Why do they put glasses on a man who can't see? Did he fall asleep in his best suit in this box, with a satin pillow and a rosary entwined in waxen fingers?

They came and arranged it all. Calls made, by whom, she's not quite sure, but someone called and someone took care of these things. All done so smoothly, quickly, neatly, and there, her husband is in the living room, laid out for all to see. She answered questions and gave them a suit, she thinks she did, maybe it was one of her sons, Phil or John. A shirt, a tie, cufflinks. All fixed up. So dapper, so right, so wrong.

That night, he came in from work, tired, a bit gray in the cheeks and under his eyes. He tried to eat the chicken Meg had roasted for them.

He managed a few bites and said *I need to lie down, Meg. I'll just go to the couch.* Meg kissed him on the head and squeezed his hand. He was wearing the sweater. It was chilly that night.

Someone sent a large carnation shamrock, sprayed in an odious green paint. It was delivered this morning, but she would let it in no further than the vestibule. It stands on a wire easel draped with a purple ribbon and gold cardboard letters that spell out *Friend,* adorned with a few cardboard shamrocks for good measure.

Her irritation with this leprechaun schlock gives way to the realization that it was sent with good intent. Someone whose name probably ends in a few vowels thought it would be just the right thing.

But no, the card says Condolences from O'Malley's Pub. Every St. Patrick's Day they color the beer green and affect some unidentifiable brogue. Gerald held union meetings there. She can't stand the sight, or the smell, of it. She can't look at another Mass card or read another letter of condolence, a testimonial to what a great man, what a blessing her husband was.

She is alone in the house where they raised their sons, entertained on so many Saturday nights, held meetings that ended with strikes planned and from which riots erupted and other men, maybe not great in the eyes of the world, were hurt, and some killed.

Alone in the house where they first heard FDR announce the war which took her sons off. Alone in the house where the commotion in the yard shook her out of her light sleep the night the Mob goons came looking for Gerald, met him at the back door and left him bloody and bruised. *Just a warning*, they told him, *next time, next time you won't be so lucky, you stupid Mick.*

They were sitting on this couch that other night, the night they came, lights flashing in the black and white outside the door.

A detective flipped a badge and entered their home. He may as well have stolen all their silver and china while he was there. He stood on her floral patterned rug, the rug where her sons ran their trucks and built their block castles when they were little boys. He left a muddy footprint on the vines in the pattern. The detective read out some words from the paper he was holding while a uniform put cuffs on her husband, led him out on that cold night, coat draped around his shoulders, his head bare against the wind.

Words like embezzlement, misappropriation of funds from the union accounts, were a distant echo, like whispers off stage in someone else's play. It must all be a misunderstanding, a lie. None of this was possible. Who would have accused him of such a thing? His life threatened so many times. The terror they endured. Every time a door slammed or glass broke, they jumped, nerves at the edge, frayed and electric.

She studied the pictures in the paper of that dark and ugly face, the face of a murderer who reigned from Chicago, who promised that Gerald was next. Maybe found in an alley. Maybe not found ever. And that smug and ambitious District Attorney who built his reputation on the backs and souls of men trying to fight corruption, trying to gain justice for the perpetual pawns in these ugly games.

They sent him to jail. Justice bought and paid for by criminals, some with records, some with law degrees. Gone two years in prison. Now gone forever.

All the years this house was filled with life, with tears, with joys, and not yet three days before the body of her husband was laid out in grand fashion.

Lines of mourners and gawkers filed through while Meg and her sons took hands and cheeks offered in sympathy.

So much chatter filling every corner of the house, guests eating the food that friends and neighbors brought, drinking what the men carried in crates and set up on the kitchen table.

Some women took a measure of the quality of the drapes, the furniture, the silver laid out on the table for their use.

He did pretty well for himself, didn't he? Not such a common man as those he blathered about, now, was he?

The kinder ones buzzed *What a shame, what a shame* through their house, their home. *After all she's been through, then he's taken, leaving her alone again. Poor Meg. Poor Meg.*

The doorbell rings. She sees through the blinds that it is the florist, but she will not get up. After a minute he goes, leaving another bouquet, another testimonial.

Mail has piled up in the vestibule. How many days has she just let it fall through the slot, not able to touch it? Bills mixed in with sympathy cards, newspapers on the porch. Her sons had to get back to work and their wives are busy with their small children.

She doesn't want them here anyway. She wants to sit, just sit and cry without anyone saying *oh dear it will be all right.* She wants to scream *It won't be all right and just let me cry, haven't I the right?*

She realizes she has been on the couch for more than two hours. A cup of tea is what she needs.

Pushing off the couch Meg goes through the swinging kitchen door, fills the kettle, turns on the gas, lights the stove with a match, then sets up a cup. The kettle whistles just as Millie puts her hand to knock on the back door. Millie is the only one Meg will welcome.

"I've taken your papers in, and put the flowers in my cellar. We don't want anyone thinkin' the house is empty and come breakin' in surprising you to your death, now do we?" Meg gives Millie a tired smile and gets out another cup for tea.

"I'm givin' you one week Meg. And then I'm takin' you out." Millie looks for Meg to disagree, to protest, but Meg smiles and says "have your tea, Millie. Oh, can your son take that awful shamrock to a pub on the boulevard? It might sell a few more beers to the thirsty men staying out all night."

"Sure, Meg. Frank'll come by after supper. He'll take it to Woody's."

Chapter Four

Millie was almost true to her word. One week she gave Meg. Yesterday she called in the afternoon and told Meg that she would be preparing lunch at her house.

"I've got in a lovely canned ham from the A & P, Meg. Since we cannot have it on Friday, you'll have to come for lunch tomorrow. I don't much like fish and I want to make an occasion of it. So, I'll expect you at one."

"One? Alright, Millie. Only because it's you. Don't you dare have any one else there."

"Just us, Meg."

"Just the two neighbor widows."

"Just two old friends."

Thursday morning Meg is up at 6:30, same as she's done for years.

She doesn't look at the empty side of her bed. She slips on her blue chenille robe and heads down the stairs to make coffee. One slice of toast, with a little butter and jam.

The coffee perks in the glass button of the aluminum pot on the stove. Meg turns off the gas, gets the milk and sugar and pours herself a cup.

She will wait until the coffee cools before pouring the rest down the sink. She thinks she might buy one of the small percolators she has seen in the A &P.

The right size for one person. Maybe. Or maybe I'll just learn how to measure out enough for me.

As she washes up the few dishes, round and round with the dishcloth on the small plate that only had crumbs to dirty it, she sees the note, as if it is right in front of her, as close as the faucet.

Typed unevenly: Banfry—79 Forest Parkway. Blue shutters, loose knob on front porch banister. Careful.

Tucked under Gerald's undershirts, wrapped in a handkerchief. The Holy Family on a prayer card was lying on top of the note. Gerald's touch of protection. For her. Whatever he did, he did for her.

The running water has been getting hotter as she stands with the cloth in her hand, watering the flowers on the plate. Just before it scalds her she pulls away.

She sweeps the kitchen floor, dusts the living and dining rooms, then starts up the varnished banister.

Once upstairs she goes into the little bedroom that Gerald had used as an office. Papers are piled on the narrow bed against the wall. She sits in the chair at his desk.

She is too tired to cry. Wrung out. She never did ask him if he was guilty or innocent.

He didn't use those words. He used the word 'betrayed'. Betrayed by his assistant, someone he trusted. Trusted with the fact that Capone had a gun to his head. That this wasn't bribery, it was life insurance. All the salary Gerald never collected, that was rightfully his, was nothing compared to this bit of life insurance. Justified. There was no question. He was an honorable man.

After the police took him that night, during the trial and when he was sentenced, the papers were full of him.

Oh, how the mighty have fallen. The whispers in church, in the shops on the avenue.

The sympathetic smiles, the sneers. They almost looked the same. But she always rose above. Always held her head up. She would not play victim for them. She would not be disgraced.

There are always those who love to see a local hero fall. Too big for his britches. Tsk, tsk-ing from their comfortable well-stocked kitchens, with their tight mouths and even tighter hearts.

Better the trouble that follows death than the trouble that follows shame.

Nasty, narrow minded fools!

All the years he was on fire for justice for the working man, the oppressed, those on the edges of the world who cleaned up after the rest of us.

She thought of all the good he did. All the jobs he saved. The working conditions and wages improved. The speeches he made that got them fired up and emboldened to change things, to claim their rights. She was proud of him then. She will be proud of him now.

Meg knows that her husband was framed.

Framed by the District Attorney looking to make a name for himself. Framed by the Mafia, angry that they couldn't make him fall in line. Framed for holding out so long when others caved to the pressure.

They don't know how long he resisted. How long he would not get dirty. Even with the threats against his life. When they left another man the goons thought was him for dead in a dirty alley in Chicago, then he compromised. Compromised, not colluded. Real life was not spelled out in a textbook. Real life was lived threat to threat, power play to power play.

Meg wonders why he kept that note with their address. They both knew he could be killed at any time. But wrapping that note inside a handkerchief with a prayer card of St. Joseph, that was not only evidence, it was a plea.

That gives her a chill. He was brave. *He was protecting me. I will protect him. My beloved. My husband.*

Over the years, though, she saw him wear down, the fire go out of his words.

Little resentments at the lack of gratitude, the men who did nothing to further their own state but expected him to carry their burden.

The deserving poor. She knew that sometimes he said the deserving poor with the emphasis on deserving rather than poor.

Yes, she could see that sometimes, when he was tired and spent, when he had no money left because he had given so much away, sometimes, then he fell from his ideals and thought they deserved to be poor.

For drinking their paychecks and living in squalor. For not wanting something better for their children. For not seeing a bigger picture. And then he would recover and begin again.

Meg sits there a little while longer. She smiles and wipes away a few tears, good tears.

He was vain. Oh, yes, he was vain. He liked a new suit. He liked his shoes polished and sharp.

A good silk tie with a gold bar. He liked the way he sounded, the echo in the halls and the roar of applause, the standing ovations, the press write-ups.

He liked seeing himself on the front page with the mayor. Yes, he was vain.

Meg and Gerald had a deal, a pact. For better or for worse. The better was worth the worse. She will remember that.

Meg takes the crimpers out of her hair and carefully places them in her top drawer.

Purposefully, carefully she works her fingers through her hair that is more silver than it was last Easter.

She hadn't noticed it so much until now. She rather likes it; it suits her.

She slips her navy dress with the white piping from the cushioned pink hanger, then chooses two stockings from her lingerie drawer. She unwinds the red lipstick from its gold tube and dabs, dabs, smacks her lips, then blends it with her right pinky.

She smoothes the front of her dress, sweeps two fingers of white cream that smells of roses and caresses it into her hands, corrects a twist in her left stocking. She is almost ready.

Meg walks down the stairs to the living room, standing taller than she has these several days. Her black wool coat, white silk scarf tucked artfully over the lapel, and gloves pulled over her fingers.

Now she is ready.

Chapter Five

Sheila
August 1954

"DARLIN', WOULDYA MIND VERY much bringin' me beer?"

"Of course, Mr. O'Grady."

"Well, that's a good lass, then."

Sheila Lynch smiles at the old man with the exaggerated brogue. He came over decades ago, but he lays it on thick for the girls in O'Riordan's as if he's stepping into a play set among the rolling hills of Eire.

She plays along because he's a good tipper and a regular customer; at least three times a week he chats up the girls and plays the ole' boyo with Mr. O'Riordan.

Sheila shares an apartment with four girls who came over while the visas were easy and the Irish had plenty of sponsors.

This was the first part of her adventure. She was tired of life in her slow moving town where young men turned soft from too many evenings at the pub and young women, in their very short youth, town beauties, grew old and sloppy with several children in tow before they hit their thirtieth birthday.

Not for me. No, she shook the dust from her feet at the airport, determined to not look back.

"You think it'll all be like those movies you fill your head with. But it's not. There are gangs and crime and young girls like you 'r not safe anywhere. Who'll watch out for you? Who'll keep those American lads who think they can have anything they want away from you?"

Sheila bites her tongue and doesn't confess to her mother that she hopes some American boys will swagger her way and think she's a bit of something.

A week after her twenty-first birthday, she arrives. An aunt's cousin, or a cousin's aunt, she didn't pay attention to the details, sponsored her visa. From Idlewild Airport to Jackson Heights, the boys who pick her up are some degree of cousins of her cousins. Willie, the driver, barrels his way on to the Van Wyck Expressway and honks and curses like he was born here. They pull in front of a six-story apartment building.

Four girls are crowded into a two-bedroom apartment. Sheila gets the couch since she makes five. They have a job lined up for her at O'Riordan's Pub in Times Square. Broadway tourists and young actors are the regular clientele. She borrows a uniform from Colleen, who is trying on a new American name every week or so, to see which one stuck. Last week she was Audrey. Lana is her latest alias.

Years of dreaming and saving, now she is here. Lying on the couch that smells like cigarettes and beer with the street traffic and sirens blaring through the dusty screens, she feels part of some drama.

With the sun creeping up the side window through blinds she awakens to a concert of doors banging and spoons clanking against cups of coffee. Colleen is demanding that Mary Margaret get out of the bathroom so she can get in. Each of the girls sleeps in rollers and then spends twenty minutes spraying AquaNet on their immovable hair.

America. Home of the brave. Land of opportunity. Noisy, smelly, crowded, and oh how she loves it.

Colleen's cast off uniform is so tight Rose spends her whole shift sucking in her belly hoping the zipper doesn't break. She knows she has to do something about this situation fast. And it has nothing to do with buying a larger skirt. Colleen shares some of her little white pills, so tiny that a hundred of them fit in a little compact.

Here, these'll help you lose some of the potato around your middle and get the lumps off your backside.

That and seven cups of coffee get her through her shift each night and down two sizes in six weeks. It has an added benefit of keeping her alert and edgy on the subway from Times Square to Jackson Heights after midnight.

A butterfly shedding her cocoon, that's what I am.

She's a little frightened, but bigger than that is her determination to not turn into her mother and all the women at home. Their entire lives revolve around church, kitchen and nursery. She wants something more alive, more dangerous, more real.

She wants to dance with a handsome stranger. She wants to go to cocktail parties and stand on a balcony overlooking the lit up city with a martini in one hand and a cigarette in the other, laughing and being clever with people whose lives are bigger, shinier: better.

Since she doesn't know how to make that happen, she decides to learn by observing the women in New York who know how to walk and dress so men notice. Those women seem to shrug it off with complete indifference. She practices her 'couldn't care less' face in the mirror.

The girls in the flat do the tease and sprayed look, with regular doses of peroxide to various shades of unnatural blonde. Sheila though, aspires to a darker look, sleek and angular. She wants to move like a dancer, like Leslie Caron. She buys red lipstick and black eyeliner and leaves off the rouge.

Her hair is a problem, though. She's an ordinary brunette with an unruly wave held in place by a barrette. That has to go. Black hair dye and V-O 5 along with a short haircut of elfin wisps move her toward her new look.

She needs a black pencil skirt, black tights, a white tailored blouse with an oh-so snug fit and a collar she can snap to rakish effect. Shoes, hmm. Heels or flats? Both, of course, one for the more beatnik look, and one for here-I am-boys look. All she needs now is to learn how to smoke and drink. Sheila figures this is part of her education in becoming a real American girl.

She practices flirting with the middle aged old men who stop in for a drink and a look around before heading to Penn Station or Grand Central to catch the trains to the suburbs where a wife and a couple of kids are waiting dinner in a new development. She imagines they are accountants or insurance agents or bankers. There is a uniform grey look to them: inexpensive suits, wingtip shoes, a newspaper tucked under an arm and a sigh when the beer is done.

Sheila pictures them walking out of O'Riordan's on their own yellow brick road of mortgage payments, braces and pushing a lawn mower across a yard every Saturday morning for the next thirty years.

Chapter Six

January 1955

Sam comes into O'Riordan's when he has a few dollars to spend. He's in an off-off Broadway rendition of Othello, playing Iago in a church basement. First time Sheila sees him he still has black greasepaint in the hollows of his cheek and down the side of his nose, with a residue of gray powder in his hair. She points out the smudges and offers him a damp towel to wipe them off.

Every few months when there is bound to be some new girls working at O'Riordan's he shows up with splotches of stage makeup on his face, or part of a costume unshed. It's a very effective conversation starter.

A week after he starts working on Sheila, Sam invites her for a drink.

"Sheila, some buddies of mine go to this place in the Village. They say the music is hep. Interested?"

"When you say 'interested', what exactly do you mean?"

"I mean, would you like to go with me sometime? Tomorrow night?"

"I work till midnight."

"Perfect. The scene doesn't get going till then."

She brings her tight black skirt and turtleneck to work. She changes in the ladies room and re-applies her lipstick and adds another coat of eyeliner.

Sam is waiting for her outside, a lit cigarette pinched between his thumb and index finger. When he sees her he gives her the once over and takes a long hard drag followed by a flick of the burning tobacco into the gutter. He offers his elbow. She takes it and tries not to stumble in the tight heels. A gust of cold wind hits them as if on cue, so she pulls in close to his side.

They take a cab downtown. Maneuvering the winding slate steps to the basement club is a bit of a challenge. The tiled vestibule with a clogged drain holds the stale smell of wet tobacco, vomit and urine. She suppresses a cough.

Sam holds the door for her into the smoke fogged room. Tiny tables and cracked linoleum floors are barely visible in the weak light of candle and a dim spotlight on the musicians. The saxophone and trumpet player pour out their pain in long notes followed by complex riffs while a sleek languid woman sings heartbreak, holding the microphone with open fingers, her mouth close as in a whisper to her lover's ear.

Sheila wants to look beleaguered by life, as if she knows something deep and soulful. She wonders if she'll ever be that interesting, that complex, that meaningful.

She fears she'll always be green and boring. Sam lights a cigarette for her. She takes a puff, then rolls the ash in the stained tray, doing her level best not to look the novice she is.

Sam puts his arm around her shoulder. Leaning into him, inhaling the smoke, inhaling the scotch, inhaling the whole show, she knows this is the next step.

On the cab ride back to her subway station Sheila slides under Sam's arm, his leg pressing into hers. In one smooth move he oh so gently strokes her neck, circles her ear and finds her lips with the tip of his finger. She turns into his face and meets his mouth with hers. She doesn't pull away when his fingers sweep over her breast. This is encouragement. He moves his hand under her skirt to the top of her stockings. The cab pulls up to her subway entrance just as he dares a finger onto the skin in the gap between the stocking and the garter.

"Sheila, meet me at The Wilton this Saturday at eight. In the bar."

"I'm on to work. I'll try to get one of the girls to take my shift."

"Do that. See you then."

He stays in the cab. She fumbles for a token in her pocket and holds tight to the railing because her knees are shaking. By the time she gets to Jackson Heights she is breathing steadily enough to walk the two blocks home, hardly noticing the budding blister on her heel.

Chapter Seven

March 1955

Sheila wrings out her bras and panties in the bathroom sink, hanging them alongside Colleen's on the shower bar. With the back of her wet hand she wipes away tears. She's not sure if she is more frightened than sad.

Terrified comes pretty close.

He was charming, I'll give him that. Like the lads at home, just with better teeth and some money in his pocket.

He told me his name was Sam. Sam Dean. Second cousin once removed from James. He said that with a smile and I knew he was lying, but I gave him credit for making me laugh. And he did. He made me laugh. He'd come in twice a week when I was working at O'Riordan's, always sit in my section. He'd order a hamburger and scotch rocks.

He took his time with his fare, twirling the French fries in the little pool of ketchup he made on his plate. Made a fuss over how juicy the burger was. Best burger in town, he'd say. He'd catch my eye and summon me with his index finger, always a smile, always a wink and ask for a refill on the scotch, not so many rocks this time, lass. He threw the 'lass' in with a wink.

I should have known better. I did know better. He was a faker, a phony, full of blarney and malarkey. Yeah, he was full of something.

And now I am. Full of him. And him nowhere in sight.

Sheila collects her last bit of pay from O'Riordan's. "Ah, you girls. You come over here with dreams in your head to marry a rich American and then you take up with the same sweet talkin' lad you could've met if you'd a stayed put."

"Mr. O'Riordan, I'll thank you very much for my pay. And then I'm off. And you can save your pretty speech for the next girl."

~ ~ ~ ~

That night plays over in her mind, like bad background music. *When he dropped you at the subway, you should have known. Why, why did you meet him at the Wilton?* Now she has to listen to herself as if she is her own mother.

It wasn't the Waldorf. It was an old hotel whose best days were long gone. Sam mumbles something about this is where so and so would meet for drinks and a rendezvous. On 'rendezvous' he raises his eyebrow and gives her a little wink. He may well have said Laurel and Hardy met here for all she knows. She doesn't want to ask who the famous people were; she just goes along with it.

The place smells like it hasn't been cleaned since before the war. Low lighting and candles are a big help to fake some atmosphere and hide the stains on the carpet. Three vodka tonics persuade her it's not so bad. It's got character, she tells herself. And history. *My history, anyway.*

She hopes dinner is part of the plan for this evening. She hasn't eaten since an apple at lunch. They stay at the bar. When she finishes her second vodka tonic, she looks up at the mirror behind the bar. A young girl with dark hair cut Peter Pan short with too much eyeliner looks back at her, once plump cheeks sunken solemnly into her face.

She thinks this face tells the world she knows something about life, about men. She sips her third drink, and looks directly into Sam's eyes while he fingers her knee under the bar. *It's time. Time to know what I've been rehearsing for.*

"Hey, baby, one of my buddies from acting class got me a room key. We just have to not fold down the covers." He is caressing her very slowly, tracing his finger inside her elbow and down the soft underside to her palm while he whispers this.

A tremor runs through her gut, tightens her chest. She has to think to take a deep breath and act more sober than she feels.

He takes her arm and leads her to the corridor. Two flights up on a rusting elevator. Thank God no one else gets on.

Sam turns the key in the lock, then switches on a lamp. The shade is torn. "We don't need this, now do we?"

They take a few steps in the near dark. The street lights cast illumination and shadow through the sheer curtains. She can pretend she is anywhere. Anywhere but here.

Sheila feels sick; she pushes it down. The bed creaks as she sits. She tries to look casual. She tries to look knowledgeable. She tries to hide whatever nerves she has left that aren't compromised by alcohol.

He's quick to get out of his jacket and pull her sweater over her head. She shivers as she sits there in her slip. Her shoes are still on. She can hardly move.

She has no idea what to do. No soft caressing gentleness now. He pushes the straps of her slip down below her bra, then with his hungry mouth he goes right for her breast while a hand unhooks her bra.

She's on her back now, still unable to move without his moving her. Her skirt is still on. He pushes it up over her hips then tugs at her panties. The garters holding the stockings are attached to this so he upends her backside and pulls.

In one brief flash she pictures herself, slip bunched down around her waist, skirt bunched up around her waist. Everything else exposed. She squeezes her eyes shut and holds her breath.

He pries open her legs and fumbles with himself. She won't look, she just feels him directing her limbs. She lets out a yelp as he pushes himself inside her.

This can't be what the girls were talking about. This is all wrong. He pumps and pumps for a few seconds, a few minutes, who knows. Her face is pulled in pain, tears drip into her ears. She faces the window, stares at the half open blinds. A line of cars two floors below honk in an uneven rhythm as Sam lets out a final grunt and rolls off her.

Sheila pulls her skirt down over her hips and the straps of her slip to her shoulders covering her small breasts. She is sore.

"First time, huh." He states as he lights a cigarette.

She can't answer. She is still facing the window, her back to him, knees hugged to her chest.

"Gotta take a leak." He rolls off the bed and heads to the bathroom, leaving the door open. She grimaces at his noisy relief when he lets out a long "aaah". Not so very different from that noise he made just before he rolled off her.

"It gets easier, the girls say, a few more times and you'll know what you're doin'. Relax a little. Let yourself get juiced, if ya know what I mean. Makes it smooth. Some girls really like it and they can't get enough. You'll learn. Hey, I gotta go." This he says while he zips up his trousers. He's looking for his shoes; his socks are still on.

"I told the fellas I'd meet them tonight." He looks at his watch in the square of light from the bathroom "Holy shit, I'm gonna be late." He opens his wallet and takes out a few singles.

"Here's some cab fare. This should get you to your subway, at least. I'll see you at O'Riordan's in a few days, 'kay? It was fun kid—see ya around."

As she's lying on her side, not speaking, not crying, just breathing through the thick air that barely gets to her lungs, she wonders why she never noticed his low class accent before. Did he always speak like this? Or just after he got what he came for?

Sheila hasn't said a word, hasn't made a sound. When he slaps her on the rump in farewell the thin skirt pulled tight over her hip is not enough to eliminate the sting. She pictures the cow in Mrs. McKenzie's yard. Useful for certain necessities, but not as prized as the family dog. With this mockery of affection, he leaves. He whistles his way to the elevator.

If she could move she would put on her panty girdle and stockings that are still clipped to the garters. But she cannot move. She doesn't want to move ever again.

After fifteen minutes, an hour, she can't tell, she wills herself to move, to get up. Go to the bathroom. She is so sore that it takes a long time to pee, but eventually, she manages to let go.

Sheila runs the water, cold, colder, coldest. She cups her hands around her face and just lets it soak her skin. Looking into the mirror, she is surprised she recognizes herself. The thick mascara she applied to look sophisticated, dangerous, knowledgeable, runs in black streaks down her pale face.

She wants to go home.

Chapter Eight

May 1955

"Where's that number for Ma's cousin?" Sheila is desperate. She and Colleen upend Sheila's shabby suitcase onto Colleen's narrow bed. Tucked inside the elasticized pocket of the case, Sheila's mother had written her cousin Meg's address and telephone number. A tiny pewter miraculous medal is attached to the note paper, a length of Christmas ribbon pulled through the chain and tied in a bow.

"What am I going to say to her? What if she think's I'm common? Oh, sweet Jesus, I am common!"

Colleen has her arm around her friend. "Pull yourself together, Sheila. If you're common, then so am I."

"You too? Are you..."

"No, I was lucky, that's all. I never saw him again, just like your lad. We're the ones who pay the price, Sheil, not those hinky bastards. They can just come and go as they please and no one's the wiser. Jaysus, what kind of system is that? Does God hate women so much that we get to carry all the blame?"

Sheila doesn't have the energy to engage in her friend's tirade about the unfairness of the universe and who gets to do what. She's busy enough trying to figure out how she is going to get through the next several months without dying of embarrassment.

Colleen stops talking when she notices Sheila's not listening.

"Sheila, it will be all right. You're not the first girl this has happened to. If your aunt can't help you, we'll find one of those places nuns run in the country, far away from the city."

At this solution, Sheila cries even harder. Everyone at home knows about those Magdalene houses and the awful things those girls suffer. If that prospect wasn't enough to keep a girl's legs closed, nothing was. That option is terrifying. Shame and more shame. How could she ever look at her parents again? Would they even let her speak to her own sisters, or would the disgrace be too much?

She is pacing, pacing around the little apartment. Feeling queasy, she tries to eat some dry crackers and cola. She can't keep even this down. Nerves or morning sickness? Who knows? Colleen tells her to take to her bed and get a little sleep.

The girls don't have their own phone in the apartment. So Colleen takes the note, goes to the drugstore on the corner and calls Meg Banfry. The glass and wood telephone door squeaks shut as she puts coins in the box.

"Mrs. Banfry? Hello, I'm a friend of Sheila Lynch. I believe her mother is a cousin of yours."

"Why isn't she calling herself? Well, Mrs. Banfry, Sheila is in a spot of trouble and she is too upset to call you. She's afraid you won't want to see her if, well, if you, oh, Mrs. Banfry, don't make me say it."

For a few long moments Colleen holds a silent phone, praying Mrs. Banfry will have something good to say.

"Bring her around? Oh that would be grand, Mrs. Banfry. Tomorrow will be just fine. Thanks ever so much, m'am. We'll be there tomorrow."

~~~~

"This wouldna' happened at home." Meg is lunching with her cousin Kathleen after Colleen called.

"What's that you're saying? Do you think the boys at home are any better than the American lads?" Meg Banfry demands.

"What I mean is, first whiff of suspicion from the ma an' the da wou' be marching over to the lad's house an' the priest would be called an' there'd be a ring on her in no time." Bridie Reilly wags her finger at her two lunch mates as she describes the familiar scene.

"And a leash around her neck. And every year that slim hipped lad would grow larger around the middle from all the beer in the pub after work and she would grow rounder every year with him filling her up with another baby. She'd look fifty before she made thirty, if she lived that long, and lose her teeth and her looks and her own twin who left for New York or Boston wouldn't recognize her. Nah! We'll do something for the girl."

"Whatever do you mean we'll 'do something' for the girl?!! I'll have nothing to do with that kind of sin!" Kathleen shrills.

"I suppose one can get used to a little scandal an' then not mind as much another scandal. There are places for girls like her."

Bridie sniffs as she lifts her cup of tea to her mouth in a failed effort to hide her pinched grin, her right eyebrow raised as she glances at Meg.

Bridie was not supposed to be part of this conversation between Meg and Kathleen, but as was her way, she overheard the two women talking and just pulled up a chair without so much as a 'how do you do' and poured herself a cuppa.

Meg ignores Bridie's attempt to provoke her. Meg turns toward her cousin Kathleen, "sometimes you're as thick as your faded red curls. I'm going to meet with her. Maybe I can figure something out."

Bridie declares, as if it were the right thing to do, "Someone will have to tell her mother of course. It will break her heart, but it has to be done."

"Bridie O'Reilly, don't you dare. I'm the girl's closest relation here. I will handle this situation. You keep your big mouth shut." With that, Meg gets her coat and goes home.

~~~~

Colleen and Sheila walk up Forest Parkway, glad for the bit of exertion the hill calls for. It will give Sheila a little more exercise to calm her nerves. The house that matches the number on her mother's note has a front porch with three wooden steps. Colleen rings the bell.

Meg opens the door for the two girls. She knows right away that the girl with the oddly colored black hair with brunette roots is her cousin's daughter, not only because she can see the family resemblance, but because she looks terrified.

Colleen holds out her hand, "Mrs. Banfry, I'm Colleen and this is your cousin, Sheila."

Meg reciprocates Colleen's forthrightness, then takes Sheila by the hand, leading the two young ladies into her living room.

"I've prepared some sandwiches for us. Come into the dining room."

Colleen starts her one woman show of commentary and tales before they can reach the table. She has them laughing and smiling with every dramatic hand gesture and imitation of the various New York accents from cabbies to the butcher and the baker and the boys who stand on corners and whistle at the girls, "bold as can be, don't you know," and winks at that because she doesn't so much mind the bold as can be fellas who line the street corners of New York evaluating the 'talent' as the girls saunter by.

By the second cup of tea and the third triangle of a ham sandwich, Sheila's shoulders loosen enough for her to sit at a natural angle for the first time in weeks.

Meg reaches across the table to take Sheila's hand. "Colleen, I haven't heard such delightful blather in years. The gift of gab was laid heavy on you in your pram, now wasn't it?"

When the girls leave to go back to Jackson Heights, it is with the understanding that Sheila will return tomorrow with her belongings.

~~~~

"What a lovely linen—"

"Open it Sheila."

Inside the lace is a thin platinum band with engravings all around and two tiny square cut sapphires in the center.

"Try it on. We have to keep the tongues from wagging around here. I bought it several years ago in an antique shop but I never could get it over my knuckles."

It fits almost perfectly. Sheila holds her left hand out in front while her right hand runs through her very short hair with the odd black tips, a temporary reminder of her trying on a new American life.

"One more thing, Sheila. We need a bit of a story to explain your presence here with no husband in sight. What if we say he's still over, working, saving money for a better start here?

He sent you ahead of time once it was arranged that you could bunk with the girls in Jackson Heights and they had a job for you. You didn't know you were expecting until after you arrived and so here you are."

Sheila nods her head at Meg, trying to understand the ruse that her cousin is inventing for her, glad that someone is taking the lead.

"You're not showing yet, but we'll have the cover in place when the questions start coming. Right now, you are here to help me out with light housework and keeping me company since Gerald passed last year. How's that?"

This is the closest they've come to mentioning the baby. No question about a due date or how they will manage the situation once the baby arrives. Meg has asked no questions about the man involved or if she ever hears from him. She has opened her home, come up with a cover story and given her a ring. Sheila does not know what comes next, but she feels that whatever it is, Meg will be there.

Chapter Nine

"Frank. Frank."

"Got it up here, Ma."

Before hanging up the kitchen extension, Millie puts the receiver to her ear. Not eavesdropping, exactly, just wants to make sure Frank picked up the extension.

"Hey, Frank—it's Joey—meet us at Woody's 'bout 9? The guys will be there, 'course."

"Yeah, aren't they always? See ya later, Joey."

"So, Frank, what's up for tonight? Any plans?" Millie asks her son, hoping to sound like she has no idea.

"The usual, Ma. Me and the guys. Woody's, play a little pool, ya know."

"Isn't there a picture playing on the Avenue, Frank?"

"Sure Ma, there's two. On the Waterfront and Marty. Which do you think me and Grace Kelly should go to, Ma? Am I more the Marlon Brando type or the Ernest Borgnine type?"

"Oh, Frank, do you know how many young ladies are just sitting home waiting for a nice boy to call?"

"I'm not a boy, Ma."

"I know that, Frankie, but you're my boy. I want you to be happy, find a nice girl, have a family someday."

Instead of speaking, Frank just looks at his mother. The scar on his cheek reddens. He touches two fingers to it, then turns toward the door.

"Gotta go. See ya later."

~ ~ ~

"Millie, so sorry to call you on a Saturday morning, but do you think your Frank could take a look—we've no lights, I'm afraid, and I'm not sure what to do."

"Of course, Meg, I'll ask him right away."

Millie opens the door to Frank's bedroom at the top of the stairs. The venetian blinds are pulled tight and the plaid curtains that have been there since Frank was in high school filter the bit of light that squeezes through the slats in rectangles of green and red.

Frank's Con-Ed work clothes are thrown across his desk chair, each of his boots kicked to two ends of the room. His left arm is extended over his head under the pillow, his legs splayed beneath him in an elongated V while his right hip is embedded in the sagging mattress.

"Frank, Frank, dear" she tentatively touches his shoulder.

"Hmmph, hmph. What?" One eye tries to open as he mumbles his question.

"Frank, Meg called. Her lights are out, could you...."

"Sure, Ma. Soon's I get up." He rolls away from her, face to the wall.

"Frank, its 10 o'clock. You should be up by now."

"Got in late. Be up in a bit."

Millie leans in, sees the dusty growth on his face, the stale odor of beer substituting for Old Spice.

"Frank, please, she needs her lights."

"Ma, it's the day. It's sunny. I'll be up later. Later."

Millie phones Meg.

"Frank will be over in a bit, Meg. He just has a few things to take care of, Okay?"

"Sure Millie. He's a hard working man and it is Saturday, I do hate to bother him."

"It's no bother, Meg. He'd be happy to help."

Millie hangs up the phone, dropping the smile she'd been wearing even though Meg couldn't actually see her over the phone. Somehow it helped her voice to be cheery if she forced her cheeks to retract.

"'Morning Mrs. Banfry—Ma said your lights 'r out."

49

"Frank, you are such a dear—on your day off still fussing with electricity for your helpless neighbor."

"Not a problem Mrs. B."

Frank hadn't shaved this morning, despite his mother's numerous suggestions.

Sheila is at the stove heating the kettle.

"Frank, I don't believe you've met my niece. Frank, this is Sheila. Sheila, Frank."

Frank starts to extend his hand to the girl in the dirndl skirt and peach sweater. He pulls it back to wipe his right hand on his pant leg.

"Nice to meet you. Frank Rasansky. I live next door."

Sheila takes his hand, smiles, averting her eyes while he still has her hand, just a moment longer than a usual first time greeting.

"Just making some tea, care for any Frank?"

"Nah, that's okay. I just had coffee. Mrs. B, I'll be in the cellar. You probably just need a new fuse."

Next door Millie is shaking out the small rugs from the brick stoop outside the kitchen. Her hands smell of Spic'n Span from mopping the kitchen and bathroom floors. Every Saturday for more than thirty years Ray had always found something to fix, like a broken screen or a squeaky hinge.

Ray had a heart attack the night they celebrated Frank's discharge from the Army. Frank graduated from high school in '45. All his friends were waiting to be called up, and just like boys they hoped the war would linger long enough to get some action. All the mothers, of course, prayed everyday for an end. There were too many stars in too many windows in the neighborhood.

But before Frank and his best friend Tommy were called up there was the Fourth of July. They started out at Victory Field with fireworks and hot dogs and beer. Lots of beer.

Frank and Tommy were best friends since first grade. They would be in the army soon, so the older men handed the boys cold beers from the ice chests. Big crowds were celebrating this Fourth of July because so many sons, brothers and husbands would be home soon. It couldn't be much longer until we finished up in the Pacific.

Millie had constructed a scene in her imagination: someone shouted 'Hey there's a party on the beach'. Frank had Ray's car, the 1935 black Ford, tires a bit thin because of rationing, but still a sturdy ole gal. Frank and Tommy yelled 'Woohoo!!', jumped in the car, a beer in hand and three more on the seat between them.

Down Cross Bay Boulevard, over the bridge, right to the beach, just a few miles on a summer night. Beer, girls, just lettin' go. They were off to the Army soon, right? The girls might even give them a good send off.

Millie filled in the gaps of the story while she and Ray waited in Frank's hospital ward that night. Over the bridge, faster, a little faster, then "Boom!" just as they dared the red light a truck made a left turn and they met. Formed a crumpled T.

Tommy was thrown through the windshield and smacked head first into the side of the truck before his body broke on the asphalt. Frank was projected on to the big steering wheel.

The medics had to pry his fingers from it. Pieces of windshield sliced his face, his left leg pinned between the door and the seat, broken. Some ribs cracked against the steering wheel. But still, he was luckier than Tommy. They covered Tommy with a blanket when they took him away on the stretcher. Frank got to the hospital unconscious, but breathing.

Frank's leg and ribs healed pretty much. They did the best they could with his face. A couple of gashes sewed up almost evenly, just a faint scar after a few years. But the scar from the edge of his lower right eyelid, over the cheekbone, halting at the corner of his mouth was deep and ragged. Even now, ten years later, the scar tugged his eyelid down, pulling at the delicate skin around his eye.

The Army took him, though. Just seven weeks later, long enough for his leg and ribs to mend. Didn't send him overseas. But they did train him. Electrician. Got him a foot in the door with Con Ed when he came out. Good steady job. A livelihood.

He's got more than a lot of young men, Millie tells herself. So many in worse shape. Boys from the war who will always be in a wheelchair. But Millie knows. Frank's real scar is Tommy. That one hasn't healed yet. Don't know that it ever will.

Millie had just lifted the last of the small knit rugs to shake out over the railing when Frank returns from Meg's.

"Ma, you didn't tell me Mrs. B has a houseguest. You keepin' her a secret on purpose?"

Millie starts to protest. "Well, Frank, it just, uh, slipped my mind."

Frank leans in and kisses his mother on the cheek, then taps her gently on the side of the head. "Must be gettin' old, Ma."

Frank smiles at Millie and gives her a wink, then takes her hand to twirl her around the top of the small stoop while whistling Rock

Around the Clock. He swings open the aluminum screen door shuffling a few dance steps. A moment later Millie hears the shower running and Frank's off key voice singing over the water. It's been more than ten years since she heard her son sing.

Chapter Ten

Sunday, June 26, 1955

The 6:30 is the first Mass of the day. Fr. Downey is the regular priest. He stands outside the sacristy door sucking on a cigarette and nodding to parishioners before he goes in to vest. He hurries through the Latin so he can get to his coffee and maybe a roll later from Schmidt's bakery and break the midnight-to-Mass fast.

There is no music. The sermon is short and vague. The altar boys a bit more disheveled than the crew that works the 9:30, hair barely combed, mumbling their memorized syllables, hoping they get it right enough to avoid a raised eyebrow from Father. Not that Fr. Downey is likely to raise an eyebrow at them. He's mumbling too, only he's better at it.

Sheila sits in the back, in the last pew, behind the green marble pillar under the choir loft. It's cool and dark here. She sits next to a window of the Annunciation, hoping to borrow a little grace from that maternal scene, though she knows her virtue is nothing like that of the Blessed Mother.

She cannot go up to receive Communion because she hasn't found the courage to go to confession. She knows she has committed a grave sin, maybe even a mortal sin, but she is here, every week, because she doesn't want to add to the tally that already has her standing one foot inside Hell's gate. She'd like to get closer to Purgatory, but her courage fails her in the minutes before Mass begins while Fr. Macelli sits in the confessional, a bare green light bulb glowing, waiting to cleanse the slate of those wishing to receive Communion this morning.

This time last year Sheila was home with her parents and sisters, planning her great escape. She was going to be a sassy American. Confident, capable, stylish. Not tethered to husband and children until after she had done some living. Some glamorous, even dangerous living. Her mother's warnings were dismissed without concern. *Not me, Mother. I want something more from life.* Her something more landed her here, sitting in the back pew, pleading over and over *I confess to almighty God that I have sinned through my own fault, through my own deeds. Kyrie elieson. Christi elieson. Kyrie elieson.*

Next week. Next week I'll go and get this over with. But the promise itself makes her tremble. She gets through Mass fingering the beads in her sweater pocket, racing through the Hail Marys.

Chapter Eleven

"Mother, how long has this girl been living here?"

"Just these past few weeks, dear. You'd know that if you came by more often."

"Yes, but who is she? Where are her people?"

"Her people, Phil? I'm 'her people'. She has a family on the other side; in fact, she's the daughter of a cousin of mine. Her husband will be joining her as soon as he gets enough money together."

"Oh, and when was the last time she saw this husband?"

"Well, I don't know that, dear. I haven't asked her. Seems a little nosy."

"How long has she been in New York? A few weeks, a few months?" Phil's voice rises to what he assumes is an appropriate pitch to convey his disapproval of his mother's behavior.

"Mother Banfry, I spoke with her in the kitchen just a while ago." Maureen interjects quickly, eager to get her own bit in to the confrontation. "She made a reference to going to Central Park last summer, then she got flustered and twirled that ring around her finger. Last summer! Now it's June. I hesitate to say, but she looks about four months gone, if you'll pardon me. I'm not the only one who can count, you know."

"Mother, how does that look?"

"Look? Phil, what are you trying to say?"

"Well, Mother, we have to think of what this looks like. What kind of example does this set? Here you are taking in a perfect stranger with some mixed up story and from the look of things they'll be two of them in a short time.

"Yes, mother, how does that look? Aren't there places for such girls? Don't you think the neighbors will talk?" Maureen couldn't help but present her argument.

They left hanging in the air the rest of what he was thinking, but Meg didn't need to be psychic to fill in the silence. *Haven't we been the subject of enough talk, Mother. Enough scandal?*

Mother and son exchange a glance that acknowledges the words left unsaid. But Meg breathes in, looks straight at her son, and smiles.

"Why Philip, dear. I believe I can invite whomever I wish to be a guest in my house. I hope you enjoyed your little visit. It was so nice to see little Jimmy. What beautiful eyes he has, don't you dear?" Meg hugs her grandson and lifts him to her lap.

"Mother, really, why don't you listen? You can't have a girl like that around here."

"What? A lovely girl, with fine manners and so handy around the house? She's such good company, son. That kind of girl?"

"You know what I mean."

"I'm afraid I do."

Without them realizing the movement she has walked her son and daughter-in-law to the front door.

She hands Jimmy to his father. "My, this little boy is getting so big, aren't you Jimmy? Have a safe trip home, now. Take care."

"Mother."

"Bye, now."

Meg locks the door behind them. *When did he get so prissy? Since he met Maureen? No, he always cared about appearances. Perception is reality, he'd say to her, smiling his way through his father's trial. Angry that the stain on his name might ruin his life. He kept his distance from his father those last few years. Pleading too busy with work and family to come for dinner. Too busy to sit next to a convicted felon. He wouldn't say that to his father's face. He just didn't come around.*

Chapter Twelve

Maureen, Phil and Jimmy settle into the front seat of the Buick for the short ride home.

"Well, you won't say it but I will. I'm glad we don't live in the same parish as your mother. What must her neighbors think?"

Phil grunts an assent.

"At least my brother married the girl he got in trouble. What kind of fellow did this Sheila take up with that he won't even do what's right by her?"

Maureen pulls her little boy closer on the big bench seat. She kisses Jimmy on the head and says, "you will always do what's right, my little angel, won't you? You will always make Mommy proud, I know you will."

He looks up at her with his big blue eyes.

"Say, 'yes Mommy I will always make you proud'"

"Yes, Mommy. I make you proud."

"That's my good boy."

Chapter Thirteen

On that first Monday after Sheila and Frank meet, she is standing at the kitchen sink filling a pot to boil the potatoes. Frank walks up the drive, turns toward Meg's window, sees Sheila and waves. She waves back.

"That Frank, regular as clock work. Five forty-seven each working day that back door slams a bit and I know Frank is home. It's nice to know a good man is around, don't you think?" Meg is at the table peeling the rest of the potatoes when she asks Sheila if she agrees.

"Oh, uh, right, Aunt Meg. A good man." Sheila is a bit distracted.

Tuesday Sheila is at the sink again, washing out the tea cups. She glances at the clock. 5:45. How long can she wash the same cup? Meg doesn't comment on the water running that long.

Up the drive he walks, turns and waves. She waves back.

On Wednesday Meg prepares a pitcher of fresh lemonade, fills it with ice, gives Sheila two glasses and asks her to string the beans on the front porch. It's 5:43. "Take your time, dear. Oh, and offer Frank a glass as he comes up from the avenue. He'll be glad of it after a long day." Meg tries to make that sound like an afterthought. Sheila blushes just a bit. She knows what Meg is up to, and she doesn't mind playing along.

Not more than two days goes by without Meg inviting Millie and Frank for supper or Millie inviting Meg and Sheila for supper. They play cards. They laugh. Frank and Sheila clear away and wash the dishes together. Frank finds things to repair at Meg's house, a little painting, a little plumbing, a little reaching high to get things from the top shelf so Sheila doesn't risk falling from a step ladder.

Sometimes Sheila almost forgets that she is carrying a child, a child of a near stranger at that. Sometimes Frank forgets that his leg is lame and he sports a scar across his face. Sometimes there is a moment of silence after the laughter, a moment of silence when their hands touch or they brush past each other clearing away the dishes. They are anxious to regain their equilibrium and keep the smile going, and usually they do.

The Fourth of July is on a Monday this year, making for a three day weekend of barbecues and fireworks Saturday, Sunday and then Monday night the real show is on. From Meg's front porch they can see the skies light up from the celebration at Victory Field on the other side of Forest Park.

Sheila is on the front porch with Meg and Millie, enjoying chips and Cokes. She keeps adjusting to make herself comfortable at six months along. Children run with their sparklers spinning round and waving them like magic wands.

"Where's Frank tonight?"

"Ah, he doesn't much like the Fourth, Sheila. Bad memories."

The sprinkler is running on the little patch of lawn to dampen it in case someone's firecracker decides to ignite on their bit of green.

"Looks soaked enough, Aunt Meg. I think I'll turn the water off." Sheila goes around to the side of the house to turn the spigot.

Frank is heading toward the aluminum cans with a bag of trash.

"Frank? Frank, how are you?"

"Ah, okay, Sheila. You? You feeling okay?"

"Can't complain. The fireworks are lovely Frank—why don't you join us on the porch to look at them?"

"Nah, it's not my thing—"

"Well, how about some lemonade or a Coke? It's so very hot."

Sheila turns her head toward her left shoulder. Frank can't resist the look of concern in her face.

"Okay, but not out front."

"The back steps will fit us I dare say."

"Allright."

They sit together on the back steps of Meg's house, sipping Coca-Cola, looking up occasionally at the fireworks. Sheila jumps as a cherry bomb explodes in a garbage pail on the other side of the house. She impulsively grabs Frank's arm. He squeezes her hand.

They exchange a look; a shadow falls over their faces as the moon rises. Even in the moonlight Sheila can see that the scar running from Frank's eye to his lip is reddening. Slowly, tenderly, Sheila touches her cool fingers to the mark, then cups her hand under his chin. They don't speak. After a few moments Frank pulls himself back and asks:

"So, any word from back home? From your husband?"

"Frank," instead of turning away, she looks at Frank straight in the eye—"Frank, I've been telling a fib". Her eyes fill, she wipes the tears with the back of her hand. "I don't know what I'd do without Aunt Meg and your mother, and, well, you."

Frank hasn't let go of Sheila's hand.

"Well, yeah, I couldn't think why any man would be separated from you this long, especially, well you know."

"Yes, with a baby coming". She turns into Frank's shoulder. He puts his arm around her.

"I was a fool, Frank. Thought I'd be a 'real' American girl—working in O'Riordan's—the music, the laughter, businessmen and actors coming in. This one fella, charming, smooth, full of blarney, got my head spun around. He took me for drinks a few times, one thing led to another and here I am. Never saw him again."

Sheila is still nuzzled in Frank's arm when she confesses this, wanting to know the look on his face. She feels his head shift so he can see her.

"I'm so sorry for you Sheil, but if I'm not being too selfish, I'm kinda glad you're here with Mrs. B—we've all got stuff, ya know—I've got stuff I'm not too proud of."

"What kind of stuff, Frank, if I may ask?"

"Well, why I don't celebrate the Fourth like everyone else." Frank pulls back a sniffle that threatens to turn into tears. "Ten years ago I killed my best friend. We were drunk. We were going to be called up any day. I was driving, we were laughing, singing, drinking—I didn't see the truck coming because I felt, well, I felt 18—18 with our lives ahead of us. Tommy crashed through the window and died when he hit the asphalt—this scar— that's to remind me of how stupid I was and the price Tommy paid for my stupidity."

Frank and Sheila sit on the back steps for the longest time, Frank with his right arm around Sheila, Sheila holding his left hand on her lap.

"Frank?"

"Yeah, Sheil?"

"I've been thinkin,'" Sheila pauses. "I think, maybe, that we have to meet each other in Purgatory before we can understand anything of life. I mean, I think we have to get kicked out of Eden before we can get to Heaven."

"Hmm," Frank nuzzles the top of Sheila's head into his neck. "Purgatory's been looking a lot brighter these last few months."

Chapter Fourteen

"What if she gets a letter in the next few days telling her the sad news of her husband getting conked on the head while working the docks and the poor fella' tumbled into the water and drowned, and now she's a tragic young widow..."

"Oh, Meg, you're always one for the stories."

"It's my birthright, Millie. Land of saints and scholars. And storytellers. Just can't help it."

The two old friends look at each other and laugh.

Besides, the last time we had a party around here was for Gerald's wake. A wedding would be much better, don't you think, Millie?

Millie raises her Coke bottle and the two women toast.

To life.

And dear friends.

Amen.

~~~~

The wedding is small. Colleen comes to be Sheila's maid of honor and witness. Just the five of them in the rectory.

They had to explain the situation to Fr. Downey and Sheila had to go to confession to be absolved of her sin. A fresh slate, a fresh start.

Meg and Millie prepare a roast beef dinner for their celebration. They have a lovely white cake from Schultz's bakery and a bottle of champagne for the toast. Millie takes a photograph of them, Sheila standing with a chair in front to cover her belly. This is a picture they can send to her parents. Explanation to come later.

October arrives with the trees starting to turn orange, gold and red. There are great piles of them on the lawn. Sheila loves to rake them. It's a soothing thing to do. Make great piles, then scoop them up in handfuls for the trash, leave some on the lawn for a touch of bright carpeting. She is raking one morning about nine, the breeze is cool after the hot and humid summer. She is wearing one of Frank's sweaters since none of her own fit. Any day now.

The pains start. She get both Meg and Millie to help. Millie calls into the ConEd office to get a message to Frank who's out at a job site.

Both women take Sheila to Mary Immaculate in a cab. It's not far, just a few miles. Sheila holds both their hands. They will stay with her as long as they are allowed. That's not long. Frank arrives in the afternoon. He's so worried about Sheila, but they don't let fathers in. So he waits with Meg and Millie. They wait. Hours. Finally, at ten-thirty that evening, a doctor comes out to the waiting room.

"Mr. Rasansky, you have a beautiful little girl. Your wife is recovering now. You can see her, but just for a few minutes."

Frank rushes to Sheila. She is so worn out, so pale.

"Sheil, I've been here all day."

"I know, Frank. The nurses told me. I knew you'd get here."

"I saw the baby. She's beautiful. She's got some lungs on her Sheil, a real lively little girl.

"A little girl. What could be better than this.? He holds her hand and speaks close to her face.

"Margaret Camille?"

"Yep, Margaret Camille. After two wonderful grandmothers. My mother and Meg will be so proud."

"Sorry, sir. You will have to leave now. Your wife needs her rest."

"My wife, my beautiful wife. Our beautiful daughter."

Chapter Fifteen

Maureen

Maureen and Phil chose their house largely because of the oak tree. It was set back near the middle of the small yard, wide and strong and formidable. Phil could barely wrap his arms around it. It was a comfort, that tree. It seemed to stand for the natural order of things, a certain justice and logic. It shaded the house nicely in the summer and when it snowed the branches held the magnificent white crystals. The weight of the snow and ice pruned the tree of its weak and dead branches, which crashed to the ground to be covered in the blanket that built itself right over the fallen wood.

The kitchen faces the backyard. Maureen would sometimes bathe her children in the sink. As she squeezed the cloth over them, their oh so soft skin slippery under her fingers, she would gaze at the big tree as if it was their guardian. Strong and sure and present.

They married in 1948. For the first two years they were relieved to not have children. They were warned by the priest before the wedding that under Church law they were to have as many children as they could bear. If they wanted to space their children, they needed to have compelling reasons to do so. The only method they were allowed, under penalty of sin, was the Rhythm Method.

Maureen was working and Phil was getting established in his practice. They were saving for a house. After they moved in, they thought it was time for a child. If there was too long a time without a child, tongues would wag and whispers would start with suspicions that they might not be 'good Catholics'. That kind of speculation could ruin Phil's practice.

They made a good team. He was a young attorney and she was the lovely wife: pretty, elegant, pleasant. She was an asset to Phil, witty at social events, giving a listening ear even when someone cornered her and droned on about some matter about which Maureen cared nothing. She kept the house and prepared interesting dinners from recipes in Ladies Home Journal.

Toward the end of 1950 Maureen was pregnant. Though her pregnancy had its difficulties, it wasn't too bad after the first few months. She tried hard not to put on much weight. She was horrified to see what happened to some of her friends who had children and began to resemble brood mares, going wide in the hips and soft in the belly. Maureen was determined to get her figure back. Motherhood was not going to change her, much. She was well warned from losing her looks, and thus, her husband's attention. With the growing population of young women working in offices, sensible wives knew danger when they saw it.

When Jimmy was born, she had her week stay in the hospital. The first time Maureen saw her baby, a nurse handed him to her in the recovery room and then whisked him off to the nursery so Maureen could get some rest. A week in the hospital with the baby brought every few hours for a bottle was almost pleasant. The nurses did the diapering and the swaddling and carried the little squealers away before the mothers grew too tired.

Jimmy was a week old when Maureen had her first day alone with him.

She settled in with him, positioning her arms in the rocker, a pillow supporting the little fellow. This morning, before Phil left for work, she made up a batch of bottles, mixing and stirring and pouring a days supply of ecru colored stuff that made her nostrils pinch when she smelled it. She warmed the bottle in a pan, squirted a little on her wrist to test the temperature and gathered up her hungry son.

She held him, squirming, crying, until he caught hold of the rubber nipple and settled into a rhythmic gulping. Soon, he was satisfied. Not quite ready to give up the bottle, but soothed enough to study his mother's face.

He held her pinky with his tiny fingers. Strong. What a wonder. Someone so little can grab on so tight. His lashes were drying from his hungry cries, fanned out like a star. He was content now. With her free hand she stroked his cheek, velvet against her finger.

Mother and son were all there was to the world. The two of them, bound, caught up in larger arms, graced in a haze of violet light.

Something opened in Maureen. Where, she could not say, but somewhere in her body, in her soul; a movement, an enlargement. The only way to find this place was this, holding her tiny child in her arms, letting him break her heart.

The intensity, the consuming protective passion for this child, almost annihilated her in its fierceness. It could not be possible for her to love anything or anyone else the way she loves this child. No one's heart could be that big.

He was her delight. Every first, when he rolled over, when he held his own bottle, when he pulled himself to stand, when he took his first steps, said his first words were celebrated with applause and big hugs. He loved to please her. She loved that he did.

When Jimmy was six they had settled into the expenses of the house enough to have a back porch built in the yard. From the cellar stairs to the driveway side of the house, the frames were laid, cement poured, the roof and walls secured and the screens set. Two Adirondack chairs and a child's size table for Jimmy made the room.

These were good years.

Maureen was glad she was not one of those overly fertile women who was pregnant every year or two producing a brood of unkempt children with scruffy shoes and tangled hair and a faint scent of unwashed skin about them. Maureen was proud of her slim waistline and her one perfect little boy who always had a bedtime bath and freshly laundered, pressed clothes to wear.

When Jimmy started school, her days began to get a little long. Jimmy could do so much for himself now. He wanted to go off with his friends after school more and more, and of course, she had to let him. She didn't want people to think he was a momma's boy. Momma's boys grow up to be pathetic men, she knew. It pained her to let him go. One more child might be okay. She hoped she would have a girl. No other little boy could take as big a place in her heart as Jimmy.

Rose arrived when Jimmy was eight. This pregnancy was a little more difficult than the first, but Jimmy was in school so she could rest during the day. Rose was a beautiful baby, too. *Of course,* Maureen thought, *what other kind of baby would Phil and I have?*

The times she watched Jimmy playing with Rose were moments of grace. *This is perfect, this is love,* she thought. All the romantic poetry in the world pointed to this. Maureen's heart was glad when Rose fixed her sights on Jimmy and everything he did made her laugh. She smiled broadly when he came into her sight. He helped her walk and practiced words with her. He built up towers of blocks and knocked them down, crashing a toy truck into them to his sister's delight.

A few months after Rose's first birthday Maureen began to feel ill. She had quickly regained her figure, but now her skirts were getting tight again. She took some little pills that all the women who wanted to be slim took. They razzed her up, a bit, and cut down on her appetite. But she was so tired all the time. She didn't remember being this tired when Jimmy was little.

The doctor told her she would be having a summer baby. Middle of August. Maureen wept.

Chapter Sixteen

Priscilla Marie Banfry arrived at three in the morning in the beginning of July 1961. She was six weeks early. Her lungs and heart were weak. She would have to stay in an incubator for several weeks. The doctors told the exhausted parents they can only wait and see.

Maureen went home when her week was up. Phil's mother Meg came and stayed to look after Rose and Jimmy. Maureen slept for the first few days home. She kept her room dark; the summer heat made the air thick and re-used. She won't allow the window to be opened. She can't stand the summer sounds of children playing and cars going by. A week passes and she has not yet gone to see her baby daughter in the hospital.

Phil pulls her up out of bed and runs the bath for her. They will go to the hospital together and face the child's situation. Maybe it won't be so bad. Maybe. There's hope. There's always hope.

When she is seven weeks old, Priscilla comes home. She is a red-faced child, colicky, fussy, unhappy. When Jimmy and Rose were infants Maureen had a bassinet next to her side of the bed so she could quickly get to the hungry crying baby in the middle of the night. A bottle and some rocking usually got them to go back to sleep.

Priscilla, though, is relentless.

Her crib is in another room. Maureen's nerves are raw, exposed, frayed. She is afraid of what she might do to the child if she has to try to sleep in the same room. Meg comes a few days a week to be a relief, to stay up and rock the baby so Maureen can recover. But Maureen is not recovering.

The doctors say she has a bad case of the baby blues. The baby blues. Sounds so innocuous, almost pastel. A euphemism for the midnight blue of a moonless night of what has her in its grip.

There are emergency runs to the hospital. They leave Jimmy and Rose in the house to sleep as they wrap up the congested baby. Sometimes she will have to stay for days. That's good news. If Priscilla can stay they can go home and get some sleep. When they clear her lungs quickly and send her home, Maureen cries.

By the time Cilla is three, Maureen has tried to resign herself to this life. Cilla is smaller than other three year olds and delayed in some of her development. But she has good days. When she has more than a week of good days, Maureen knows what is coming and braces herself. A week is a gift that can be taken from her at any moment. She can't trust it. A sniffle, a little cough, a runny nose and then the fever, congestion and the emergency room.

They take her in. Maureen feels that her life is a series of emergencies and then recovery and re-set for the next emergency. The doctors and nurses are diligent in their work on this child. Once in a while, when the crying and the coughing start, Maureen hesitates. She hesitates until she forces herself to go in, start the vaporizer, the pounding on the tiny back to get up the mucus. Sometimes while she sits in the rocker with Cilla, she wonders what life would be like if this were to be over with.

Jimmy is thirteen now. Never home. Doesn't bring his friends over. He says he doesn't want to risk bringing extra germs in the house. Rose is five. She can tie her own shoes and get herself dressed. She can pour cereal and even manages the milk when the bottle isn't too full. Most importantly, though, she entertains Cilla.

Their favorite place to play is on the back porch. It's early summer; the girls have their own little table and some plastic cups and bowls. Maureen sits with them in this little enclosure under the broad oak and savors the warm summer breeze filtered through the green leaves. Just breathe it in and out. The Valium helps keep the anxiety subdued. Anxiety is the first sign of trouble.

Rose knows it's her job to keep Cilla happy. They are playing house with their dolls in their make believe kitchen. When Cilla grabs something Rose wants she has learned to let it go, not hit her like she wants to, not grab it back. Cilla loves playing with her big sister and Rose loves having a little sister to play with, to boss around. These moments are good. But, right now Rose has the red plastic saucepan because she is making spaghetti for their dinner. Cilla wants it. Rose tries to give Cilla the blue one. No. Cilla doesn't want the stupid blue one.

Maureen closes her eyes. *The girls are going to fight. That's what little girls do; they fight when they both want the same thing. It's okay. It's not important. Let it go.*

Cilla complains, "Mommy, tell her to gi' me it!"

"Keep it, okay," Rose hisses, trying to avert Cilla's whine.

But it's coming. The breathing, the Valium, the telling herself it's nothing, None of that matters now. Maureen whispers under her breath *I'm sorry* to the girls, but they can't hear her. The darkness comes over her, like the veil the Italian widows wear when their husbands died. She pictures them, the dark women she saw as a child, traveling in twos and threes, going to church with their rosaries dangling from their fingers or working behind the counter in the deli with the cheeses and salamis hanging in netted string. Their mourning was a way of life, a vocation. They had each other in this sisterhood. Maureen, though, is alone in her darkness. Her angry, unreasonable darkness. The kindness she felt for her children just a moment before the veil descended is gone now. There is only this cold rage.

Rose tries to make Cilla laugh to show her mother everything's all right. But it's too late. Rose knows it's too late. She snuffles up the tears that are threatening. She looks at her little sister with disgust and wonders how she can be so stupid as to not know what makes their mother mad. Rose will be sent to her room, alone. If Cilla is punished she'll start crying and then she'll get congested and then she'll get sick. Then it will be worse. The house will be dark and everyone will have to be quiet. They will have to stay away from Mommy. But Cilla never seems to get that. She cries until Mommy picks her up. She cries until she gets what she wants. And she gets what she wants so she doesn't get sick.

Rose knows she has to get away from the porch and into the house fast. But she's in the corner where they have set up the boxes to be a stove and refrigerator. Maureen gets up and takes two steps toward Rose, grabs her arm, tight, and swats her bottom. Hard. She doesn't want to cry, but she can't help it. When her mother lets her go Rose swats Cilla because it doesn't matter now. This was all Cilla's fault and it doesn't matter if Rose hits her because Cilla's going to cry anyway and the house will be dark and Rose will be alone in her room.

~~~~

Rapunzel, Rapunzel let down your hair that I might climb the golden stair.

Rose is alone in her room with the large brightly illustrated book of fairy tales opened on her bed. There is the brick tower as tall as the trees and the lovely young girl with a braid as long and thick as the tower leaning out, longing for her rescue.

Rose wonders if the wicked woman who keeps her captured can make herself look like the lovely Rapunzel when she goes out in the world, stealing her identity and then turning without warning into the witch. The townspeople don't trust the beautiful girl. She might be soft and lovely, kind and smiling one minute and turn into the wicked witch at any time. The magic must wear off, Rose figures. First the eyes change from a clear blue to a smoky gray and if the townspeople aren't watching she will be mean to them. The more clever ones get out of her way as soon as they notice the change in the eyes.

Chapter Seventeen

The first time Rose felt the promise, she was five. She was in her bedroom on a Sunday morning, in a pretty dress because she and Jimmy and Dad had gone to early Mass. Mom was home with Cilla, who was fussy and crying.

Rose was sitting alone on the floor in her bedroom just under the window, a big book of fairy tales open in front of her, with brightly colored pictures of a lovely young girl, a castle and a handsome prince cutting through the forest to rescue her.

Sunlight brightens the page, bleaching the picture. She looks up. The light enters her, fills her. Fills her inside and out. She is light. All of her is infused with beautiful primrose tinged light, like a yellow rose with a delicate rim of deep pink on the tips of the petals.

A hymn runs through her brain, words she knows substituted for the lyric: *soul of my savior santa by my chest*.

Rose looks up into the sunlight pouring in through the window. It's Jesus. Jesus come to tell her she is chosen, special. That He will always be with her.

There aren't any words, exactly, but she feels there is a promise. She is sure of that. Promise that she is special. Promise that she is protected. Promise that she has a very important role to play in life and that her path will unfold before her.

The smell of bacon and eggs coming up the stairs draws her down. She climbs up onto a chair and waits for someone to notice that she is filled with light. Mom is busy at the stove trying to keep the bacon from burning, Jimmy is pouring orange juice and Dad has a portion of the paper folded in front of his face while he drinks his coffee. Cilla is lying in the playpen just outside the kitchen, quiet for once.

"Rose, eat your eggs before they get cold." Most of the scrambled eggs fall off her spoon before they reach her mouth. When no one is looking she scoops some up in her hand, then has to wipe the butter off her fingers on the tablecloth. Her bacon stiffens on the plate and, just because, she smashes it with the back of her spoon.

Chapter Eighteen

MAUREEN CARRIES THE STROLLER down the brick steps and secures the brake. She settles Cilla in the seat, zipping her into her harness. Rose holds onto the handle, at her mother's side.

They are taking a little trip down to the corner deli to get some milk, bread and bologna for lunch.

Cilla grasps the bar in front of her with both hands, delighted with the spinning pinwheel that is secured to the stroller. "Wee, wee,wee" she says, looking back to her mother and sister to share this wonder. She has bluish circles around her eyes, just a little. The doctor advised Maureen to get her out in the sunshine, get a little color on her pale skin.

Mrs. Duffy is ahead of Maureen at the deli counter. Karl, the owner, says, "Ja, ja" when Mrs. Duffy orders three quarters of a pound of ham bologna and a quarter of a pound of Swiss cheese.

"Oh, Mrs. Banfry, how good to see you and your little girls." Rose smiles at Mrs. Duffy, but she is looking only at Cilla, who is trying to keep the pinwheel moving in the still air of the corner store

Maureen answers her neighbor, trying to get her attention away from Cilla. "How are your boys, Mrs. Duffy?"

"Oh, good, good." She straightens up after her unveiled examination of Cilla. "You know what boys are, always running around like wild Indians. They bring so much life to the house."

Maureen feels assaulted with Mrs. Duffy's comment. She is sure that this is a slight, a pity, directed at her because she has a sickly child. Maureen stands a little taller, picturing the Duffy boys, all five of them, running around the streets from the minute school let out to well past the time the men paraded down the streets from the LIRR station, ready for dinner.

Karl saved her "vat can I get for you, Mrs. Banfry? He asked, dropping the notes of the 'Ban' down low and swallowing the 'fry" as his voice rose to the question.

Mrs Duffy took it upon herself to run her hand along Cilla's face, ignoring the scowl the little girl answered her with.

"Bye, bye."

"Bye", Maureen mumbles, just loud enough to not be rude.

Maureen can't tell anyone how she feels. She is supposed to complain, just a little, and then laugh it off and say how wonderful the children are, what a blessing, blah, blah, blah. She wonders how many other mothers are lying. She thinks she captures a glimpse with some of the women once in a while, but then that look is quickly withdrawn, replaced by a sort of smile that is supposed to reveal nothing. If someone says, oh, you look so tired, she just waves it away as part of being a mother.

The black opaque curtain that sometimes wraps itself around her, sucking her will, her goodness, her light, must remain secret.

It had been so easy with Jimmy and for a while with Rose. She had everything. A handsome husband, a home, enough money. This was what she had worked for all her life.

She had it because she deserved it. She set about having a life that was different, better, than the one her mother had. Her mother had five children. Her mother wore housecoats and cracked rubber soled shoes, her stockings drooped around her ankles. Her mother didn't take care of her appearance and let herself get fat. She gossiped over the fence with the other women and laughed too loud.

Maureen set out to have more. From the time she was a little girl, the youngest child with four brothers, she wanted things to be nicer. She had hand-me-downs from cousins. She was grateful for the school uniform because others wouldn't have to know that she didn't have new clothes. It didn't occur to her that most of the children wore their siblings or cousins cast offs. She would look longingly in the windows of the shops on the avenue while her mother stopped and caught up with a neighbor out doing her shopping. The shiny new shoes, the crisp, ironed dress in royal blue over a petticoat. That's what she wanted. And she decided that she would have that.

Someday.

She went to work in big firm in Manhattan when she finished her course at Miss Brown's Secretarial school. She shopped carefully. The war was on, so everything was rationed. But she did her best to look professional everyday. She knew how to mend her clothes and darn her stockings in the tiniest of stitches. Her gloves were always clean and her shoes shined.

By the time she met Phil after the war she had worked out the bones of a life plan. She had selected a china pattern and a silver setting. She had been buying one piece at a time, careful to hide them in her closet. She knew her mother would laugh at her for her airs and la-di-da ways.

But she set up her house the way she wanted it, adding a chair here, an ottoman there when the budget allowed. She kept to a schedule all the years she had just the one child because he was easy and healthy and cooperative. When he started school they had a regular routine for homework and play and dinner and bath and bedtime. She'd tape his spelling tests with a gold star on the refrigerator along with his drawings.

When Rose came along it didn't take long to get back into a routine, one that accommodated two children. She put Rose in a carriage and took walks around the neighborhood, proudly showing off her pretty little baby. Before Rose turned two, all that was over with the arrival of Cilla.

She carries her burden alone. Phil makes himself scarce, staying late at work, with meetings to run, hands to shake, events to be seen at, all in the name of work. Has to keep his practice going by getting out and cultivating a clientele; a clientele with enough money to meet his bills.

Maureen has no sister to confide in. She has few friends of a confidential nature. Maureen has set herself apart, above, the other women. She works to maintain her wall of respectability and confidence, worried that if she admits weakness everything will crumble beyond redemption.

~~~

"Mrs. Banfry, yoo-hoo, Mrs. Banfry." Maureen turns toward the voice. It's Sunday morning and she is leaving church with Phil and all three children. Cilla has just turned six and she has grown stronger over the years. The crying spells have lessened considerably, which, in turn, has granted some peace to the family. They've been able to attend Mass as a family almost every week.

"Yes?" Maureen turns to see a very tall woman, about sixty, she guesses, approach her.

"Mrs. Banfry, I'm Nancy Proctor. I just wanted to tell you what a lovely family you have and, well, I know this might sound a little strange, but I was over on Rockaway Avenue, at the Catholic Store, to get something for my grandson's first communion, and, for some strange reason, I saw this", she reaches into her large shiny handbag and pulls out a small box, "and, well, I felt I was supposed to get this for you, for your little girl."

Maureen puts Cilla's hand into Phil's so she can receive the gray velveteen box. Inside is a small Miraculous Medal. Maureen looks at the figure of the Blessed Mother on this tiny thing smaller than her pinky nail, marveling at the detail of the face and the folds in the gown and the letters encircling her. Maureen knows those letters spell out 'Mary conceived without sin pray for us who have recourse to thee' because her elementary school nuns taught her this when they studied the lives of the saints in preparation for Confirmation.

She doesn't know what to say. She looks at this woman, just one woman among the many faces she has seen every Sunday for years now, never having had a conversation with her that she can recall, and here she stands, this almost stranger, handing her a gift for her little girl. A gift of a symbol of faith, of miracles, of hope.

Mrs. Proctor squeezes Maureen's hand while Maureen tries to get out the words 'Thank you' but cannot because of the tears in her throat.

"You have a lovely day, Mrs. Banfry." She turns and walks away.

When they get home from church Maureen clasps the chain around Cilla's neck. Rose watches this and wonders why no one ever gets her anything special. Cilla cries and gets what she wants. Rose already has everything, so she's been told. She doesn't need anything special. She goes to her room and reads.

Maureen sets about preparing Sunday dinner. Cilla climbs up on a chair in the kitchen. "Why don't you go play with Rose, Cilla?"

"I want to watch you so when I get big I can cook, too."

Maureen turns around from the stove to look at her youngest child. Cilla is smiling at her mother. Maureen goes to Cilla's chair, bends, and kisses her dark curls.

"I love you, Cilla."

"I know, Mommy."

Chapter Nineteen

The sisters play in their room. They play in the little landing at the top of the stairs. They play on the slightly bigger landing at the bottom of the stairs. The stairs are mountains to climb or rooms in a castle or the houses they brought into being with their little girl imaginations. They transform shoe boxes and appliance boxes into sinks and refrigerators and stoves; into beds for their dolls and desks for school or work. Crayons and magic markers and construction paper and tape are the materials to make a castle, even if adults can't figure what they are until the girls tell them.

The yard and the back porch are great play places if the weather is good. In the fall they partition out rooms from the fallen leaves. The tree could be the tower where Rapunzel lives or Sherwood Forest with Robin Hood and his Merry Men shooting arrows at the evil Prince John and the Sheriff of Nottingham.

For hours they are fine. When Cilla is sick Rose moves everything into their room. If the vaporizer is running, they pretend that a comb or a plastic toy case is an airplane and the steam is the fog of London and they are detectives looking for the bad guy. If Cilla is asleep or in the hospital Rose makes believe her sister is there, changing her voice and place to cover the absence.

Part Three

1970 through 1990

Chapter Twenty

In the summer of 1970 a new curate was sent to St. Maria Goretti's. He was fresh out of the seminary and the aromatic oil of ordination surrounded him, like an aura.

They were introduced to him as Father Joseph. The new people friendly Vatican II church called for first name familiarity for this crop of priests.

His below the collar wavy hair and preference for the new alb of ecru linen without the fuss of lace and embroidery helped him look like Jeffrey Hunter in <u>King of Kings</u>. To complete the portrait, his deep blue eyes were set off with dark circles and his ascetically thin body hinted at long nights spent in prayer and fasting.

He invited the small weekday congregations to join him at the altar, where they'd hold hands during the Our Father. He prayed the consecration slowly, with a hint of pain, or was it awe, or something close to ecstasy? The cup of sacred wine, the blood of Christ, was handed one to another after he broke the bread with his long artist fingers reaching out through the extended sleeves of his tunic.

The handful that attended his early Masses found something in his presence almost familiar, but not quite. Something holy. Something sacred. Some wisp of memory, of ancient longing.

Whatever gifts of the Holy Spirit the pastor, Monsignor Dunleavy, was given, seemed to have collected dust over the decades since his ordination. He was not burdened with the post Vatican II call to open wide the windows of the church with fresh ideas, with a return to the Gospel and being Christ for one another.

His investment was in Holy Mother Church, Magistra, that stern matron with rules and standards of behavior that were always out of reach except for the truly exceptional. Magistra made sure the confessional lines were long on Saturday afternoon and the congregation approached the communion rail with fear and trembling in what passed for a state of grace. A perpetual nagging doubt as to one's standing with God made for some rigid and careful practitioners of the faith, exchanging observable behavior for an open and loving heart.

Monsignor Dunleavy favored the old set of vestments. He wore a black cassock and a lacy alb, something you might see on your grandmother's dining table. He tucked a grayish handkerchief in his sleeve, which he would pull out and loudly blow his nose into during the consecration, somehow managing such toilette while he kept his thumb and forefinger pinched in the proper liturgical posture.

When he distributed communion it was difficult not to notice the crepe skin and moles dotting the back of his hands. His nails were a tad too long and curved slightly over the top of his fingers. You had to put out of mind that he recently emptied the contents of his nose into his shabby hanky, hoping that the holiness of the consecration wiped away any bacteria.

He had a favorite sermon that he would somehow manage to bring up nearly every Sunday: the danger all the young people were in surrounded by the temptations of this decadent age.

Chapter Twenty-One

April 1972

"Wosey, Wosey!! I haf to tell you somfin'!!"

"Okay Cilla, what is it?" Rose has grown tired of Cilla's demands on her time and attention. She knows she's pushing her away, but she figures it's for her own good. She needs friends her own age and Cilla very definitely does not fit in with Rose's friends.

Rose needs some space. She wants to be normal, not the girl with the sickly sister, and 'oh what a nice girl she is always protecting Cilla'. Rose just wants to play with makeup and be able to go to the middle school dances and meet boys like her friends are doing. She doesn't want to babysit her prickly little sister any more.

They share a room, of course. Cilla has been home in bed with a cough and a cold for a few days, but there's nothing new with that. She seems to get a cold every six weeks or so and their mother, looking more and more tired, has the routine of the medicines and humidifier down after more than eleven years of constant practice.

"Wosey!" She still can't say the R correctly. Rose rolls her eyes impatiently.

"What is it Cilla?"

"Wosey, 'member when we played at Grandma's in those pretty dresses? And the tea parties? Wasn't that fun, Wosey?"

Rose is in a hurry to get to school, but she looks over at her sister and Cilla seems even smaller than usual. Something moves in Rose so she gives Cilla her attention.

"Yes, Cilla, that was lots of fun. A long time ago. Now we're big and we'll do other things."

"Wosey, I'm going to always play wif you at grandma's, always."

She coughs again and Rose yells down the stairs. "Mom, Cilla's coughing a whole lot."

"Coming, Cilla." Their mother's voice is tired, worn out. "Rose, you'd better get going."

After she checks her peppermint lip gloss in her mirror, she goes over to Cilla's bed and rubs her dark curls. Her head is hot.

"Cilla, I'm going to tell Mom you have a fever."

"Okay, Wosey—Wosey—I'll see you later and maybe we can play together."

"Sure, Cilla." she says to her very little sister, but she's thinking of how she can get out of it. There is a basketball game this afternoon and she and Sue are going to watch the boys play.

Chapter Twenty-Two

MAUREEN FINISHES HER COFFEE as Rose leaves for school. She hears Cilla coughing, but she's been pretty good lately. She didn't send her to school this morning because last night she started with the coughing, again. But, she's become a little more independent.

Maureen is exhausted. Even though she was able to sleep last night, it feels as if her sleep account for the last eleven years is past due. She pours another cup.

She stands at the bottom of the stairs to listen. Quiet. She pictures Cilla asleep. She looks so little when she's asleep. So peaceful. And pretty. Like a doll. If only she would sleep more, Maureen thinks, I wouldn't be so exhausted and crabby.

She tip-toes up the stairs and just peeks in at the door. All quiet, just a little catch in her breathing from the congestion, but it sounds more like a web of mucus than a thick wall. She goes to get dressed, wondering if she will have time to take a shower. The thought of standing under the hot water to soften the kinks in her neck and shoulder is so inviting. Cilla is stronger now. They've been through so much and lately Cilla seems to be able to handle the coughing by herself. She's learning. She has to learn how to take care of herself, of course.

Maureen is grateful for the hot water beating on her back, her face, her head. Just to stand here with no one calling her name, no one demanding something from her. This is luxury. This is all the luxury anyone could want. The soap feels so good. Just stand here holding the bar in cupped hands, close to her face. So good. She's always telling Jimmy not to waste water with long showers, but she doesn't care about that now. Doesn't care if the water bill is outrageous. When the hot water turns cool, the luxury is over.

She gets dressed and looks in again on Cilla. She stands over her bed and sees that her forehead is damp. Cilla coughs now from a deep place in her lungs. Deeper than it was just before she stepped into the shower. Taking a pillow from Rose's bed, she lifts the sleeping child and lays her at a better angle. She's burning up. Maureen runs cold water over washcloths and hand towels and places them over her daughter's forehead, her neck and chest. She pulls back the blankets and wraps her ankles and feet in the compresses.

She's more comfortable now. Maureen lies down on Rose's bed, next to Cilla. She thinks about her hair being wet from the shower, but she has to lie down. The shower has made her drowsy and she has to close her eyes. She has to.

It's past noon when Maureen wakes to the sound of Cilla coughing, hacking. She pulls her little girl up, slapping her back like she's done so often, too often to count. Cilla opens her eyes and looks at her mother.

"Mommy?"

"Yes, dear?"

"Do you see it? It's so pretty and blue and cool."

Maureen opens her arms to get a better look at Cilla. Her lips are turning blue. She lifts her, runs her to the room across the hall and calls the ambulance. They know the address. They will be right over.

Jimmy is walking in, home from his classes at St. John's.

"Call your father, Jimmy."

The ambulance pulls up. Maureen is at the door, waiting. She has managed to wrap Cilla in a light blanket and continues to slap her back to keep the mucus from solidifying in her exhausted lungs.

Chapter Twenty-Three

"Banfry Law Firm, may I help you?"

"Jenny, tell my dad Cilla has been rushed to Mercy Hospital. He's got to hurry," Jimmy Banfry gives his urgent message to his father's secretary.

"Oh my God, Jimmy. Right away."

"Mr. B, Jimmy just called. He sounded awful. He said Cilla has been rushed to Mercy and you've got to get there fast."

Phil Banfry takes this latest emergency in with a sigh. He's almost used to these emergencies now. They've been through these countless times in the last eleven years. More like status quo than emergency.

He finishes some prep for a trial coming up next week. An hour after he gets the message he leaves for Mercy.

Chapter Twenty-Four

Rose and Sue hid their new, suck-your-gut-in-to zip-up jeans in their school bags along with stretch polyesters blouses so they didn't have to be at the game in their gray plaid jumpers and blue knee socks.

Tommy Masters bends down to adjust his sneaker, looking up at them sideways, raising one eyebrow, and just very slightly raising his head in their direction. They are cool until he starts running again, then they turn toward each other, giggling.

"Rose. Rose." She turns her head as her shoulder is gently touched. She's met by the deep set blue eyes of Fr. Joseph wearing his Roman collar and a blue cardigan. He came over from the rectory to the auditorium where the girls are watching the boys in their CYO play against St. Pius.

"Yes, Father?"

He speaks slowly, deliberately, holding her eyes with his so she will understand that this is important.

"Rose, there was a call to the rectory from your brother. Your family is looking for you."

"Did something happen, was there an accident—what happened!!?"

"Rose, it's your sister. Your family is at Mercy. They asked if someone could drive you there."

Sue pipes in, "Rose, my mom will. I'll call her now."

Fr. Joseph sits outside with them while they wait for Mrs. Rogan to drive up in her station wagon to take them to Mercy Hospital.

"Priscilla Banfry?!" Rose yells to the gray haired lady at the information desk.

"She's in Pediatrics, dear. Just take this elevator to the 4th floor. Room 445."

She races down the hallway and stops short at Room 445.

"I don't understand." Her mother's voice is thick, her throat filled with unshed tears.

The doctor places his hand on her shoulder and says, "Mrs. Banfry, her lungs were worn out. It's amazing she lasted this long, and that was due to your love and care."

Maureen Banfry sits in a chair next to Cilla's bed, holding her small hand, the IV's still attached, the monitors, mercifully, turned off.

Jimmy is standing at the end of the bed, fingers touching the foot, just to touch something. Phil comes in moments after Rose. He goes to stand next to his son.

Their eyes are filled. They sniffle and turn away when they need to wipe their nose. Rose stands just inside the room, watching. She cannot speak. She watches this scene as if she's not there; it's like something on a television screen.

No one notices her standing there until a nurse comes in and asks her to move, please. She takes a few steps to put her hand on her mother's back. She stiffens under Rose's fingers, pulls herself together and does not look at her daughter. She does not look at her husband or son. She stands up, holding her back straight, her face set, more stone than flesh.

Without turning her head she says. "Well, Rose, you won't have to complain about what a little pain your sister is anymore."

She turns and walks out. Rose stands next to her baby sister, her Cilla. Her hand is cold and her skin is turning blue.

"Come on dear. Its time to go." The nurse escorts them out of the room. Sue and her mother hug Rose in a big embrace.

She follows her silent father and brother to the car. Her mother is sitting in the front seat. They drive home, wordless.

Chapter Twenty-Five

Cilla's funeral draws a big crowd. Rose's entire seventh grade class is there, of course. And Cilla's fourth grade class. Along with neighbors, friends of her parents, relatives and her father's business associates. Her father is involved in local politics so men who think they are somebody, like the local assemblyman and state senator, put in an appearance. Monsignor Dunleavy presides with Fr. Joseph assisting.

"We gather this morning to say good-bye to one of God's little ones. Priscilla was with us only a short time, and much of that time was spent in suffering.

"Because of the love and devotion of her dear parents, little Priscilla was with us longer than any of the doctors predicted when she was born so small and weak, more than eleven years ago.

"Maureen and Phil Banfry have been exemplary parents to little Priscilla and to Priscilla's brother and sister. They have lived their lives emulating the example of the saints in their tender care of this chronically sick little girl…"

Monsignor drones on like this in his professional funeral Mass voice for several minutes more.

Rose sits in the front pew of the church next to Jimmy. Cilla's casket is covered in the white linen of the new Mass of the Resurrection that has replaced the Requiem Mass with its somber music and dark purples, black vestments and altar cloths.

The songs are all upbeat and full of hope. But Rose wants to cry. She leans her head against Jimmy's arm when he sniffles and wipes his nose with the sleeve of his jacket.

Their parents sit together at the end of the pew, within touching distance of Cilla. Her father is slumped a little, though every once in a while he makes himself sit up straight.

Their mother sits straight as if her dress were made of cardboard with a metal pole attached to her spine. She took a hat from the back of her closet for the funeral. Black felt with a webbed veil that she pulled down over eyes, not for any dramatic effect—no, to suggest that or even think that would be to misinterpret her altogether. The veil and the hat are something to hide behind to get her through this ordeal.

Monsignor's homily goes on with what wonderful parents they were; devoting all their time and love to this precious little angel that God gave them for a short time. He never actually says anything about Cilla. He keeps calling her Priscilla, which no one in the family has called her since she was a baby.

He never says anything about how every achievement was monumental; going from a tricycle to a small bicycle with training wheels; reading Dr. Seuss books; figuring out her arithmetic homework without help.

He doesn't say anything about her less than charming personality traits, like her directness and blunt honesty. She didn't lie. Rose didn't think she could lie. When she didn't like something or someone, she didn't hold back. The family thought they had to smooth things over and be charming to whoever she most recently offended.

Sitting through this canned homily that has nothing to do with her real little sister, Rose wants to scream, *Monsignor, you've got it all wrong. Cilla was a pain in the neck. She was rude. She was funny. But she was always my sister, my playmate, my pest who followed me around and just didn't fit in anywhere. Please stop talking! You didn't know her at all. You patted her on the head and said 'God Bless You' on Sundays.*

But, of course she doesn't. Her parents would be mortified. Besides, she doubts they are listening to a word he says. He keeps going in that priest voice of his, repeating a sermon he delivered too many times in his long career.

The pall bearers from the funeral home carry Cilla, and the family follows. Her mother does not take the arm that her father offers. Jimmy and Rose look at each other when they see that, their brows creased in confusion.

As they are getting into the limousine to go off to St. John's Cemetery, Monsignor Dunleavy leans to Rose's ear "Now, young lady, it's up to you to take care of your mother. Don't give her any trouble or cause her to worry. She's been through so much already. You need to be an extra good girl."

Rose nods her head and mumbles "yes, Father" and gets in next to Jimmy.

A luncheon was arranged at Trinity Restaurant on Jericho Turnpike after the cemetery. All the cousins and uncles and aunts are there, drinks in hand, eating sandwiches, catching up with the news of the latest addition to the family or who got into what college and yes, of course, we have to get together soon, not wait until there is another funeral.

What a shame, such a shame. The poor little thing. They always knew it was coming though. This kind of conversation buzzes throughout the restaurant.

Rose weaves in and out, getting hugs and kisses from aunts and uncles she hardly recognizes, wiping lipstick off her cheek every so often. Her dad is holding a Manhattan in his left hand so he can shake hands with all the well wishers with his right.

She sees Jimmy talking to the cousins who are college age like him. Cilla and Rose were the youngest cousins, so there is no one her age to talk to. She looks around for her mother. Doesn't see her. She asks several aunts if they have seen her mother and all she hears is *why no, dear, I haven't seen her.*

Grandma Meg rescues her from her search. She takes her arm and sits her down next to her in one of the booths. Meg asks a waiter to bring Rose a Coke and a sandwich.

"Rose, your mother asked the limo driver to take her home. She told your father to stay with you and Jimmy. She couldn't go through with this chatter. She needs to be alone for a little while. Are you okay, Rose?"

Rose shrugs her shoulders at her grandmother and leans into her. She breathes in the sweet scent of her powder. Next thing she knows, the restaurant is nearly empty. As she wakes she sees her father's brother, Uncle John. He drove in from Pennsylvania for the funeral. Car keys in hand, he's ready to take them home in his station wagon.

She hasn't touched her lunch and Meg hasn't moved since she wrapped her arm around her.

Chapter Twenty-Six

MAUREEN CANNOT GO TO the luncheon after Cilla's funeral. What is that? A party, a family re-union, a free lunch.

Just three days ago, when she woke up to the hacking cough of her little girl, Maureen knew this was different. This was more like those terrible coughs from when she was very little, but deeper, stronger. They'd had a reprieve of sorts, for more than a year now. Cilla had been going to school fairly regularly. She was in the fourth grade, a little older than her classmates, but she was so little, who would know? When she couldn't attend school, Maureen would help her keep up with the assignments the teachers had prepared at the beginning of the year. Maureen had the teacher's version of the texts and Cilla, the student's. She read ahead so she could explain the fractions and divisions and the history lessons so Cilla wouldn't be too far behind.

Coming out of the nap on that awful day, Maureen became the ferocious tiger mother. The tiger mother was so long in coming with this child. Tiger mother appeared rather quickly after Jimmy was born, and then when Rose was born. But for so long Maureen wondered where that fierce I-will-die-for-you love was with this littlest and weakest of her children. Oh, and that darkness that accompanied her since before Cilla was born. Was that the substitute fierceness? Was that what animal mothers felt when they left their weakest pup out to be eaten by predators? This made her shudder. The darkness that descended and ate at her soul was bad enough, but the terrible guilt of realization that she didn't love this child enough, and consequently could not give the love she had once felt so fiercely, so terribly, to Jimmy and Rose sent her deeper into an abyss that had no bottom.

But the tiger mother did appear. Slowly, peeking out in those moments of quiet, the rare moments at first when Cilla was so young, building with such tiny bits as she managed to grow, as she made it through another life threatening episode. Was that it? Was there some part of her that could not invest fully in this child because she knew that her weakness meant she could go at any time? That realization horrified Maureen. It was so uncivilized, so primal. And she knew it was true. It was easy to invest in Jimmy and Rose. They were perfect, healthy, competent children. She could project her hopes and dreams onto them and they would not disappoint. But what hopes and dreams could she project on this unfinished child, this child who came too early and had weak lungs and a weak heart? This emptiness in her own heart made her shudder to realize that she was defective as a mother. She was the weak one who didn't have enough room to take this needy child deeply into her heart.

So she worked on it. She set about to fall in love with this little girl who demanded so much and seemed to give so little. All right, she decided. Whatever she gives, whatever smile or thank you or look of gratitude this little girl gives, I will take and I will nurture. I will make myself remember when I am exhausted that those little gifts matter. They mean more than they would seem to a more cynical heart. They mean everything, everything.

And they did mean everything. She moved from not loving to total devotion. Now there was little space to love Jimmy and Rose and Phil. They were the strong ones. They had to live on whatever love she had given them to this point. It had to be enough. They could get love from other people. They were lovable. She decided that Priscilla was only lovable to her. She decided that no one else could love her, that this weak and crabby little girl was her burden to bear, and hers alone.

And now she is gone. She had poured all her love and devotion, though late in coming, into this child, and now she is gone. She had gotten out of the habit of loving anyone else and all that remained once that tiny child was placed in the ground was dark emptiness.

And so the anger that she felt toward God since she was pregnant with Cilla (*which God? The imperious judge who keeps close account of all the little black marks next to your name? Or this new God they are promoting—the all loving, warm and fuzzy Jesus God who picks you up and carries you like a little lost lamb and says everything is all right, everything's fine?*) rises up and becomes her only voice. Alone in the house while the others have lunch and drink and shake hands and catch up with cousins and aunts and uncles who have done nothing, nothing to relieve her burden when this little girl was alive— she screams NO!! She cannot, will not, trust God again.

Chapter Twenty-Seven

Jenny Tagliani and David Cellio, Phil's young assistant, sit together at Cilla's funeral, along with Jenny's parents and several neighbors. It breaks her heart to see her boss so devastated. Stunned. Mrs. Banfry looks like she will crumble into a million pieces if anyone touches her or even stands too close.

Jenny expected her to be weeping and weak kneed, hanging on to her husband and gathering strength from him. She is sure that's what she would do if it were her child who died and her husband was as strong and capable as Mr. B.

She feels so bad for Jimmy and Rose, watching them process up the aisle behind their parents, following little Cilla's white casket, covered over in the white linens. They look like they were hit so hard by this, their faces slack in grief. Rose holds on to Jimmy's arm as they make their way to the front pews.

David drives Jenny to work after the funeral Mass. They have to keep the office running and the phone answered. It is a silent ride.

~~~~

"Hiyaa, uh, 's Mista Banfry in?"

Jenny looks up from her typing to see Joey Checkers leaning into the office. He is wearing one of his signature plaid jackets; today a loud green number with silver threads woven into the pattern. His tan sans-a-belt pants strain at the belly. She flashes a smirk thinking he should have updated his wardrobe thirty pounds ago.

"Mr. Banfry is out for a few days. Family funeral."

"Yea-ah, dat's why I'm here. I got this condolence card for him. You make sure he gets it, huh, sweetheart."

Jenny sighs at this clown. Her father put in his time handing out pamphlets and addressing envelopes for primaries and general elections at the local Democratic Club which earned her this job as Phil Banfry's secretary at his Queens Boulevard law office.

Jenny could have interviewed at any of the big companies in the city when she graduated from Dominican Commercial, but her father convinced her that this would lead to opportunities down the line.

She takes the bus and subway in from Rosedale, more than an hour most mornings. Sometimes she wonders if Mr. Banfry will ever offer to pick her up or drop her off since they live so close, but that might be uncomfortable. Besides, most evenings he has a dinner or meeting to attend.

"And, uh, sweetheart, it's for his eyes only. Understand?"

The gum-bah in polyester hands her a large manila envelope well sealed with packing tape. Jenny can feel the outline of an oversized Mass card inside, but it's thicker than the others that have been arriving for the last few days.

"Sure, I'll put it with his personal, private mail collection, okay?" She wishes she were chewing gum so she could pop it right now.

"T'anks a lot sweetheart. I'll be seeing you aroun.'" A wink and a thumbs up, and he's gone.

Jenny takes the magnetized key from under her boss's desk drawer, unlocks the file cabinet, places the stuffed envelope in the file marked P. She leaves a note on his desk: *Mr. B, Mass card in file drawer under P.* That should do it. Jenny looks at her watch. It's 11:30. David, who is due to graduate from St. John's Law school in June, is working in his small office, door closed. She grabs her bag; lunch comes early today.

Chapter Twenty-Eight

Monday of the new week, the week after his daughter died, the week after he looked at her pale face on a white satin pillow, small body in her First Communion dress to look like an angel, he supposes.

Why do people always say when a child dies that she was an angel, always delightful, patient in suffering, prematurely holy, sure to be with the saints now?

His Priscilla was not a darling sweetheart of a little girl; she was irritable, cried too much, threw things when she got mad and demanded everyone's attention, day and night. She was exhausting. He was exhausted.

This morning he kissed Maureen on the forehead where she lay in bed, back turned to him, not even a sound in acknowledgment that he existed and was now leaving for work.

She's been like this since they came home from the funeral lunch at Trinity's. The house dark, blinds drawn, only the sound of the clock on the piano to mark the silent moments.

Jimmy changed out of funeral clothes into jeans and a sweatshirt and left, walking off in silence, hands in his pockets. Rose went up to her room, closed the door, got into pajamas and pulled the blankets up over her head.

Phil stood in the living room then went to the kitchen and got a bottle of Jameson's from the cabinet over the refrigerator, and poured himself a double. He sat in his chair while the sun lowered in the sky, casting long shadows through the blinds, onto the empty couch and coffee table, across the silent television screen.

This is a new week and there is work to be done, calls returned, cases handled. No more middle of the night emergency room visits with a weak and sallow daughter. No more starting the workday after returning from the hospital just long enough to shower and have a cup of coffee.

No, now maybe there was normal to look forward to, though he can't remember what normal feels like. Phil sits in his Buick behind his office building, car in park, but still running. Just another minute. Okay. Go up now. Go up and start the week.

~~~~

Jenny's left shoulder holds the phone to her ear as she jots a message with her right hand. Another condolence call. He nods to her as he opens his office door. A minute later, Jenny walks in with a stack of messages from the week he was away.

"Oh, before I forget, that polyester guy with the belly—Joey Checkers—he left a big Mass card and told me it was for your eyes only. It's in the file drawer under P."

"P?"

"P for plaid, or polyester, or pest or punk..."

"Very funny, Jenny."

Jenny is almost the same age as Phil's son. She's too smart for this job and someday he'll tell her, but she's good at what she does and he needs her.

Young and full of life and possibilities. With a great smile to greet clients. She needs to get out of here soon, go to Queens College, take some night courses. When he was in his early twenties, he thought life would look quite different in middle age than it does now. But Jenny's smile almost makes him forget some of his troubles.

Phil thumbs through the messages. Most he can just ignore, some he has to answer.

He takes the file drawer key and goes to P. He recognizes the handwriting at once. Panic spreads out from his heart, stifling his lungs, tightening his gut, his arms and legs tingling with dread. He feels the outside of the package for the thick rectangles he knows is cash. How much? He doesn't want to know.

Charlie Gagliardi sent it over with his brother-in-law Joey. The Planning Commission meeting is Thursday. Gagliardi and his people want a variance to open a nightclub/bar on Northern Boulevard on a block that's zoned for small stores.

The community has organized a protest to forbid the bar on this block. They say there are too many bars, and a nightclub would bring down the neighborhood. It would turn the area into a neon mess with crime, drugs, fights.

Phil had met with the citizens committee and indicated that he would side with them—though he was careful not to promise anything. He had learned the subtleties of polita-speak years ago—be vague, smile, change the subject, shake hands—and choose your words carefully.

At 4 o'clock Phil tackles another file. He's in no hurry for the day to be over. He doesn't want to think about how Maureen spent her day. Just for a second he lets himself wonder if she got dressed today, or even got out of bed. He pushes the thought away. There's no meeting tonight, so he'll have to go home eventually.

Jenny buzzes him at 4:11. "Mr. B, Rose is on the phone—she says it's an emergency."

"Rose?"

"Dad, I came in from school and found Mom on the couch, passed out. I called Dr. Miller and he came right over. She's in Mercy. In the psych ward." Rose is crying into the phone.

"Jimmy's not home. You're not home. Dr. Miller told me to wait for you. He called an ambulance and went over to check her in himself."

Phil holds the phone, breathes slowly. His fist tightens on the desk, jaw clenched. He feels the red of anger boil up to his forehead. Great. Another scene with an ambulance flashing in front of his house. Neighbors gossiping. Just what he needs.

"Okay, Rose. I'll be home in a little while. Stay calm. Everything will be all right."

Phil gathers up all the condolence cards into his briefcase, patting the Joey Checkers delivery twice. Then he heads out to deal with Maureen. Good thing Rose and Jimmy can take care of themselves. Phil's all out. Of tears, of grief, of sympathy.

"Jenny, can you hold the fort down tomorrow? Maureen's not well. I'll call."

Jenny looks at him steadily. "Sure, Mr. B. Anything you need."

Chapter Twenty-Nine

Phil drives straight to Mercy Hospital. The psych ward is a separate building from the main hospital, the place where Cilla died just days ago. The security guard checks his I. D. , then buzzes him through the heavy metal doors.

Maureen is down the end of a long hallway. He stops outside her room to take a few deep breaths.

She is in a hospital gown, soft with countless washings. Her back is to him and he looks at her bony spine beneath the loosely tied gown. She had such a lovely back long ago, strong and supple. They had danced, his hand on her spine, directing her with fingers, like playing the flute. They moved so beautifully together. She was almost regal. Proud, proper, with just a hint of passion under those blue eyes.

Her shoulders are curved forward now, her hair a tangle. She is folding, unfolding, refolding a corner of her bed sheet, while looking blankly at the pale pink wall, tethered to an IV.

"Maureen. I'm here."

She doesn't look at him.

He sits in the chair in the corner of the small room. The drip, drip, drip of the IV has all his attention. The sun is setting and throwing long shadows across the bed, the tiles, his wife. He should get up, talk to a doctor, a nurse, an orderly. Someone. But what can they tell him? She's depressed? Despondent? Worn out? He knows these things.

When a nurse comes in and gently pushes Maureen down and covers her with a warm blanket, he is stirred enough to leave. There are papers he has to sign, talk to the doctor on the floor. He nods his head and scribbles his name, vaguely trusting that what they are telling him is good for Maureen.

When he gets home, Rose has fallen asleep with the television on. There is no food in the house. He wakes his daughter and they go to eat at the diner down the road.

Thursday comes. Jenny reminds him of the zoning meeting about the proposed nightclub on Northern Boulevard. He wants to bow out, plead family emergency, but the practical part of him knows people will only put up with so much family interference before they look to someone else for leadership.

The bills have arrived for Cilla's funeral. "No, rush, Mr. Banfry, no rush" they said so kindly when he made the arrangements. In small print at the bottom of the bill, it reads, account due within thirty days of notice.

The doctors think that Maureen will need some long term care, but that would have to be at another facility. There's a good one on the eastern end of Long Island. Insurance covers eighty percent. What's twenty percent of long term care and how long is long term?

He got a reminder call from Gagliardi's people this morning. "See you tonight". Phil's headache threatens to turn into a migraine. He downs some Excedrin with his coffee.

What will he say tonight? That he met with the developers and they promise to have an understated appearance, that they will contribute to the local park, pave over the cracked basketball court and put up some new hoops?

That, he believes now, he will tell them, after meeting and negotiating, that this developer will be good for the community, help restore it? There have been no such meetings. But he's in this far. What are a few more un-truths? Phil thinks those concessions are an easy bet. Some concrete and basketball hoops are pocket change to Gagliardi.

Chapter Thirty

David Cellio is an eager young man, getting ready to graduate, then take the bar exam in July. He works days in Phil Banfry's office and after graduation he'll take a bar prep course at Queens College in the evenings. When he's not busy with work he's reviewing test material. His mother is considerate enough to prepare a bag lunch for him so he doesn't have to spend time or money getting his own. He usually eats at his desk with study material fanned out in front of him.

He's not entirely caught up in studying, though. He looks at Jenny, noting her deep brown eyes and long dark hair.

"Hi, Jenny. Just wondering if you'd like to have lunch." He asks this with a catch in his voice, a little earnestly for such a simple request that co-workers share their lunch hour.

Jenny has just emerged from Phil's office, cheeks flushed, eyes filled with warmth. David takes this as a good sign that she might be interested in him and asks his question.

"Sure, David, sometime. I have to get this motion typed up." She's a bit distracted, holding the bundle of papers close to her chest.

April gives way to May, then June. Mrs. Banfry is away somewhere on the eastern end of Long Island. It breaks Jenny's heart to see Mr. B look so lost, like the life has gone out of him.

She knocks on his office door.

"Excuse me, Mr. B, but what should I do with this invitation to the Catholic Lawyers Guild dinner at Anton's? Should I send your regrets, or what?"

"What's the date, Jenny?"

"Next week, Thursday evening."

"I'll think about it. Let you know in a bit. Oh, and thanks Jenny for handling everything."

"Sure, Mr. B" She doesn't add "I'd do anything for you." Not aloud, anyway.

~~~

Phil Banfry's aftershave reminds her of the sweet smokiness of brandy. Last Christmas her parents opened a bottle. A long neck opening into a palm sized bowl with diamond cuts. Before he opened it, her father held the bottle up to the light of the dining room chandelier.

"Look at that refraction, Jenny. Like fiery sapphires, dancing in the sun." He poured the red-tinged amber liqueur into crystal wine glasses reserved for the holidays.

"Don't just drink it down, now. Hold the bowl of the glass, swirl it a bit, inhale."

Jenny did as her father suggested.

"Inhale, inhale, let the amber magic fill your nose, warm your lungs. Then, take a sip. Just a sip."

She figures he's about 5'10". His full head of light brown hair has just a touch of silver on the sideburns, over the ears and a spray of silver through the crown. Mr. B is mature and experienced; in his prime. He's in his early fifties, but his abdomen is tight. He stands tall and greets everyone with a firm, warm handshake. When he goes over a brief he positions himself behind her chair and folds over her. With his warm arm not quite touching her, he points out the paragraphs that need re-wording. She has to remind herself to pay attention.

~~~

A half hour after Phil took the message about the dinner from Jenny, he emerges from his office.

"Jenny, see if David wants to attend. I think I'll go. Yeah, I'll go. And Jenny, RSVP for three. That is, if you'd like to attend too. You should mingle and meet some people. After all, you keep the business going."

That is the liveliest she has seen her boss in weeks. *Dinner at Anton's, what do I wear?*

Chapter Thirty-One

The following Thursday Jenny arrives at work in a simple black dress. Jenny's mother insisted that she wear her pearl necklace for the dinner. She tucks it under the front of her dress, because it's just too fancy for a day at work. Later she will display it over the dress. She has her dangly cultured pearl earrings from the little boutique in Green Acres Mall. Those will stay in her purse until this evening. Them and the small bottle of White Shoulders perfume she borrowed from her mother. Her good shoes are in a bag, along with a little multi-colored wrap to dress up the outfit for dinner.

They drive over together, Jenny and Mr. B, that is. David takes his own car.

David wears a crisp white shirt, freshly ironed this morning and the sharp pinstripe tie his mother handed to him along with his lunch. "Remember, David, shake hands, look people in the eye and you'll do fine."

He was hoping to get some alone time with Jenny. Well, if not alone, at least to sit next to her at Anton's. But Jenny sits next to Mr. Banfry's left and David to his right.

Men and women come over to Phil Banfry's table, extending condolences and pats on the back. His recent set of hardships makes him the main attraction at this dinner. David turns in his seat to listen to tonight's speaker, but he can't concentrate. Jenny hasn't said more than three words to him after they found their table. When the speech is over, David leaves. He's shaken enough hands tonight.

David has been waiting for Mr. Banfry to say something about taking him on as an associate after the Bar Exam. With nothing specific to point to, David finds he has a growing dislike for his boss. He tries to push such feelings aside because Mr. Banfry has been through so much lately. But that touch of anger keeps creeping in. He's pretty sure that if Jenny paid him a little more attention his annoyance at Phil Banfry would disintegrate. Despite his optimism, there's not much hope on that front.

The dinner is winding down. When the lights go up, Jenny realizes David has left. So, Mr. B is Jenny's ride home. Whenever her tumbler of Brandy Alexander was getting empty, a new one took its place. Three? Four?

When she stands up she's woozy. Mr. B places his hand in the small of her back and guides her out to his car. Jenny slides over on the bench seat and drops her head on his shoulder. He wraps his right arm around her. No words. When he pulls into the parking lot of the Floral Park Inn, all he says is "I'll be right back." Jenny nods. Her whole body tingles and is strangely alive even as the brandy works it way through her, loosening her limbs.

In a few minutes he comes back, takes her hand and leads her to a room.

Phil starts sending David out more and more to file motions at the Courthouse. Sends him to interview clients at the clients' place of business instead of here in the office.

Chapter Thirty-Two

When Cilla died in 1972 Jimmy had another year of college. He majored in Social Work. Once Cilla died, something in him shifted. He was released from being a dutiful son and brother. All the affection he directed toward his family turned sour. The little girl who smiled at his attempts at being funny and let him know when he wasn't, was gone. When she complained, he appreciated her honesty. She didn't try to be a trooper; she called it like she saw it, like she felt it. She was tired of being the sickly one, the delicate one who couldn't keep up with the other kids. She moaned when she hurt, she was nasty when she felt rotten. Not a little saint in training. She had no patience for the advice to 'offer it up '. Offer it up to what, to who? No, Cilla, irritable, crabby Cilla, didn't try to be holy or self-sacrificing. She didn't pretend. She didn't smile when she felt like lashing out. She didn't bury her anger; she let it out, often loudly and insistently. Cilla was Cilla. Right there, out in the open, nothing hidden or mysterious.

Once exams were over a month after the funeral, he left. Filled a few shopping bags with his stuff, got on the bus, moved in with Kathy. No good-byes. No explanations. He did wonder, though, when they would notice he wasn't there.

Jimmy and Kathy moved into a drafty apartment in the attic of an old house off Union Turnpike. They had a mattress on the floor and some thrift store kitchen utensils. He worked in a record store and she worked as a waitress in a twenty-four hour diner. It was better than living in the tomb that his parent's place had become.

Chapter Thirty-Three

Summer 1972

SHORTS, SHIRTS, SANDALS, SNEAKERS, a skirt. Into a small canvas bag Rose collects her summer wardrobe. She'll be spending the summer at Grandma's. Her mother is away and they don't know for how long.

Rose and her grandmother have an unspoken bond. Meg is quiet, peaceful. A reserve of wisdom and love that Rose can rest in. Her house is cooler in the hot summer days than her parent's house. Maybe it's all the old trees arboring the neighborhood.

There's more space in Meg's house for shaded breezes to flow through. Right up the street is the entrance to Forest Park. Rose spends many mornings walking the winding paths through the old trees. When she arrives at the carousel she stops and leans on the black enameled iron fence.

The merry-go-round is still. No noisy children, no tinny piped music. She leans on the fence and smiles.

Not so many years ago she and Jimmy and Cilla rode those horses. Jimmy, making sure Cilla didn't fall off her valiant steed, braced his arm around his sister's back. They had a running story.

Jimmy was Little John, Cilla was Maid Marian and Rose was the Sheriff of Nottingham chasing them through Sherwood Forest.

Rose practiced her evil laugh "HaHaHa!! I have you now! Robin Hood won't save you this time!" Cilla then giddy-upped giddy-upped her painted pony to safety until the calliope faded and the round and round ride came to a stop. "Again! Again!" Cilla would beg.

Jimmy fished out the ticket money from his pocket and they would once again ride through Sherwood Forest looking for the safe protection of Robin Hood.

Her bedroom at her Grandmother's house is pale blue with white molding. Some mornings she places a pillow on the windowsill and enjoys the breeze that flutters the lacy curtains and tickles her face. The abundant green leaves of the big oak refract the sunlight. Her breath follows the *shh shh* of the leaves and the birds singing on the limbs to a rhythm of peace. She falls into a lovely sleep.

The box of hats and scarves, gloves, old handbags and costume jewelry that she and Cilla draped over themselves is still here. The little girls would take the spread from the bed, pull one end over the bedposts and the other end over a chair, and have their own little land.

They brought dolls and old spoons and chipped ceramic tea cups from Grandma's kitchen and played forever. Their father would often sneak in and declare in his best giant voice "Who are these giggly girls in my kingdom?" and Cilla and Rose would giggle more behind their hands and giant Dad stood over their camp while they whispered *shhshh* until their father fell to the floor and climbed in with them. They jumped on his chest and tickled silly Dad until Mom called up the stairs "Phil, that's enough. We don't want Cilla to start coughing."

The door at the end of the hallway, next to the back stairway, has a skeleton key, tarnished, in the lock. She has never gone up those stairs. No one told her not to, but that little lock looks like a warning.

One afternoon in early July Grandma Meg asks her to go up and get a fan. Fourth of July weekend is especially hot this year, and the fan set up in the living room is not enough.

"In the attic?"

"Yes, dear. I think it's under the eaves in the front of the house. It's probably quite dusty up there, so don't breathe too deeply."

The stairs are plain wood, not stained and varnished as in the rest of the house. Light comes in through the fan vents at both ends of the house and the skylight. Children are playing outside and cars are passing down Forest Parkway; the noises that come through are *whoopedwhoopedwhooped* in a comical caricature of themselves.

Here is a treasure trove of history in this dusty room. Sheets cover armchairs, a desk, an old bureau. There is a sled, the kind she's seen in movies, that must have been her father's and uncle's. Boxes of old clothes that weren't supposed to find their resting place here, but did because they were forgotten or outgrown when it was time to get the next season's garments down. A desk with an old typewriter covered in a towel is the best find. Black enamel keys with gold lettering, the keys are stiff with disuse, but the indentation where fingers were to be placed, round with a band of metal on each one, feels so much more important than the plastic electric typewriter her parents have.

"Rose, did you find the fan?" Grandma calls from the kitchen.

"Coming."

She found the fan, an old metal thing with blades that look treacherous, right where her grandmother told her it would be.

"Gra'ma, would it be all right if I read my books in the attic. It's so cool, I mean, it's not cool, but ya know, it's so cool."

Meg smiles and says, "all right, but not in the heat of the afternoon. Mornings would be best up there. I don't want to have to tell your father that I cooked you in the attic."

She gets her summer reading books from the big library across the street. *Johnny Tremain*; *A Girl with a Pen*—a biography of Charlotte Bronte; Shirley Jackson's *The Lottery*; an annotated version of *The Merchant of Venice* and for extra credit, *Jane Eyre* to read in the attic.

Dad comes on Sundays for dinner. Sometimes Grandma cooks for them, sometimes they go out. One afternoon, Rose's fathers asks his mother "How's Rose? She seems to be doing all right. She seems almost happy. I thought she would be devastated, I thought Rose and Cilla were close. Maybe Maureen was right."

"Don't be daft Phil. She's working hard at being all right. She spends all her time alone, reading or sleeping. I get her up to go to the grocery store with me. She's trying so hard to be perfect. One day she'll crash, you'll see."

"I'm just glad she's not crashing now. Maureen is more than I can handle."

Chapter Thirty-Four

The first week that Rose is at her grandmother's, she winds her clock every night and sets the alarm to 5:30. That gives her enough time to throw on some clothes and walk over to St. Thomas for six o'clock Mass. Morning Mass is quick, no more than thirty minutes.

The church is cool, the marble pillars chilled overnight, the light dim as the sunlight slowly makes its way through the reds and blues and greens of the saints in the windows. It is an extension of early morning sleep, a gentle awakening from one dream to the next.

The second week Rose has a little more trouble getting up at five-thirty, so she bargains with herself, if she runs, she can wait until 5:40.

By week three she sleeps through her alarm. Grandma tip-toes in to stop the bell.

At eight thirty, quarter to nine, then nine, she makes herself get out of bed. She doesn't want to be lazy. She wants to get all her reading list finished, not waste the summer.

White bread, toasted to a golden brown, with real butter and strawberry preserves and a glass of milk for breakfast. There's a note on the kitchen table from her grandmother: "Gone to the Avenue. Be back soon." Grandma's wire pull cart is not on its hook at the back door, so Rose knows she is grocery shopping.

She brings *Johnny Tremain* to the attic. There is an area rug rolled up behind the chairs covered in yellowed sheets. She unfurls it, revealing a floral patterned wool rug. There are some patches of wear on it, but its still pretty.

Then she takes an armchair, shakes the dust off the sheet and positions it on the rug, in the spot the sun shines best into the attic. Perfect reading room. She opens *Johnny Tremain*, starts the first chapter, then falls asleep. When the red hardback book falls to the floor, she startles awake. She goes downstairs to help Gra'ma when she hears the kitchen door.

While putting away the cereal in the pantry, Rose sees a flashlight. A heavy black metal thing. Pushes up the switch. It lights.

Sometime in the dark of night, Rose quietly makes her way down the back staircase, careful to avoid the planks that creak. She retrieves the flashlight, goes upstairs. At the landing she lifts the old brass knob, so quietly, *please be quiet*, turns it and steps on the bare wood step. Round beam of light emanating to a cone shows her the steps. One, two, three...thirteen.

She's a spy, an undercover agent on an important mission from the government. If she doesn't succeed, countless lives will be lost and liberty gone. She must be quiet. Tiny little steps. Phew! She makes it. All the way to the chair, uh, the boat in the middle of the lake.

Rose feels at home in this almost spooky atmosphere. It's meant for a make-believe world. All these items out of time and place gathered under the dust, years of untold stories in them.

She sits cross-legged in the chair. Closing her eyes just a little and there's Cilla, on the floor, waiting for her sister. Rose smiles at her. Won't they have fun up here?

The real Cilla would never be allowed in this dusty place, but Rose's Cilla is. Her Cilla is strong and funny and adds to the stories that Rose starts. She is not pale and cranky; she doesn't wait for Rose to make up all their games. And Jimmy is there too. The Jimmy who was on the carousel; the Jimmy who was their big brother making sure the two little girls were safe. The Jimmy who is funny and laughs and tells corny jokes. That Jimmy.

"Cilla, what's it like?"

"Wosey, it's beautiful. The carousel is here and I don't haf to have tickets to ride it."

"That's great, Cilla."

"Are you sad?"

"Guess so. I mean, I miss you. I'm living here now, with Gra'ma. Everything is different now, Cill. Mom had to go away. Jimmy moved in with Kathy, Dad's always at work. Glad I have Gra'ma."

"Gra'ma's nice."

"Yup."

"I want to play with you."

"I do too, Cill. I'm sorry I didn't play with you more."

"Wosey, we can still play you know."

"Yeah?"

"Here, in Gram'a's house. Like we used to."

"Sure Cill. I'll get the box of scarves and hats and junk."

"Will you read to me?"

"I only have these books I have to read for school—no pictures."

"That's okay. I like when you read to me."

So Rose reads to Cilla; the adventures of Johnny Tremain, brave boy in the American Revolution. Then Rose reads *The Lottery*. She decides to skip the ending and hopes Cilla doesn't notice. She thinks *Jane Eyre* and *The Merchant of Venice* are books she will have to read to herself—so many words, she'd never get through it if she had to read them out loud.

Chapter Thirty-Five

AT THE END OF July, Jenny knocks on Phil's door and enters. She closes the door quietly.

"Mr. B— Phil—I'm late."

Phil Banfry looks up over his glasses at Jenny.

"Late?"

As he looks at her, she begins to cry.

"What are we going to do?"

"Maybe it's just nerves, Jenny. Maybe you're just a little off schedule."

"I've been sick in the mornings for a week now." She cannot hold back any longer. She slumps into the chair in front of Phil's desk.

"Okay, Jenny. It'll be okay." Phil thinks of the abortion bill New York State passed so recently. It was the subject of the speech at the Catholic Lawyers Guild. *Is that an option?* He looks at Jenny. So beautiful, so soft. And pregnant.

He doesn't go over to comfort her. He remains behind his desk. *Shit. How will this look? Can't hide a pregnancy forever.*

She sits in that chair. No arm around her shoulder now. She fears she's on her own. She looks up. He doesn't look back. He's swung his seat around to face the windows. After a few minutes she dries her eyes, breathes deeply. Leaves his office.

"Hey, Jenny, you okay?"

David stands in front of Jenny's desk and looks at her with tender concern.

"Oh, David, yeah, just heard that a great uncle died. I didn't know him very well, but, well you know, sometimes life seems so fragile."

"Sure is. We have to make the most of it, don't we?"

"We sure do. David. How 'bout sharing a sandwich today? I know it's early, but I don't think he'd mind if we took an early lunch."

Jenny knows she has to work quickly. Pregnancy seems to have made her more clever, calculating, desperate. She touches David's hand at lunch and leans into his arm on the walk back to the office. He hasn't said anything about a date. She has to move this along.

"Hey, David, I'd was thinking of seeing *The Heartbreak Kid* this weekend. It's a Neil Simon, and he's usually funny. Don't you think that sounds good? Charles Grodin and Cybill Shepherd are in it."

"Oh, yeah. I hadn't thought of movies much lately. Bar exam is in two weeks."

"A little break is probably good for your brain, or so I've heard."

"Okay, then. So, you and me, Saturday for *The Heartbreak Kid*?

"That's a great idea." She gives his arm a little squeeze.

Jenny Cellio. She tries it out in her head a few times. Sounds kind of nice. Like a pasta dish or a dance. *Jennicellio!* Sure. She'll make it happen.

David is surprised at the affection Jenny pours on him. She holds his hand all through the movie, slipping her arm through his and snuggling close, the side of her breast against his biceps. He's getting more confident of a good night kiss. When she moves in close to him in his car after the movie and before they start back to her parent's house, he is surprised and a little confused by the hunger of her mouth over his. She's working her fingers around his neck, his ear, his throat. He puts his confusion aside. He's twenty-six years old and he hasn't had a date in two years.

"Let's go somewhere." She whispers into his ear.

"Uh, huh."

There is a park a few miles down in Baldwin, near the water. A full coverage of thick summer leaves on some mature trees becomes their little love nest.

Chapter Thirty-Six

JENNY'S PARENTS ARE GOOD at throwing a party together quickly. Family gatherings are a way of life for them. All the aunts will bring a few dishes for the buffet, an uncle or two will bring in a few cases of wine and her grandmother will bake a large cake.

Monsignor Dunleavy lectures them, of course, in their Pre-Cana meetings. *No way to start a marriage, with such a sin on your souls. Pre-marital sex is forbidden and I know both of you know that. Think of the disgrace you have brought upon your families.* Jenny is smart enough to look appropriately chagrined. She has to get through this part so they can get married. Her cousin's dress needs to fit.

The last weekend in September comes quickly. Jenny's mother helps her get dressed, neither of them meeting each other's eyes much lately.

"You don't look like the happiest bride I've ever seen."

"I'm happy, Ma."

"Try a little smile, then. This is all quick for David too. You're not the first couple in history to have this kind of a difficult start. In time, it will work out."

"I know, Ma." Jenny manages a smile.

"Do you love him, Jenny?"

"Yeah, I love him." Which him she doesn't need to tell her mother.

"He's a nice young man, Jenny. Be good to him." She pats her daughter on the back and leaves her questions alone.

Jenny is David's good luck charm. He used to think that all the best things in life happened to other people. Other guys got the girl, the good job, the family. Before he met Jenny he didn't dare hope that the woman in his life would be so beautiful. He was king of the world.

Soon after he and Jenny announced their engagement at the office, an associate of Phil's offered David a job in his firm over the Nassau border in Mineola. He receives a wonderful starting salary, enough so he and his new little family can afford an apartment and Jenny can leave her job.

Chapter Thirty-Seven

October 1972

Monsignor Dunleavy meets Rose after school and summons her to his office. He pushes his black framed glasses into place on the bridge of his nose. His index fingernail is long and ridged. As he adjusts his glasses, a flake of dandruff falls onto his black shirt.

"Rose, how would like to get some office experience on Friday afternoons after school?"

"Well, uh, I'm 13 you know, Father."

He laughs. "I don't mean to go off to some big office in the city, Rose. I mean, how would you like to work in the Rectory answering the door and phones? When you're not busy you can get some studying done."

"Just on Fridays, Father? 'Til what time?"

"From 3 until 6 o'clock. Then you'll be free to have dinner with your family."

"I'd have to ask my parents…"

He holds up his hand, then places it on her shoulder. She holds back a shudder. "Don't worry about that Rose, I've already discussed it with your parents and they think it will be wonderful for you."

"Oh, they didn't say anything to me."

"I asked them not to until I had worked out a schedule with the Parish Secretary. You can start tomorrow, Rose. See you then." He leaves before she can say yes or no. Tomorrow after school she will start her working life. Three hours in the rectory answering phones and doorbells.

Sue is waiting for her at the corner.

"What'd old crepe face want?"

"I hafta start work tomorrow. At the Rectory."

"Eew. Why'd you say you would?"

"Old crepe face and my parents had it all worked out. No one asked me."

"Is he goin' to pay you?"

She laughs at Sue. "Sure, probably in Rosaries and holy cards."

They get half way down the block when Sue yells out—"oh, the ole' bastard! Fridays is when we get to go to 8th grade Youth Group starting next week. He doesn't want you to go! He's such a creep."

Rose stops at the curb, sits on her schoolbag. She doesn't want to go home. Sue sits next to her. The leaves on the trees are beautiful. They just watch them fall, turn, turn, turn to the ground. Sue gathers up a bunch like a snowball and throws it at Rose. They play at leaf fighting for a few minutes, then fall on the ground laughing. It's time to go. Home.

Rose's mother has returned from her summer rest. Now that she's back the house is disturbingly quiet. Rose dares not break the silence because her mother is probably sleeping. Or just sitting in the living room, arms folded across her chest. A cup of "tea" on the coffee table. Today she's in the living room. Rose mumbles hello and heads straight to her room.

Lying on her bed, looking at the shadows on the wall, she hears her mother get up and go to the bathroom. Quickly, Rose tip-toes down the stairs and goes out the front door. She should do some homework, but she can't concentrate. So she walks. Blocks and blocks into Valley Stream where she doesn't know anyone, where all the houses look just a bit tidier, the streets a little nicer.

There's a deli on Rockaway Avenue where she gets a tuna on a roll and a can of coke. She walks over to the little town square near the Long Island Rail Road where there are benches and eats her solitary supper. It's getting dark. Time to go. Home.

Chapter Thirty-Eight

Thanksgiving means a four day weekend. Four days without the distraction of school. Four days in an unnaturally quiet house.

The morning of Thanksgiving Rose's mother sits at the kitchen table, drinking coffee. There is no smell of onions and thyme and celery. There is no large bird to fit in the oven, no stuffing to make or potatoes to peel. No cinnamon scented apple pie to look forward to.

Maureen announces, when Phil and Rose are within hearing distance, that she has decided that they will not celebrate Christmas this year out of respect. She leaves it at that. Respect. Strange word to use to place the blame. Rose looks to her father to speak up, to protest, to say something like, "you know, we still have Rose to take care of, Maureen. Doesn't Rose deserve Christmas?" But he doesn't say anything. He just takes his coffee cup and leaves the kitchen.

Maureen then goes back to bed and stays there for the rest of the day.

Phil gets some fried chicken. No one even puts it on plates, they just let the greasy meat stain the cardboard bucket. Jimmy is at Kathy's family for dinner. So it's just Rose and her dad and a football game droning in the background.

December is gray and cold. More days than not it rains, then sleets. Rose gets a lot of use out of last years boots, the fleece lining is flattened from wear and they are just a little small. The halls outside every classroom are lined with wet boots and small puddles. Everything smells damp.

Christmas lights go up at the mall. The family across the street has a Nativity, a large plastic Santa and two snowmen crowded together on the small lawn. The lights outlining the shape of the house blink, on and off, on and off for weeks before it is actually Christmas.

The week before Christmas, the sky is a deep blue-gray at three in the afternoon. Rose sits at her bedroom window, arms folded on the sill, her chin on top of her hands. The street lights come on at four and the flakes fall. She is drawn into watching the flakes play in the dim yellow light in its funnel to the ground. It is their spotlight, their moment of glory before they mix in with the millions of other flakes that make up this crusty blanket. Wind whistles in through the space that has opened between the window and the house over the years. Just a small space, enough for a cold wind to work its way through.

Tonight I'll get some money from Dad. He doesn't get home until after eight. No explanations anymore. Rose had a bowl of cereal for supper. Her mother shuffled out still in her robe, gets some water and a pill, goes back to her room. No greeting. No *how was your day?* No *did you get your homework done?* No *are you as lonesome as I am, Rose? Are you in as much pain as I am? Do you want to talk about it?*

Phil comes in smelling of cigarette smoke and beer.

"Dad, I need some money for a project."

"How much? Will twenty do?"

"Nope, I need more."

He hands her three twenties. "Will this do?"

"Sure."

Rose and Sue walk over to Green Acres Mall the following day. They have to get across Hook Creek Boulevard which is strewn with deep potholes, now filled with icy water. No one driving a car seems to think they need to slow down for two girls trying to get across. The cars go by with a *swooosh* in the black and white sludge where it snowed yesterday.

At least Sunrise Highway has a light. If they get there in time they can make it all the way across, but the lights seemed to be timed to make pedestrians stand on the narrow cement divider waiting for the next light, cars zipping by just inches from their backsides. Their knit hats are pulled down over their foreheads, gloved hands in coat pockets. And, because they are thirteen year old girls, they let out a little scream as they run across the highway.

Newberry's basement is their favorite place to shop. It is stocked with all kinds of cheap things, toys, face cream, a sewing department, yarn in all colors and Christmas decorations. Rose wants to buy some Christmas.

There is a little tree with wire arms and green scruff that looks like small toilet brushes. There is a string of lights attached. This will fit in a shopping bag, so Rose gets one and then a few ornaments, including a Santa, a nativity and star for the top.

She gets a pair of gloves for both her father and brother, and long knit scarf for her mother. Rose wants to get a little girl makeup kit for her sister. Sue sees her put this in the little basket. She doesn't remind Rose that her sister has died.

"Now you go to another department Sue. I want to get something for you. Meet you at the cash register, but don't look."

She chooses a pale blue brush, comb and hand mirror set for her friend. Rose takes two. One she will wrap for Sue, one for herself. She needs something to open on Christmas morning, even if it's alone in her room sitting under the tiny tree on her nightstand.

On Christmas morning, Rose looks across at the empty bed. She puts on her robe and fuzzy slippers and takes the two gifts from under her tiny tree. First she opens her brush set and gushes *thank you Cilla,* in a whisper and then a giggle. *Now open mine.* Cilla is so happy with the little make-up kit. It comes with a small yellow plastic bag, real lip gloss that turns in the cylinder, a quarter sized round of blush and a blue crayon shaped eye shadow. *Rose we can play dress up!*

Yes, really, daahhling. We absolutely must. It would be just dreadful if we didn't, daahhling!

"Rose, come on, I don't want to be late for Church." Her father calls up the stairs. She quickly dresses and fixes her hair with her new brush.

~~~~

1973 begins with a sunny, cold week. The temperature never gets out of the twenties, but the skies are clear and bright.

Once school starts back up Rose has to return to her Rectory job. Three hours of social isolation, answering the front door and the telephone and instructing parishioners to sit in the cold folding chairs while Father Joseph or Monsignor comes for them.

While Rose sits in the rectory waiting for the bell to ring her classmates are across Brookville Boulevard in the old parish hall playing ping-pong and listening to music as an introduction to the youth group they can join when they are high school freshmen.

There are a few other girls who work the after school shift the other four weekdays. In the beginning of March Monsignor stands in front of the desk where Rose is doing her homework and presents her with a proposition.

"Rose. I was thinking about taking you and the other girls out for a treat, as a 'thank-you' for working here."

Rose looks up from her math book, not knowing what she is expected to say.

"Uh, that's okay, Monsignor. You don't have to do anything special for us, I'm sure."

"Nonsense. I was thinking a trip over to the natatorium in Valley Stream might be a fun outing for you girls."

Of all the possibilities for a 'thank-you' treat, going swimming with Monsignor would never have crossed Rose's mind.

"The natatorium? It's still winter, Monsignor."

"That's what's great about the natatorium. It's a heated, indoor pool. How about this time next week? I'll let the other girls know."

Without waiting for an answer, because, she guessed, it wasn't really a question, Monsignor left to call the other girls and tell them they have a date.

Chapter Thirty-Nine

Paul David Cellio was born in April of 1973. A year after Cilla died. Jenny, painfully aware of the irony, stores this in her heart, right up there with all the deception and maneuvering of the last several months. He's a beautiful six pound baby, a month early by David's calculations, but at six pounds, that's a good weight for a child born a few weeks early.

Paul's eyes are blue. Sometimes baby's eye color changes over time.

David is a proud papa. He assails his workmates with photos of the squirmy newborn at every opportunity. Paul's baptism is a bigger event than their hastily arranged wedding. Both sides of the family rent a hall. David's mother helps Jenny dress Paul in the baptismal garment that David wore as an infant. "From father to son. Someday his child will wear this, God willing." Jenny cries.

She's not quite sure if the Cellio's family embracing of her and Paul is a blessing or an added weight to her guilt. They love her, even if the wedding was rushed. They were so relieved that David had it in him to win a girl, any girl, and such a pretty one as Jenny was almost too good to be true.

They all make such a fuss at the big baptism party. What a beautiful child, what a beautiful child, they couldn't say it enough. Cousins would say among themselves, good thing he looks like Jenny, such a handsome little boy.

Jenny is terrified of the day when every one will know just by looking at them, that Paul is not David's son.

That fear and the knowledge that she has thrown away her chance to marry a man she's madly in love with by getting involved with Phil Banfry is something she just has to ignore. She's in battle mode now, trying to stay a strategy ahead of the truth. She must be alert, all the time. Relaxing her vigilance over every word and reference to who Paul might resemble in the family can lead to her undoing. She is exhausted. She aches. Every joint hurts. Her energy is almost depleted.

But she works hard at keeping a smile on her face when she's with the big family. She works hard to make David happy and proud of their little boy. David loves this child immensely. Oh, the things we'll do together, just wait, he tells the little smiling child. Oh the fun we'll have.

Jenny watches this lovely interaction and she feels the tears coming. Dishes need doing and laundry needs folding. She leaves the two of them to bond. It's so important for fathers to bond with their sons.

When he's at work, Jenny spends so much energy weaving a new version of the truth in her imagination. David is a good man. A little plodding, but he's sensible. He saves money, he's home every night for supper. He doesn't drink or gamble or chase women. He's not exactly handsome, but he is neat and clean. He's a perfect husband. All the things Phil is not. Phil is full of passion and power and full speed ahead, damn the consequences. Phil has a presence. But David is here.

She prays to fall in love with him.

Chapter Forty

April 1973

Fr. Joseph is in charge of the youth group because he's young. Msgr. Dunleavy had practically blackballed Rose from the eighth grade group by arranging her job at the rectory. But there were things even he couldn't prevent. The eighth grade retreat was the Monday after Easter.

They meet in the parish hall for an informal Mass around a folding table covered with a white cloth. They sit in a circle for the readings and homily, which was a give and take between Fr. Joseph and the kids.

For communion, Fr. Joseph arranged with one of the mothers to bake some flat brown bread. After the consecration Fr. Joseph takes a small piece, hands it to the kid next to him and around the room they go. Same with the cup. They all take a small sip of consecrated wine while sitting cross legged on the floor of the old building.

It was the most beautiful Mass she'd ever been to. Before or since.

Fr. Joseph gives some talks, they have some sharing activities with sheets of paper, magic markers, clay and finger paints. In the afternoon Fr. Joseph makes time for confession. Rose waits her turn and sits on a folding chair next to him behind makeshift room dividers.

"Bless me Father, for I have sinned. It has been two months since my last confession." Words memorized since first grade gets the process started.

"What would you like to talk about?"

Here she hesitates for more than a minute. Her only plan for this confession was to rattle off her usual list of venial sins, like being disobedient, lying a little, being angry. But this conversational tone that Fr. Joseph uses steers her in a different direction.

"Um, well something's been bothering me."

"Yes," he says, encouragingly.

"Well, let's see." She presses the bridge of her nose to hold back tears. "Fr. Joseph... an older man, well, um... You see... he exposed himself to me. Now, I don't know if it was an accident, and I don't want to make a big deal out of it, and I probably shouldn't have said anything, but I don't know what to do. I can't tell my parents, they'd just yell at me for having a dirty mind..." these last verses fall out of her mouth faster than she can control.

He leans over, elbows on his knees, palms holding his face. She tries to look at him, but she's scared. Scared he'd tell her she has an active imagination and she shouldn't presume things.

"Rose. Was it a relative?"

"No."

"Do you come in contact with this person often?"

"Yeah, I kinda hafto."

"You 'kinda hafto'?"

Now she can't hold back tears. She tries so hard to control it; she wipes them away with the back of her hand. Fr. Joseph hands her a tissue.

"Can you tell me about it?"

She makes herself look into his eyes. They are deep blue and the expression on his face looks like a holy card. She wants so much to trust him; she wants so much to trust anyone.

"He took me and Miriam and Danielle over to the Valley Stream pool last month. He said it was an outing to thank us for our work in the rectory. None of us wanted to go, but we didn't know how to get out of it."

Fr. Joseph nods his head, "Go on."

"So the girls went to the women's locker room to change and he went to the men's, of course. Then before any of us went into the pool—we really didn't want to go swimming, I mean it was still cold outside and the indoor pools, well you know, they smell like chlorine and mildew, but like I said, we didn't know how to get out of it."

"Slow down, Rose, no one is rushing you."

"He went and got us some hot dogs and cokes from the concession stand. A picnic in March in a stinky pool. Anyway, there we were, in bathing suits and big towels wrapped around ourselves. His towel was on the seat beside him. He only had his bathing suit and his cracked black leather shoes, no socks. He came back with the tray of food, dropped the napkins on the floor next to me, so of course I bent down to get them.

" He, he.... his legs were open and the, um, the netting in his bathing suit was torn and well, you know."

There was no holding the tears back now. She is so grateful for the noise her classmates are making in the rest of the parish hall.

"Oh, Rose. I'm so sorry." He reaches out to touch her knee, but pulls his hand back before he makes contact.

"Is there anything else?"

"Well, yeah, and I don't know how to handle this. Just last week, it was Good Friday, so I didn't have my uniform on, just my regular clothes. I wore a blouse I had from last year and I guess it was a little small for me, but he came into the rectory office and stared at me, at my, um well, he stared and started yelling at me. 'Young lady, how can you wear such a tight blouse? Do you know what you do to the boys in your class looking like that? Do you know what they will think of you? Modesty is a young lady's highest virtue. Does your mother know that you wore that here today? Hasn't she been through enough without you parading around town like that?'

Rose tries to relate this incident to Fr. Joseph, but as she speaks she wonders if she should keep it to herself. Monsignor was right. She's supposed to be modest, she's supposed to wear clothing that is loose and hides her figure. And maybe, she was thinking, maybe, what happened next was an accident, something that anyone would have done, that only she with her dirty mind would read into. She lowers her voice to a whisper, feeling exposed.

"Then he said 'Put a sweater over yourself. You can't look like a trollop and work here.' He took off his sweater and put it on me. And he buttoned it."

That's enough. That's too much. I shouldn't have started this. This isn't confession. I just sinned in confession, gossiping about a priest. Oh, God. Me and my big mouth.

Her head is bent, eyes closed tight. She can feel purple throbbing heat in her face.

"Go on, Rose, is there something else?"

All she can do is shrug her shoulders and nod yes. She can't speak. She can't tell this handsome young priest what the old man with age spots on his hands did next. She can't tell him that as Monsignor pulled the lapels of his sweater together over her chest that his hands lingered as he checked to see that her breasts were not discernible through the wool.

They are both silent for a few minutes.

"Father, am I doing something wrong?"

"God, Rose, no. You haven't done anything wrong. Now, listen, and please do what I say. Do not go back to work there."

"I don't want to ever go there. I never wanted to go there in the first place. He arranged it all. He said he suggested it to my parents but no one ever asked me if I wanted to work there."

In the silence she gathers the strength to speak.

"My parents think he's great—bringing morals back and all that. He always talks about my parents as wonderful examples of good Catholics, but, but … I don't have any choice, Father."

Fr. Jospeh's head is bent. His fingers arched under his chin. Then he blesses her.

"Father, you didn't say the absolution prayer."

"Rose, you didn't confess any sins, any of your own I mean. Everything's good. I'll pray for you, Rose."

Chapter Forty-One

May 1973

There will be a Spring Dance on May 4. Rose has saved her allowance and gets herself a dress. There will be a disco ball and band of local teens will provide the music.

Tommy Masters walks Rose home from school once in a while, well, just to the corner, she doesn't want her mother to see her talking to him. He makes sure she's going to the dance and asks if she will dance with him. "Sure." She tries to sound nonchalant.

"Okay, tomorrow night then."

She has to erase the happiness from her face so her mother doesn't catch on that she has anything to be excited about. She packs her dress and shoes carefully into her schoolbag and figures she'll wait till morning to casually mention that the Rogan's have invited her to supper and to stay over so she won't be home tonight.

Her mother just mumbles "oh, all right. Be good and don't make a nuisance of yourself, Rose."

Tommy Masters looks sharp in his dark Huk-a-Poo shirt and denims. When *Color My World* comes on, all the girls say "ooow" as if on cue and the boys rush to find a partner.

Tommy is right at her elbow and they do the slow song embrace. For all the time she has spent thinking about how that first slow dance will be, this is better than she had imagined. He is confident. He takes her hand, turns her around, then wraps his arms around her back. Rose nervously places her hands on his shoulders. He guides her head forward so her cheek lay on his chest.

Before the song is over Rose spots Monsignor Dunleavy walking in her direction. Fr. Joseph intercepts him and pulls him away from the dance floor. Tommy and Rose disappear into the crowd.

Chapter Forty-Two

Rose hasn't acted on Fr. Joseph's advice to resign from her job at the Rectory yet. Since the dance on Friday night, though, she feels bolder.

She heads straight from school to the rectory, knocks on the office door and is relieved to find that only Mrs. Hollander, the Parish Secretary, is in the room.

"Excuse me, Mrs. Hollander, I just wanted to let you know that I won't be working here anymore." Rose speaks quickly so she won't stumble on the words.

Mrs. Hollander lowers her glasses down her nose. "I'm sorry to hear that Rose. But I think that's a good decision."

"What's a good decision?"

He is standing at her back. She can feel the sound waves of his words assaulting her from behind.

Mrs. Hollander takes the lead. "Rose was telling me how busy she is with schoolwork, so she won't be able to come on Friday after school from now on." Rose looks at Mrs. Hollander gratefully.

"Nonsense, Rose. I hear your grades are fine. There's no need to leave. Put your books down right here." He indicates a desk. "In fact, I have a few errands I'd like you to do. We are running low on typing paper, Rose. Go down to the basement and bring up a box for Mrs. Hollander."

"Yes, Monsignor." Her assent comes out so quickly, years of training taking over to drown out any protest of her own instincts.

She is in the rectory basement with its cheap wood paneling over the rough cement walls, looking for a place where boxes of typing paper might be kept. There is a closet under the stairs. She lifts the small latch, pulls the cord for the bare bulb overhead and sees what she is after.

As she struggles to lift a box, heavy footsteps sound from overhead. Maybe if she's quiet he will leave.

"Rose!"

No such luck. She steps out of the closet, holding the box of paper in front of her.

"I want to show you these," he waves something in his hand, "before you go."

Still holding the box, she steps out, rests it on one of the metal folding tables a few feet in front of the closet.

Monsignor fans out several photos.

Rose swallows her breath when she sees them. They are photos of very young, very nubile girls in pleated plaid skirts and tight white blouses. In the first a girl is leaning over a desk, the roundness of her bottom peeking through. Either she has on panties that have ridden up or nothing at all under that skirt.

The next photo is the same girl, from a front shot. Her blouse is tight, so tight it's bursting and her large dark nipples are erect and pointed directly into the face of a young man, an innocent victim of this evil voluptuous pawn of the devil, Rose supposes.

She's trying to pull away from these pictures but Monsignor points to the next and then the next. Variations on the same theme.

Rose wants to cry. And run. But she doesn't. She is stuck to that basement floor, her legs heavy, her rubber soled oxfords melted into the green and black linoleum tiles.

"I'm showing you these pictures for your own good, young lady. Soon you will be starting at Mary Louis and I hope you never consider dressing like some of these girls do. Oh, don't think these are fake. I have it on good authority that there is an element at even the best schools who behave in this disgraceful manner."

She manages to nod her head in agreement.

"Never, ever disgrace your school, the church, the Virgin Mother of God in such a way. These kinds of girls are no good. They drive the boys wild. The boys cannot be held responsible for what happens to these girls."

Rose thinks she nods, but she isn't really sure.

"Because of girls like this, the boys know that all the girls look like this under those uniforms. All girls carry the sin of Eve within them, ready to be unleashed at any time if they are not constantly on guard."

The muscles in her face are pulled tight, in pain. She tells herself to breathe, but she can't.

"All of you are Eve offering the apple of sin to Adam. How could Adam resist the apple when Eve held it so seductively between her breasts?"

With 'breasts' a little spittle flies from his mouth to her cheek. She wants to wipe it away, but she dare not move, dare not draw any more attention.

"And you are all Eve unless you choose to be like the Virgin Mother of God. No man ever touched her or looked on her with lust in his heart because she always dressed in the highest modesty, her eyes cast downward in her humility, in her consciousness of the sin of Eve that all women carry."

While holding her face muscles taut Rose wonders: Even her? Did she have to put up with this from her rabbi?

"It was the sin of Eve that imprisoned all mankind. Caused wars and famine and plague. You are charged with correcting this sin of your kind, of women. You need to prepare yourself for convent life, the highest form of service a woman can give to God."

Each sentence, each syllable he gets closer to Rose. She can smell his stale breath, his grey teeth behind his chapped lips, which he licks with every other breath, takes over the width of her eyesight.

"Before you go, Rose, before you go, I want to bless you."

With his right hand on the back of her head and his left on her shoulder he pulls her close, forehead to forehead. The box is between them. "May the blessing of Almighty God, of his son Jesus Christ and the Holy Spirit, keep your mind and body a pure and holy temple in the manner of the Virgin Mother of God and our patron saint, the virgin martyr Maria Goretti. Amen."

He releases her.

"Now, bring this box up to the office."

He waits at the bottom of the stairs for her to proceed ahead of him. Since she is wearing her uniform jumper and knee socks she does not want to go first. But she has to.

She is clenched so tightly it's difficult to walk. On her third step up he follows. When they get to the top of the stairs, in front of the closed door, Rose feels his finger tug at the bottom of her panties to cover the rounded flesh that has escaped the elastic. She stifles a scream. One of his fingers has wandered further in.

"What did I say about this?"

She opens the door, hurries into the office to Mrs. Hollander, drops the box, grabs her books and leaves.

~~~

Rose runs down the cement steps in front of the Rectory, around the corner past the side of the church. The root of one of the large trees has broken through the sidewalk. She catches the toe of her oxfords on the crooked growth. Her arms go wide, the books scatter as she falls. Skirt flies up as she lands on her knee. Her right knee and hand take the brunt of force. Automatically she pulls the skirt over her exposed panties before she can even process the wounds.

Dirt and cement particles embed in the flesh of her palms. Her right knee is torn, cut deeply with a sharp edge of the gnarly root. Any effort to hold back tears evaporates now. She gathers her books, pulls up her knee socks and limps home.

"What did you do to yourself, Rose?"

"I was running and I tripped."

"What's the big hurry?"

"Nothing, Mom. Not a thing."

"Here, let me see that. Oh, Rose, that's deep. You might need stitches."

Maureen dabs at the wound with a warm washcloth rubbed in Ivory soap. Rose flinches when she gets close to the more tender spots. Maureen places her cool hand over Rose's clenched fist. This gentle gesture opens Rose. She is sobbing. Maureen wraps her arms around her surviving daughter and rocks her, both of them joined in this deep release.

They cry together. Maureen repeats 'my baby girl, my baby girl'. Rose doesn't know which baby girl her mother means, but at this moment she takes it for herself. She takes it for her sister.

When Maureen releases Rose she makes a sandwich and pours a tall glass of milk.

"I'll run the bath for you, Rose. Your whole body will be sore. Then we'll see about that knee. It looks like it will scar."

While Rose eats Maureen turns down the sheets and blankets, sets her nightgown on the bed, pulls the shade so her daughter can sleep. After she bandages Rose's knee, she tucks her tired daughter in, kisses her on the top of the head. "Sleep, my little girl. Sleep."

In the years to come, this is the moment Rose will cling to, this tender care from her mother at this wounding. It will pass. Her mother will be gone again. But for this one moment, she stepped out of her grief and held her Rose.

Maureen stands in the doorway of her daughter's room. Once there were two little girls sleeping here, playing here, laughing here.

Maureen fears, knows, this moment will not last, that she will be pulled back into darkness. She feels it coming even now; even now this light is fading as her little girl lies sleeping.

Chapter Forty-Three

July 1, 1973

As she lay in bed in the early morning light Rose hears her father getting ready for work downstairs. Her bedroom window is open and the air smells clear, crisp. Birds are calling to one another from the tree outside her window.

She treasures these moments alone, before she has to go downstairs and have breakfast silently, trying so hard not to wake her mother. Cilla's bed is empty, of course—Rose thought of putting things on the bed, just to change it up a bit, but she knows her mother won't allow that. It's a shrine to Cilla, and her mother is the chief worshiper keeping vigil.

Rose doesn't want another day like the days she'd had since graduation. Her mother didn't come for the ceremony, even though it had been more than a year since Cilla's death. Dad came. Jimmy came with Kathy. And Grandma Meg came. Grandma's. That's where she'll go today, if she can get out of the house before her mother wakes.

Rose carefully negotiates the stairs and waits for her father near the front door.

"Dad can I have some money for train fare?"

"Where're you going?"

"I think I'll take the train into Grandma's and spend the day there."

"What about your mother?"

Rose just looks at him, sighs deeply and raises an eyebrow.

He hands her a twenty and says "make it last".

She creeps around upstairs, putting some clothes into her backpack, closes the front door as quietly as she can and runs to the Long Island Rail Road station, takes the next westbound train that will stop in Jamaica. Since it's rush hour, there's not much of a wait.

From the stop in Jamaica Rose catches a bus down Jamaica Avenue and gets off at Forest Parkway. She has a key to her grandmother's house since last summer. The walk uphill is just the exertion she needs—not too much but enough to make her feel that she is alive. Just getting out of the house was exhilarating. Rose breathes in the air, even when the cars go by, lightened by the promise of the trees in Forest Park. The early morning noise feels like life, so different from the tomb that her home has become.

When she reaches her grandmother's, Rose goes around the back to enter the kitchen. Sheila's twins, Frank, Jr. and Tommy are leaving from the back door for their summer job at Lewis' on Jamaica Avenue.

"Hey, Rose." They say in unison.

They are tall and gangly, like only seventeen-year-old boys can be.

Grandma Meg is up, having coffee, dressed and reading the paper.

"Well, hello, dear. Come in."

Rose notes that her grandmother doesn't ask what brings her here.

"Have you eaten this morning?"

Rose shakes her head.

"Here, I have some lovely bread—I'll toast you some."

Rose places her backpack on a kitchen chair.

"I've some washing up to do, Rose. What would you like to do?"

"Do you mind if I take a little nap, Grams?"

"Not at all. Your room is always ready."

She goes to her room. Cool sheets, window open to let the summer breeze in, lacy curtains blowing. She falls asleep quickly.

Chapter Forty-Four

Spring 1974

A*LOUETTE, GENTILLE ALOUETTE, Alouette, je te plumerai. Je te plumerai le tete, Je te plumerai le tete, Et le tete, et le tete, Alouette, Alouette! Ah! ah! ah! ah!*

Around and around that little bird flies in Rose's head. She is humming the children's tune under her breath as Sister Anne Marie walks down the aisle, handing back yesterday's test.

"Rose, I expect better of you." 63 is circled in red next to her name.

Getting into The Mary Louis Academy was not enough. Rose is expected to keep up and do well. In elementary school, that was easy. It was no trouble to be the cream at the top of the class. Here all the girls were the cream at the top of their grade school classes. The shuffle of the new order is overwhelming.

Not only are all the girls intelligent, but there is a much bigger mix of background and range of 'class' from the middle, to professional, to big houses, big money, big vacations, big privilege. Queens is a lot more complicated than she knew from her neighborhood at the Southeast corner of the borough on the Nassau border. Finding a place to fit in is a challenge for which Rose is not equipped.

"Have this signed by a parent and return it to me tomorrow."

"Yes, Sister."

Rose feels the heat rise to the tip of her ears while her heart speeds up, eyes go down as she folds the paper quickly and shoves it in her notebook.

They start the next chapter. The title page of chapter eight has a picture of a bridge and a cathedral in the background. Something about future past imperfect tense. *What?* Rose is trying to look like she's listening, but she cannot hear a thing Sr. Anne Marie is saying. She hopes that writing words here and there in her notebook passes for paying attention.

But that bridge and the water and the cathedral rising up on the bank.

Sur le pont d'Avignon On y danse, on y danse Sur le pont d'Avignon On y danse tout en rond Something something something comme ci, Something something something comme ca, Et le tete, et le tete, allouette, allouette, oh, oh, oh, oh.

The bird on the bridge and the children bowing to one another and a little boy plucking feathers, torturing the poor little creature! Rose closes her eyes. She is dizzy. Bell buzzes in the hallway. Class is over. *History next, do I have my book? No, I've got to run down to the locker room. I'll be late, o god, is there a test today?*

She hasn't read a chapter in history in weeks. She likes history, especially Western Civ. She hopes she can retain enough from class discussions to fake it through the tests. The Romans and the barbarians and the castles and serfs and fiefdoms and all the wars. Every other page another war starts. And there'd be good popes and bad popes and the Crusades and so much mud and disease.

She brings her books home. Sits on her bed. Across from Cilla's bed which is lined with bears and bunnies and a little stuffed doll with yellow yarn hair. Just like when Cilla was here. Except Cilla was so often in the bed when Rose came in from school. A humidifier running and a cloud pointed at her sweaty face.

Rose opens the books, open the notebooks. Looks at the pages filled with black marks. Many of the answers are right there in the text, all she has to do is find the same sentence and fill in the missing words.

Math, though, math. Guessing isn't working as well as it was the first semester. Chemistry is a complete loss. Any answer she gets right is pure luck, some angel holding her up just enough so she doesn't drown.

But she is drowning. That angel is going to get tired of her dead weight. He's going to move on to someone who at least tries to study. She can't fool the angel forever. It's coming, it's coming. She feels the darkness of the cold water cover her face, her hair, her lungs. She startles herself with a gasp, reaching for air. She knocks the books off the bed. Another night, another waste of time. Any words she has read do not stick in her teflon mind. Not a thing. Turn the light out and go to sleep.

She has to catch her father before he goes off to work. She doesn't dare ask her mother to sign the test. *Wasting all the good fortune you've been given. You're the lucky one! You've got everything! You going to throw it all away! And your baby sister lying cold in the ground! You're always daydreaming. Get your head out of the clouds, young lady and straighten up. We're not paying tuition at that school so you can fail French. You can fail for free at public school!*

Her mother never actually says all this, but Rose is pretty sure if she saw a failed test grade she would. Dad's a better bet.

"Dad, before you go. Can you sign this?"

"What is it Rosie?" He hasn't called her Rosie in a long time.

"French test."

He looks at the paper. "Oh."

He pulls a pen out of his suit jacket and scribbles some letters.

"French is hard, huh?"

She shrugs at this. She busies herself with her backpack. They don't actually look at each other.

"There are worse things than failing a French test. Need money for lunch?"

"Yeah, Dad."

He hands her a twenty.

She starts disappearing.

She uses safety pins to tuck the waistband of her uniform skirt. She wears a big pullover, the same one every day, so no one will notice she's losing weight.

Some of the girls in school notice these things whether she wants them to or not.

"You're so lucky, Rose. Look how skinny you are. God, I wish I could lose a few pounds. How'd you do it?"

"Eat less, I guess."

She doesn't tell them that there is no secret diet, no magic pill. She doesn't have an appetite anymore. There are few family dinners and the ones they manage to have are full of tension and anger waiting to burst.

That's about the only conversation they have with her. She doesn't fit in with the nerds, those girls with hair way too long and stringy and always slightly greasy, held in a rubber band with split ends dividing up their backs. They have inside jokes and read science fiction and laugh at the most absurd things. And they get good grades.

She doesn't fit in with the popular girls. The ones with perfect hair and great shoes and always a different pretty sweater or earrings, a new bracelet, expensive handbags. They know how to walk like they own the place. They go skiing in the winter and to the Hamptons in the summer.

They date college boys who go to the 'better' schools. When their mothers come in for some presentation or meeting they wear clickety high heels, have perfect manicures and oh so subtle just done up highlights in their coiffed hair.

They wave their perfect hands around with the large diamonds catching the light and the gold bangles announcing their presence. Their daughters roll their eyes at them but it's so easy to see that they long to have the same life that Mother has.

The few times Rose squeezes into one of their tables she tries not to notice the backs turned slightly away from her and the laughter a more haphazard girl deserves as she looks desperately for someone to sit with, anyone who won't get up thirty seconds after she sits down.

Rose is becoming that girl.

Rose is that girl.

And no one notices.

Chapter Forty-Five

1977

Since Rose never knows which mother she is going to get she leaves the house quickly in the morning.

On any given day, even in the middle of a conversation, the switch from one mother to the next comes with only the slightest warning. A stiffening of the spine. A coldness in the eyes. Folding her arms across her chest. They could be going along laughing about something, and then, switch. Rose crosses a line because she never knows where the lines are. Suddenly she's gone too far or has been fresh or utters what her mother decides is a veiled insult and its over.

Rose learned young to gauge the household temperature. Before she got out of bed she'd turn an ear to the door and listen. If her parents were having a pleasant conversation, then maybe they could get through breakfast without a scene or a reprimand. Since Cilla's death, though, those mornings are rare. And not to be trusted.

When she started at St. John's she wished she could talk to her mother about her classes and the people she was meeting. Rose would get caught up in the questions, eager to share something. Occasionally, the conversation would go well. No drama. No mood changes.

But then, there it was. As if a cloud of soot rolled through the house, filling every space. The only thing she can do is escape.

No time for breakfast. She'll get that at school.

~~~

That's how she met Dennis. She'd usually get to Marillac Hall between 7:15 and 7:20. She'd park her book bag at a table, get coffee and a Danish and open a text so she didn't look pathetic. Dennis joined her in her morning routine the second week of classes.

The tables were joined in twos to make a large square. The first morning Dennis noticed her he took a seat at the far diagonal of where Rose was camped. Each morning he would move a little closer, moving from, 'hi, aren't you in my English class?' to exchanging stories.

Within the first few weeks more students gathered at their table. Morning coffee became an event, a good start to the day. Eventually, the headache that marred each morning dissipated by the second cup of coffee with Dennis.

Sure, she liked him. And it looked as though he liked her. But nothing. No 'what are you doing this Saturday night?' no 'would you like to see a movie with me?' Just chit chat and a degree of what looked like flirting.

In the middle of November the group added Friday late afternoon at Poor Richard's for a beer and an early start to the weekend. Rose wondered if Dennis was ever going to make a move.

They were chattering and laughing, competing with music over the noise of the Friday afternoon set. Their friend Ron was headed back to their table with three cold beers held together precariously in a triangle and just before he reached their table in the corner, crash! The beers were on the floor, a loud jangle of breaking glass making Rose jump. Dennis, sitting next to Rose, instinctively put his arms around her when she jumped and let out a little shriek. She turned herself toward him into this protective gesture and in that instant their relationship was on course.

"You okay?" He pulled up on her chin to ask her this.

"Yeah. Thanks."

Dennis kept his arm around the back of her chair for the rest of the afternoon. Before the little party broke up they had a date for the weekend.

Chapter Forty-Six

Meg Banfry turned ninety in 1988. They had a party at her house on Forest Parkway.

"Grams, I'm going to have a baby."

She whispered this into her grandmother's ear when they were momentarily alone in the kitchen.

"Oh, my dear, that's wonderful. Oh, please have the baptismal party here, Rose."

"Oh, okay. I hadn't thought that far ahead, but sure, this would be the perfect place, Grams."

"When's the big day?"

"We're due in May."

"May is perfect. Life is so full of promise in May."

"Grams, we haven't told anyone else yet, so let's just keep this a secret for a bit, okay?"

"Of course, dear. This is the best birthday present, Rose."

In February Rose was five months along. It was an icy month. The hill that was Forest Parkway was too slippery for Meg to navigate. Sheila would get Meg's groceries in and often prepare her dinner.

A great tiredness had come over Meg along with the ice storms. She was cold all the time. The furnace couldn't make the house warm enough.

Rose checked in on her grandmother regularly. On a Friday night, after she and Dennis had their usual spaghetti supper, Rose picked up the phone.

It rang seven, then eight times.

"Hello?"

"Grams, it's Rose. I'm just calling to see how you're doing."

"Oh, Rose. It's just so cold."

"What's your heat set to, Grams?"

"I've pushed it up to seventy."

"Well, push it to seventy-one or two."

"But that's so wasteful, Rose. My bill will be enormous."

"It's better than freezing. Grams."

"I suppose you're right."

"What I really wanted was to see if you'd like some Entenmann's. This baby is making me so hungry. What if Dennis and I come over with a cheese Danish?"

"Isn't it late for you, dear, to be bothered with an old woman like me?"

"What bother?"

"Of course I'd love to see you. A piece of Danish does sound good."

Rose puts a toothbrush and a change of clothes in a canvas tote.

"Dennis, I think I'd better stay with Grams tonight."

"What about me? I can stay too."

"I don't think we'll both fit in my old bed, but there is another bed in the small room."

"Allrighty, a sleepover at Grandma's house!"

Rose gives him a hug. "Silly."

Rose has a key to to Meg's house. Her grandmother is sitting at the dining room table, three dessert plates and forks ready for her company. The kettle is whistling.

"You're all set for us, aren't you, Grams?"

Meg looks up at her granddaughter, so full of life.

"Oh, Rose, you never looked lovelier."

Meg's blue veins are bold through her transparent skin tonight. She takes short breaths and keeps her right hand just inches below her collar bone, pressing, as if to move a weight off her chest.

When she looks done in, Rose helps her upstairs to bed.

At a little after two in the morning, Rose hears her name.

She turns on the small nightstand lamp, and sits on the bed with Meg.

"Rose, could you make a cup of tea for me? My gullet is a little unsettled."

Rose goes to make tea.

"What would I do without you?"

"You mean, what would I have done without you all these years, Grams."

Meg is sitting up with three pillows at her back.

"I like Dennis. Such a good man. He'll be a wonderful father. You know, my Gerald, oh, he was something. So handsome, so eloquent. He always drew a crowd, even if we were just having supper in a pub, he'd have an audience, telling his stories. The men would ask him what he thought of this candidate or that and why doesn't he stand for office and then there'd be a round of clapping. They'd buy him another beer."

While Meg was speaking, looking beyond Rose, Rose turned her head and looked up. She had the strangest sensation that she was watching herself in this scene, as if there were two of her and one was perched on the ledge of molding that ran along the ceiling line, watching as her grandmother handed her life's story over for safekeeping, like handing over a precious carved wood box containing all her treasured memories.

Meg offers Rose her tea cup and saucer. It lays in her palms like a gift until she sets it on the night stand.

"He would come up with something right on the spot, always an answer of some kind, always got a laugh or roar. Most of the men didn't have the kind of education Gerald had. Oh, no, he didn't go to college, but he read everything. The classics, the philosophers, history. Kept up with all the news and who was starting this movement or that.

"Gift of gab, some called it. But that sounds silly. He didn't just gab, he always had something to say. Something important. He'd stay up nights reading, thinking, writing. So the union wanted him to take charge. Well, who better? He knew the issues. He knew when the bosses were trying to get away with something, trying him out, testing him to see if he would be fooled. But, no, not Gerald.

"And when the mob wanted in, wanted a cut of everything, he wouldn't allow that. They threatened him, threatened us."

Meg pats at her mouth with the paper napkin, looking past Rose.

"They wanted to kill him, send a message to anyone else who thought they could stand up to them. They almost did kill him, you know. I was scared to death. All the time. Any little noise and I would jump. Oh, it was awful. My Gerald."

Rose had never heard any of these stories about her grandfather. Meg sips her tea, holds the cup close, still looking away.

"But they got him. Not the way they wanted to get him at first. But they got him."

Here she turns and holds her granddaughter's hand.

"You know he never took the salary he was owed from being union president. All those years, he never drew his salary. Put it all back in. So when he had to pay them— that ugly mug wanted blood, but he took the money—Gerald was ratted out, by his own man, ratted out."

Meg looks into her granddaughter's face, puzzled. She shakes her head and continues.

"That about broke his heart. Well, it did, didn't it? His heart was broken. Never recovered from that. His whole life, all that talent, giving it away so he could negotiate better contracts for the workers. And what does he get? He, my Gerald, he gets sent away."

Rose tries to process this information: sent away? Did he go to prison? She looks at her grandmother, now is not the time to interrupt her with questions. Now is the time to take this story in and keep it.

"When he came back to me, nearly two years gone, oh." One hand goes to her heart and she takes a breath, her face falls into its years, "But when he came back to me. He was so thin. So tired. And then, one night, he was really gone.

I miss him. All these years I miss him."

Meg has been holding Rose's hand through all this, this handing of her story to her granddaughter. She looks at their hands, one thin skinned, blue veined, a little brown bruise near a knuckle, the other round and soft and full of promise.

"And what about you Grams, what did you want?"

"What did I want, dear? I wanted him. I wanted a life with him. I was so proud of him. Yes sometimes I wish we could just be ordinary. Just go to work, come home, cook dinner, raise the children, like everybody else. But I didn't fall in love with a man like everybody else. I fell in love with Gerald."

She smiles, proudly, at Rose.

"He acted so confident when he gave his speeches, when he told his stories. But I was the one who knew when he couldn't sleep. I knew he paced the floors at night and worried. I saw the lines on his forehead get deeper.

"They seemed to vanish when someone came into the room and wanted to hear what he had to say. And he always had something to say, even when it was all malarkey. But they looked up to him. He was their hope. Not exactly one of them. No, he was not really like one of them because he could articulate what he thought were their needs and rights. He could write editorials and use fiery words and get them to cheer and clap and stand for him. He loved going into battle with a banner held high. This was his war."

Meg turns back to the present, back to her grown up granddaughter who never met her grandfather.

"Now you get some sleep, young lady, or that husband of yours will say I'm wearing you out. He won't let you come and visit with me anymore."

"Okay, Grams. Okay." Rose bends down to kiss her grandmother good night. Meg gives her hand one last squeeze.

Kieran was born in May and they had the Baptism celebration at Meg's house. It was bittersweet not having her grandmother there to meet her new son, but Rose felt comforted in the embrace of this old house. Her father and uncle are talking about selling the place. Rose speaks up, knowing she and Dennis don't have enough to pay a mortgage, but if Rose returns to work, then they should be able to manage.

So, that's what they do.

Marie makes a surprise appearance seventeen months after her brother arrived, but with daycare and borrowed energy, the McGuire family stakes its claim.

Chapter Forty-Seven

David Cellio stands about 5 feet 7 inches tall. By his thirtieth birthday he is developing a belly and is thinning on the scalp. His glasses get thicker and his seconds and thirds of his mother's cannolis are wearing Jenny down.

In the early days of their marriage Jenny tried to remember to smile when David entered the room. She hoped that after a while the smiling would become natural. Over the years the only natural reaction she has is to want to be in another room when he enters. She tries to keep busy. She takes long walks, then runs, trying to push away the tears.

Paul is growing to be a tall boy. He looks like he'll end up closer to six feet than 5'7". He has sharp features, a strong jaw line, straight nose, blue eyes and a headful of light brown hair. There is none of the Cellio family about him.

"Jenny, I was wondering, are you all Italian?" Mrs. Cellio asks her daughter-in-law one morning.

"Pretty much."

Jenny has been afraid of this question for a long time.

"I think one of my great grandmothers was Swiss or German, way back when."

"Oh, that must be it then. This boy has such blue eyes and he's kind of pale. I think I'll rub some olive oil into him." David's mother jokes. If only it were that simple.

"Oh well, you never know who's in your family tree." Jenny hopes that will dismiss the question.

When Paul is a little over two, Jenny decides it is time to get her bachelor's degree. She goes to Adelphi College and majors in history and education. A teaching job would work out best for her situation.

The grandmothers take turns watching the boy while Jenny is in school. David's mother loves spoiling him, so glad to have a grandson when David hadn't shown much promise in his younger years of ever marrying.

Jenny's mother sees that her daughter is becoming more and more distant. Once they would talk and linger over coffee. Now Jenny is always in a rush. Mrs. Tagliani catches Jenny look at her pleadingly once in a while, and then quickly banish that look. As much as she wants to know what is bothering Jenny, she fears her suspicions would be better off left unsaid. Who would it serve to bring such things up?

David begins to spend more time at the office. He finds that he is growing cold toward Paul, toward Jenny.

There is nothing in particular to point to, but it's just a sense of life being off kilter.

As Paul grows David is amazed at his self assuredness. He went right up to his kindergarten teacher, extended his hand and introduced himself. David was a shy child, hiding behind his mother's skirts. He hated kindergarten, threw a tantrum every morning. He wanted to stay home.

Paul can't wait to go and make new friends. He's a natural leader; other kids listen to him and go along with any game he suggests. Paul is turning out to be the kind of kid David followed around the playground when he was young. He thinks he should be proud of this quality in Paul, but he is mostly puzzled.

He eats his doubts.

At 38, David has his first heart attack.

He is told to exercise and change his diet. He does neither. He spends more and more evenings at his mother's house filling up on his favorite foods.

By forty-two he is dead. Massive coronary.

Jenny knows she killed him. She killed a good man. She used him so she wouldn't ruin her reputation and Phil Banfry's reputation. She tore David Cellio's life apart to save the wreck that Phil Banfry brought down on two families. And there is no one she can tell. And when it comes down to it, there is no one she can blame but herself.

ns br*Part Four*

2004

Chapter Forty-Eight

Madelyn Glover is a faded blonde. She has the look of a woman who has tried and failed once too often. Roots show through crisp and broken hair in an uneven pattern the morning in early January she decided to ask her boss, Dennis McGuire, to help her turn her job as his assistant into something that resembles a career. She heats the curling iron to twist her hair to disguise the dull roots. Madelyn knows she has reached the point where she has to cut her hair short or dye it. This in between is not working for her.

She drops Naomi at the before school program created for working mothers. Mother and daughter share an apartment now. It's a few miles closer to work, but a few miles further from the school than their house is, or was. The house is still there. They are not. Present tense or past tense, she wonders as she's driving. There's a contract pending; maybe some new people will have better luck staying a family than they did.

Doug left them after Thanksgiving dinner. He'd been agitated all day, but she had learned not to press him when he was like that. Often, he'd say something like *what the hell do you know about stress, I'm the one carrying the load for this family* and then take off in his car. Madelyn wanted this Thanksgiving to be nice, conflict free. She kept her questions to herself.

By the time she put the pies out for dessert, his favorite, pumpkin, and Naomi's favorite, apple, he was exasperated with, what she later figured, were his attempts to engage her in a fight.

You know I don't like this pie. I like the one from the bakery, not this frozen shit you can pretend you made because you heat it in the oven. You're no Suzy Homemaker, so don't pretend you are.

All day Madelyn had been holding herself together. She was tired now. She didn't argue with him. She sat and cut a slice of pie for Naomi and handed it to her. Naomi took the plate, looking side to side at her parents.

He tried again. *You got the pie you two like I see.* He picked up the tin and turned it over on the table, smashing it into her grandmother's table cloth; apples and crust a cobbler horror in the middle of their good china.

He stuffed some things into his gym bag. *I'm outta here. I'll get more of my stuff in a few days.* He slammed the back door. He was gone.

Madelyn sat at the table, hostess to the ruins of dinner. She poured herself a cup of coffee from the white carafe. Naomi moved her chair closer to her mother, handed her a dessert fork, put the only intact piece of apple pie between them. Mother and daughter ate their dessert in silence.

Men don't usually leave their families over pie selection. Madelyn suspected their marriage had been getting a little crowded. She wondered who the other woman is. She's curious, but not devastated. Three months later on this drive to work, Madelyn wonders if she bought the wrong pie on purpose.

As she is buttering a bagel to have with her coffee at her desk, she wishes she was one of those women who stopped eating when life takes a big turn. All her work clothes are straining at the seams and she can't afford to replace anything. Part of her wishes she cared. A stronger part wants another bite of the delicious butter soaked onion bagel.

She swivels her seat around to look out the window. From the east dark clouds are taking over the sky, moving quickly west. The guy on the radio said the storm will keep moving over Long Island all the way through Queens and Brooklyn.

~~~~

Dennis plays the oldies station on his drive to work. Traveling east on the Long Island Expressway he beats out rhythms to *Owner of a Lonely Heart* on his steering wheel. A shade of him steps into high school and college days, when the blood in his veins ran hot and he could feel the power of youth pulling him forward to the hunt: find a girl, get a job, have a family, make a mark on history.

He enters the LIE at Queens Boulevard. Horns blaring and drivers pushing their way onto the expressway, making a game of squeezing in and getting over to the left lane as quickly as possible, everyday trying to beat the previous personal best. Each morning he wags his head at this useless game. Within five miles they will all come to a standstill. It happens every morning and the guy who had to be in the left lane is just as stuck as Dennis who is biding his time in the middle lane. Every day the same dance. Every day the same impatient nuts try to get ahead and then sit like the rest of them where the LIE crosses over to the Grand Central and Van Wyck.

An announcer on the radio breaks in saying there is a storm front moving from the very east of Long Island and is expected to hit the City before eleven.

Today he plans to give Maddie an account one of the administrators usually handles. Its pretty straight forward; payments continue on the same schedule they've been on for years. He's trying to build her up, teach her more of the business. Two afternoons a week she comes into his office and they work on accounts for about an hour. He looks forward to those sessions, enjoys being her mentor and not just her boss. All the administrators have a Bachelor's degree. Maddie almost finished an Associates degree before she married. If she wants to be promoted, she'll have to catch up to the others.

Dennis smiles when he thinks of Maddie. It's nice to be needed, he concludes. Rose is so wrapped up in something lately; she barely talks to him. He drifts back to Maddie; heat rushes through him, raising the awareness of his nerve endings. He adjusts himself in his seat, then rolls the window half way down.

As Dennis rounds the corner to his office with his morning coffee in a styrofoam cup, he makes a mental note, again, to get himself a real mug for the office.

He calls out his usual greeting. "Good morning, crew. Let's see what today brings."

Madelyn pushes herself out of her chair and heads into Dennis' office before he has a chance to get started on today's work.

He is holding a 'World's Greatest Boss" mug. There is a bow attached.

Madelyn offers, "You are now free of styrofoam cups".

"Well, thanks Maddie."

"Do you know that you are the only one who calls me Maddie?"

"Really? It just seems to fit you."

"Okay, to you I'm Maddie. To the rest of the world I'm Madelyn."

"Deal."

Madelyn backs out of Dennis' office. He smiles at her, encouragingly.

Later that day Dennis gets an email reminder about the conference coming up next month in New Haven. It will be a two day affair. The newest hire often goes with him to these conferences to learn a few things and meet colleagues. All the junior officers have gone at least once. He hopes Maddie can arrange for a sitter for Naomi. This might be just the thing she needs, he thinks. He clicks *Forward*, with a message inviting her to attend.

By days end, it's arranged. Madelyn Glover will be taking a big step toward promotion and a new future.

~~~~

Rose is still sitting on her chair in the living room, observing the broken pieces of her favorite china cup mixed in the pool of blackberry tea. The puddle on the floor spreads out, down toward the front of the house. Must be a foundation shift, she thinks. She hadn't noticed the house leaning toward the street before. *Hmm.* She moves her head to catch the play of light on the shards. *I should take a picture. Nah, that will ruin the moment. Meditation in tea and china. If I painted this on a canvas, that's what I'd call it. Meditation in tea and china.*

She pulls her folded legs in, hugging them close. Once upon a time she would have hurried to get paper towels and a dust pan. *Once upon a time I thought I cared about stains and broken china. Look how pretty that is. It's beautiful, isn't it?*

The thunder rumbles and rain beats hard on the roof, on the cracked concrete in the driveway. The wind shifts and the window next to her takes a beating. She pulls the blanket closer, feeling at one with nature's force. The shards and dust of china rest in their puddle in front of her chair.

Chapter Forty-Nine

Rose finishes out the days of her leave. She has not told anyone, not even Dennis, that she has another brother, a half-brother, and that she met him for the first time at her father's funeral.

Hiding behind the pall of death, that tender space of mourning was not breached. Her family knew to keep this space. How do we know such things, she wondered, when to leave someone alone, when to intervene? A natural rhythm that needs no explanation, she supposes.

But that natural rhythm of respecting the space where she cannot be touched could become a habit; silence as a way of life. Warning all to keep away the sharp words that can open the wound, fresh as first stab. Then whatever was natural about the silence becomes unnatural, becomes a thing in itself, not connected to grief and its self-regulating end. Like her mother. She took on grief as a way of life. Cut off from the living, from those who needed her. From those she needed.

Rose wants her mind sharpened and her senses dulled. Think better, feel less. A surgeon's scalpel on her anesthetized soul. Cut away the diseased parts, let the healthy parts live. *Do this while I sleep,* she prays. *Let me awaken healed.*

At dinner she pours wine. One, two, three glasses. Dennis has a little, for her. She finishes the bottle while they do the dishes. *In vino veritas.* Finding the truth in wine? Sure, let the wine tug at the edges of the gates, pull it, slowly pull it down. Reveal the truth shivering behind the fence, ignored and abandoned. Now, *vino*, encourage *veritas* to stand, be strong, speak. These metaphors amuse her as she pours another glass.

Tomorrow, back to work.

Chapter Fifty

Rose is the last one out. As she pulls the brass handle a whisper rushes past her, through her. She rather likes the otherness of this, as if these whisperings are a sign that she is not alone, that angels or ancestors or God, even, are taking her on this dream like journey and she will be carried over the wreckage, able to view it from a safe place.

She pulled herself together enough to put on her usual 'I'm okay" act over the weekend. No one questioned it. A thought nags her. *If 'I'm okay' is an act, what am I really?* She parks this thought in the back of her head. *Later. Maybe.*

Rose holds her umbrella in front of her, against the cold wind and rain. As she gets closer to Jamaica Avenue the rails of the J line screech as a train pulls to stop. She looks up at the rusting monster that covers the avenue.

Just for a second she wonders what it would be like to fall through the tracks and land on the street or on a car stuck in the crosswalk. Would it be like a roller coaster, the excitement of disorientation and letting go, trusting in fate? Or would it be tempting fate, tempting the angels she wants to believe are protecting her?

Would she feel alive; even just a glimpse of alive? Would this damned anxiety dissolve in a rush of adrenaline? Would the adrenaline numb the pain of her breaking body as she crashed to the street?

This scene plays out in one, two, three, four strides as she walks to the stairs to board the next train. She glances up for one fraction of a second, meets no one's eye as she pictures the fall. She figures they'd notice if she went splat into rush hour traffic.

Rose slides into a double seat that faces forward, faces Manhattan. When the train leaves Brooklyn and goes under the East River she leans her brow against the scratched window. The glare of the overhead light and the backdrop of the sooty underground catch her in a dark mirror. She hardly recognizes the face.

But, no, that not's quite right. It's the face she confronts when she thinks no one is looking. It's the face she sees when she gets up in the middle of the night to sneak down for a few fingers of Jameson and the hall mirror catches her.

The bloom is off the Rose, she thinks. She tries to laugh; she wipes away a tear instead.

The thought she parked at the back of her head when she left the house is creeping forward in a rolling fog until it smacks her behind her eyes. She nods toward the question. *If 'I'm okay' has been my default act, then it begs the question. Let it beg.*

They push out of the train, closer here than they would ever allow on the street. One foot in front of the other up cracked steel tipped steps to the canyons of downtown.

Just a few blocks ahead is a hole in the ground where magnificent twins once stood. It is fenced in with names, so many names, listed in memoriam. More than two years now, but she can still taste the dust on her tongue, feel it on her face like the gray mask it was that day. Dennis and Rose found each other right here at the subway entrance.

They made their way in stunned silence blocks past the wreckage and walked over the Brooklyn Bridge, thousands of them, covered in the soot of brick and human dust.

In this shroud Dennis and Rose walked hand in hand until they reached their home. His company was a casualty of the wreckage, within hitting distance of the Twin Towers. They moved out to Long Island, out where it was safe and green, so now Rose makes this trip alone.

Her office is the way she left it last Tuesday, except for the post-it notes near the phone and mail piled high in her in-box. Returning calls will take up most of the morning.

"Rose McGuire, may I help you?"

"Hey Rose, its Sue. So the prodigal has returned to her captivity? I called you three times last week. Didn't you say you were going right back to work?

"I changed my mind. I spent the week at home."

Can you meet for lunch?"

"Sure—the Pearl Street Diner?"

"Sounds good to me. See you at noon."

Sue and Rose arrive at the same time and a booth empties just as they enter.

"Rose, um, you know you look kinda terrible."

"Uuh, my father just died." She snuffles back some tears. Sue is her oldest friend. She wishes she could tell her, tell her that after her sister died, her father took up with his secretary. Her father, a cliche.

"Yeah, that I get." Sue added, "How'd we get so old that our parents are dying? Geez, we're next up, aren't we?"

"Sue, you're a ray of sunshine."

"Aren't I, though?"

After a quiet moment, Sue changes the subject. "So, what's up with Dennis' new location? It's nice that some of the people from his office came to your father's wake."

Sue pauses, just for a moment, looks at Rose and takes the chance. "He seems to enjoy their company. He and one of the women from work seemed to be best of friends. What's her name? Margie or Maddie, something like that."

Rose doesn't pick up on Sue's attempt at sub-text. "I don't know. Something like Madelyn. Dennis seems happy to be out of the city—he keeps talking about all the new developments on the Island, great floor plans, big yards, the schools, low crime—you know, all the good reasons to get out of this crazy place."

"You'd have a helluva commute from Suffolk County."

"This job—I'm so tired of it. It's not worth an hour and half commute on the Railroad and then the subway. Nope. I'd have to be able to quit."

"Then we couldn't meet for lunch."

"Well, there you go. No move. That will be my counter-argument next time Dennis brings it up."

Tina comes over, order book out, pen ready. "Tuna on rye, lettuce, tomato, pickle. Iced Tea." She states rather than asks. Rose nods in approval.

"Grilled Ham and Swiss. Diet Coke." Sue nods even though Tina has already left to yell in the order.

"So, really, what's up?" Sue doesn't usually insist on talking like this, but today she looks as though someone whispered to her that Rose has a fatal disease.

"I thought you were into positive thinking and banishing negative thoughts before they had a chance to burrow in your brain. Isn't that what you've been sharing with me from your leadership training classes?

"Yeah, but, it's not just today, Rose. You've been looking worse every time I see you. I tried the positive thinking thing and then it hit me. We've known each other since the fifth grade and have gone through all sorts of crap together. If I have to banish people who give off negative vibes, I'd have to drop you from my list of friends, and where does that leave me? You know all my secrets."

She laughs at Sue's logic. "Well, I'm glad they didn't brainwash you completely."

Tina manages to drop the plates of sandwiches and drinks without knocking anything over.

"Here ya go, hon." She leaves the two tickets on the table.

"Okay, I'll ignore that." Sue smiles and waves her hand to draw out more information from her old friend.

"I know we've shared so much over the years, I, ah, don't think I ever told you—but after Cilla died my mother really retreated into herself..."

Sue doesn't want to discuss history, she wants Rose to think about what's going on in her family now.

"Duh, of course I knew that. Your house was always dark and sad and we stopped hanging out there."

"Let me finish, Sue. She retreated into herself even after she came back from her little 'rest'. Those cups of tea I was always clearing away?" Sue nods. "Well, I'm pretty sure she was mixing vodka with her Tetley's."

"Oh…Oh, and I assume you mean she did that longer than just a month or so?"

"Yep. At first she would just fall asleep on the couch. And then, she got angry. And mean. She screamed at Jimmy every time he came over because he was 'living in sin' with Kathy. So after a while he stopped coming around, even to check on me. Dad stayed at work longer and longer and joined every committee he could just to not be home. At least that's what I thought." She left that hint out there, but Sue didn't pick up the thread.

"Yeah, I knew some of this. But you always acted like you could handle it, like it rolled off your back. I thought you were handling everything. You amazed me. I was kinda jealous at how together you seemed."

"Seemed. I should have gone into acting. Funny, I just realized that I was orphaned when Cilla died. I never thought of that before. Lately I feel like I've been acting my whole life. I don't know what's real. I don't know what's mine or what I've just adopted to keep up the act."

"Yeah. Sounds like your mom got so distracted by her grief that she didn't see what was going on in her own house. That's something to be careful of. Maybe you should move out to the Island, it would be easier on Dennis."

"And harder on me."

"Just sayin', is all."

Rose wipes away a tear. "Stop, just stop." She commands herself. "Jesus, Sue, I have to get back to work. Tell me something funny so I can put this away."

Chapter Fifty-One

Rose usually rushes to get the 7:55 train. This morning she decides to catch the 8:05. Little thing, puny rebellion. But it's something. Yesterday's rain is finally exhausted so the walk down the hill will be pleasant. The air is fresh washed and the cars that move along Forest Parkway swoosh in the puddles.

Today she stops in the deli on the corner under the rusting scaffolding that holds up the el. She will have a cup of coffee and sip it on the train. Provided there's a seat. She walks up the chipped concrete steps as her usual train pulls out. She smiles as the doors close without her. She picks a new train and all of sudden feels she has accomplished something wonderful. Maybe it is wonderful. She feels a little lighter, breathes a little more freely.

The platform is less crowded for this train. Why did everyone need to get on the 7:55? She thinks she has opened the door to some great insight from this question. The train pulls in; there are seats. She can drink her coffee.

They chug through the west end of Queens, enter Brooklyn; move along at the height of trees. Old trees. Rose wonders what-these trees have witnessed in the faces zipping by all through the years. Some absorbed in newspapers or a novel, some looking wistfully out the window wondering if they will do this season in, season out, for the rest of their lives. The coffee is good. She sips it slowly.

At Myrtle Avenue several people exit, several enter. A man who reminds her of something steps in. Something familiar. *Do I know him?* Subtract the years, color in the gray hair to a more youthful dark blond, take a few pounds off the face and body.

So many years. She hasn't seen him since she was a kid. There was talk of him leaving the priesthood, going out west. Whispers, of course. Apparently you can't just change your mind about the priesthood without some scandal attached to it. He was so good at being a priest. Her teenage image of Jesus walking around the streets of Queens in the change-everything-seventies while the whole rest of her life was thrown into a cosmic blender and she had to find something to hold onto.

The man she thinks is Fr. Joseph is reading a book. She studies him a little longer. She won't approach him today. If he's on the train tomorrow, then, maybe. Maybe.

~~~~

She chooses a seat in the section where the man with the familiar face sat yesterday. At the Myrtle Avenue exchange he enters. The seat next to her is empty. He takes it.

"Fr. Joseph?" He looks at Rose and she can see the calculation working in his eyes, the way she did yesterday. He smiles, "Rose? Rose Banfry?"

"Yep, that's me. Its McGuire now—husband, two kids, job in the city. All that jazz."

"How long has it been since I've seen you?"

"Very long. I was just starting high school. About the same age my daughter is now."

"Well, a daughter? In high school?"

"And a son in high school. And don't forget the husband."

"Well, of course. And it's Joseph now. My life is quite different. Actually, I've been in this part of the world for more than a year. My mother was ill, in a nursing home. She died two weeks ago. I'm getting ready to go home when I clear up things at work."

"Home?" she sneaks what she hopes is a surreptitious glance at his left hand. He's wearing a silver band inlaid with turquoise.

"Yep. When my mother got ill we came back to look after her. We lived in her house for a while, but then her condition got worse and she needed to be in a nursing home. We had to sell her house to pay for the nursing home, so I have an apartment here in Brooklyn."

He pauses. His thoughtful, slow paced cadence is the same as she remembers it.

"My family grew homesick after a while. So they're back in Tucson while I stayed here for my mother. I work with Children's Services downtown, for the next few days anyway. And your parents, how are they?"

"My mother died a few years back, my father died recently."

"Ah, I'm sorry."

He was once her priest, her confessor. He knew more about her life than she did about his. Now they're just two middle aged people commuting to work. Huh.

After a moment, he takes up his book again. He seems to be able to fold himself inward and retreat right there on the noisy train. Rose opens her Daily News so as to not look like she's been left hanging. Gossip and crime. Same every day.

~~~~

Throughout her day at the office she can't shake the undertone that's been playing in her imagination. She is tired of thinking about those days; they creep into so much of her life, she just wants to move on, leave it alone, bury it.

But it is a ghost that haunts her, a ghost with the persistence of her little sister who demanded to get her own way no matter how tired anyone else was. She gathers papers on her desk, pulls up accounts, scrolls down, not seeing a word on the screen, trying to look like she's there, working, paying attention to what earns her a paycheck. It's all a farce. She wonders when she'll get caught. Her brain goes where she doesn't want it to, and she is too tired to re-direct.

Rose fakes her way through the rest of the day at work, pushing down the past, back where she'd kept it for years, letting her professional side take over. But the barrier is cracking and she doesn't know how long she'll be able to keep past and present separate.

Chapter Fifty-Two

Dennis called and said he had another meeting, so they eat dinner without him. Kieran sits at the table safe within the buzz of his earphones. Marie is telling her what she and Stella are planning for the weekend. Rose nods a 'yeah, sure' at Marie, but has no idea what she allowed her daughter to do on Saturday night. Marie's a good kid. Rose is sure it will be okay.

At three in the morning Rose sits on the living room couch, shawled in a crocheted blanket. Another night, no sleep.

Dennis is alone in their bed upstairs. Rose comes down quietly because she can't keep still any longer.

Her legs are folded lotus style on the cool couch. A calm fills her, quieting the noise that's been beating against her skull lately. She dares not move and disturb this peace, this momentary entrance over the threshold into that thin place, that step beyond the veil.

She breathes it in, breathes in the primrose light, trying to fill her lungs with this familiar substance as if the light itself were air and she could gather it, keep it in reserve. She knows these moments come when her brokenness opens the gate between here and there and she doesn't want to scare the visit away, in case it is a skittish ghost.

This gift is a grace and she knows there is a price, something more is coming, but she doesn't want to think about how it will be spent, she wants to gather now, as much as she is able, as much as is granted her.

Since she was little these thin place moments intervened, separating her from danger, surrounding her with pale light; strengthening her. They came sparingly though. In achingly lonesome times she asked for this grace; she usually had to endure without it. She would cling to the memory of the gift as consolation. Memory and imagination are her tools. And fortitude. But that is wearing thin. She is learning that her allotment of fortitude is worn out, her defenses spent. The only place of protection is this shift of perception, this retreat into otherness.

There were times she could almost step between worlds at will. Not quite, but almost. The times she'd turn her head because she thought she saw someone standing at the dining room table or speaking at the kitchen sink. Those moments hardly registered. But they did chink away at her armor until she admitted that she was between the now and the then. Or was it now, with a taste of then? She doesn't want to dwell on the questions or pin it down. It pulls away if she does that. Just accept it. Don't explain it.

Rose runs the palm of her hand over the damask. Years ago it had been covered in green mohair. They kept much of her grandmother's furniture. Not only for sentiment, but because it was still sturdy. And it belonged. Rose rather likes the connection with Grandma. She rather likes the ghosts that whisper about.

She is breathing in, breathing out. Trying not to let thoughts get in and take her down paths she does not want to go. In, out. She reaches out her hand and pats the seat next to her. Pats Grandma Meg's hand. Leans into to her, like she did after Cilla's funeral. Most natural thing in the world, right?

They sit that way for a while—she doesn't know how long. The scene shifts, so subtly, so imperceptibly that she doesn't realize it is a shift until she thinks about it later.

They are at her grandfather's wake, right here in the living room. He is laid out, hands folded, people murmuring, voices coming from the kitchen, the dining room. Lots and lots of people. There's Grandma Meg, younger than Rose ever knew her. There's her father, standing so straight and tall. And her uncle. The two brothers handling everything, shaking everyone's hand. Being strong for their mother. Being their father's sons. Competent, in control, professional.

Shift again. The night before the wake. He, her grandfather, is on the couch. He calls: *Meg. Meg.* But it's barely a whisper. She comes from the kitchen, drying her hands on a linen towel. *Gerald, would you like your coffee out here or in the kitchen?* A few steps more toward him. *Gerald, GERALD!!* She takes his hand and collapses to her knees in front of him. *Gerald, oh no, Gerald.*

Rose is there with her. Before she was born. She can't tell if she is standing, or sitting. She just knows she is there with Grandma Meg. In her heartbreak. At her most tender spot. And here she is with Rose.

She wonders if she were to tell Dennis that she sat with her grandmother tonight, though she has been dead for years, would he look at her like she was a stranger, or worse, too strange? Probably not. Maybe a little. He'd listen. Get her a cup of coffee. Tell her she's so tired from her father's funeral. Grief takes time. He'd say the right thing.

No, I am not ready to tell Dennis. This is mine.

Chapter Fifty-Three

Dennis comes home late, again. He whistles in a little after ten. Rose has already gone to bed. He slips in next to her. She doesn't do anything to let him know she's not asleep She isn't ready to tell him about her morning crack up. She plays the scene again and again, like a video on instant replay.

Joseph sits next to me on the train. I manage a smile, a weak one. I'm is so tired from being awake last night keeping company with Grandma. Joseph tilts his head and looks at me. I look back.

"How've you been, Rose? Sorry I was a little distant there yesterday. You're a blast from the past and you've had an effect on me, if you don't mind my saying."

Since he is leaving in a few days, I'd better ask some questions before it's too late.

"I don't mind you saying—you kinda resurrected some memories for me, yourself. Can I ask how long you've been out of the priesthood?

"Sure. I left not too long after I was kicked out—or more politely 'transferred'—from Maria Goretti. A few years after that. I suppose I should thank you."

"Thank me?"

"Well, your, um, situation, propelled me into making a pest of myself at the diocese. I talked to some bureaucrats down in the Chancery. They thanked me for my concern and before you could say in nomine patre I was out. They sent me to Brooklyn where they told me there were real problems I could put my 'youthful' energy toward."

"You spoke to the diocese? For me?"

"I tried to get to the bishop but his bulldogs didn't allow that. After two years of banging my head against the wall, I asked for a leave of absence. I went out to Tucson to a retreat center for ruined priests. That's where I met my wife, and history, my history, changed."

I sit for a few minutes, taking this in. Then I turn to face him.

"You tried to speak to the bishop's office for me?" I say it again, because, well because it's like a trapdoor coming loose.

"You and a few others. I saw that Dunleavy was paying too much attention. He did seem to focus in on you. Maybe because your family was going through a hard time and there was no one to take care of you, I don't know. I don't get it."

We sit a few minutes in a silence that hovers between the uncomfortable and the familiar. I have one foot in the past, stuck in drying cement, while some part of me is trying to pull out, flailing and directionless. Here is this man I haven't seen in years, prying loose memories I tried to keep buried.

"These past few years with all the dirty secrets pouring out of every diocese, bishops and cardinals trying to brush everything under the carpet; it made me sick. Well, that's the thing these days. So many people feeling adrift, rudderless. I hope something good comes out of all this." Joseph shakes his head as he says this, then turns to look out *the window.*

Feeling sick. God, that's about right. I've been feeling sick for so long I don't know what feeling good is anymore. Secrets. Yeah, dirty secrets. Dare I tell him what I recently discovered? Not yet, I haven't even told Dennis. Should I tell the kids they have an uncle out there. Another uncle. He looks so much like Jimmy, before Jimmy started drinking, before he and Kathy divorced.

As much as I want to talk to him, I'm afraid. What scabs would be ripped off? I cross my legs, hold on at the knee. The scar from the fall I took the day I quit the Rectory is ropy beneath my fingers.

But, God, oh, God, I want to know that I'm not alone in this abandonment, this feeling sick with the church.

All the trust invested in it; the history, the hierarchy, the traditions and sacraments. The right and the wrong, sin and salvation. The nuns and the priests. The whole wonderful, terrible, awe-inspiring, piercing, transformative, incandescent, demanding great mythology of it.

And all those rules and warnings, mostly about sex. The obsession with sex. The obsession fed the great dragon behind the church doors. The dragon that consumed them, twisted them, turned some priests and nuns into monsters. Turned parents into shrieking fools and hypocrites. Turned children into prey.

But I don't want to think about it anymore. I want to be done with it all. Just move on. But I have to know more. I turn to him, almost touch his arm, but don't. A little cough will do. He looks at me, his turquoise eyes encourage my speech.

"Well, I know this isn't confession, but I haven't been able to enter a church for more than a year now, except for my father's funeral. After the abuses from priests coming out in the news from Boston, and then, everywhere—feels like volcanoes keep erupting—I just *couldn't go."*

With one subtle move he rests a warm palm on my arm while his other hand releases the tight fingers of my fist. My hand feels so small in his, so safe. I can continue my confession.

"I wasn't able, I mean, it felt like a force field that was so much stronger than me, that wouldn't let me in. I have two kids in high school, Marie is in the youth choir, but I can't even go to hear her sing."

The light pressure of his hands on mine is stronger. Just. The warmth flowing from him runs through my veins. It reaches my heart. My tight, tired heart. I close my eyes and breathe. Breathe. My words come now, not afraid, but relieved, finally released. My complaint is free from rebuke and the accusation of self-pity.

"My parents made such a fuss about attending Mass every Sunday, no matter what. Even when my mother checked out of my life she got herself off to early Mass on Sunday and then came home and went back to bed. But she fulfilled her obligation."

Joseph nods his head to let me know he is listening.

"I read the accounts of all the altar boys and the girls who were really abused and I feel I'm not in their league of suffering—I just had to deal with a flashing and some obsessive behavior from the pastor telling me I was an occasion of sin just for being a girl, just for being me. And he with his hungry eyes checking to make sure I was not leading anyone into sin like the girls in his pictures, and some touching. Minor league stuff in this horror show."

The anger rises in my voice. But the anger is safe. I can tell him and not worry that he will dismiss such a little complaint. I don't want to cry, don't want my mascara to run. Joseph moves in closer, our legs sharing heat. His touch is warm and strong and gentle. A wave of love radiates from him, all through me. I didn't know how much I needed that.

Lying in bed, her back to Dennis, the end of that scene plays over and over, loud and persistent:

When we come to the last stop in Brooklyn, just before going under the East River, Joseph turns his head and whispers in my ear, so close I feels his breath on my neck, I feel the syllables separately. "Rose, thank God it wasn't worse than what you did go through. But it's all part of the same problem."

He pauses for a thoughtful moment. "Listen, there are so many places of grace in this world, so many graces that can heal the hole in your heart."

His hand is still on my forearm, only now he is so close that his arm presses into my side as he whispers this benediction.

"When I went out to Tucson all those years ago, I would sit outside my room, wrapped in a blanket. Looking at the sky, the jewels of stars, the clouds that passed in front of the moon, the smell of the desert flowers, the sound of a coyote in the distance and the cicadas in the long grasses—that was a gift of grace, Rose. I go back there in my mind when I need to, and yes, I need to quite often. And in a few days, I'll be back with my wife and children. I pray that you have such moments of grace."

We are under the river now, the lights in the train sputtering on and off, mostly off. We sit there, arms together, our legs from hip to calf pressed close in the tight seats, the electricity between us strong, neither moving for those minutes under the river, not moving until the train rumbles to a halt, brakes screeching, passengers filling the doorway, waiting for them to open so they can rush into the crowd.

We rise slowly when the train is almost empty, nodding our heads in farewell, not speaking. Ah, the warmth of his breath and closeness of his cheek as he moves to me. His soft lips press into my warm face. A lingering. A life raft. When he pulls his face away the energy of his tender kiss is branded on my skin. Can anyone else see the freshly burned brand that mingles with all the nerves in me, all the way to wherever that center is, the center where I am most real?

"M'am? Eh, eh, M'am?"

"Yes?" I take my hand from my cheek.

"M'am, this is the last stop. Everyone has to be off the train now. Have a good day."

I stand in the all but empty train car. The conductor takes me by my elbow to the door. I have the stairs to myself and melt into the foot traffic. One foot in front of the other, all the way to my office. I get a cup of coffee, take two aspirin out of my purse and pretend to work. My head is pounding. I'm dizzy. I make it to the ladies room in time to throw up this morning's bagel.

When I look in the mirror I see how pale I am. Still, I feel the imprint of Joseph's lips pressed against my cheek. I look close to see if there is a mark. But there is not. There cannot be. I haven't figured it out yet. Another moment, then I'll catch up. Then I'll know that no one else saw Fr. Joseph because he wasn't there.

I keep looking in the mirror, looking for an answer, looking for a question, even. Slowly, but not slowly enough to protect me from the punch to my gut, I realize that the barriers I thought I maintained had vanished. Last night watching my grandfather's wake with Grandma Meg was one thing. A graced moment under cover of darkness and near sleep.

But this, no this is not the thin place of comfort and strength. This is daytime, rush hour, the real, concrete world of dirty handrails and *body odor. The walls of the ladies room telescope in on me; the face looking back from the mirror is stunned.*

She went down to Personnel and requested an immediate leave of absence.

Chapter Fifty-Four

On the way out to work on Wednesday morning, Dennis tells Rose, as if an afterthought, "oh, yeah, you know I've got that conference tomorrow up in New Haven— it's over late Friday night, so I'll be home Saturday."

"Oh, did you tell me?"

"Sure, I told you a few weeks ago. You probably forgot."

"Mmm. Probably. You'll be home tonight, but not tomorrow or Friday night. Got it."

"Have a good day." He leans in to kiss her; she turns her head and he gets a cheek.

"Mmm. You too."

When he leaves, she lets out a sigh. Now its the kids she has to fool. Another half hour till they leave. *God, I'm so tired. I just want to get back in bed.*

This is the third day of going through the motions of getting ready for work. Shower, blow dry, makeup, clothes. Rose turns the shower on, but she sits on side of the tub. After ten minutes of running the water she reminds herself to turn on the hair dryer. Every breath hurts. Every thought is work. She tries to keep her inner drill sergeant alert, but it is so difficult. Pretending takes so much energy.

When Marie yells out "Bye, Mom" Rose notices that she has been holding her left hand over her mouth and her right arm is wrapped around her belly. When the door slams, she lets out a long breath.

The bed, the soft thick quilt, the cool cotton sheets and pillow. It is everything she could want right now. Everything.

Chapter Fifty-Five

MADELYN IS WAITING FOR Dennis in the lobby of the Marriott. She checks her hair in the reflection of the glass doors. Yesterday after work she spent two hours at the salon getting her hair transformed to a more believable honey color and a chic, smooth cut. She invested in some new clothes to premiere at this event. Sophisticated dark trousers, new shoes and a coordinated jacket and blouse go far in disguising her flaws. She hardly recognizes herself.

She wonders if Dennis will recognize her.

Dennis comes through the revolving doors scanning the lobby. His brow is pinched, eyes focused. To his left, nothing. Down the middle to the registration desk. Nope. To his right. He scans over Maddie, then immediately comes back to her. Smile is returned with smile. He walks over to her, his step brisk, arms open. "Well, look at you." She stands and he motions for her to turn around so he can see the full effect. "Wow."

Madelyn does a little curtsy. Dennis gestures a slight bow. He extends a folded elbow. She takes it and they walk in.

The conference has begun. A day of meetings, note taking, shaking hands, exchanging business cards. Dennis had fifty cards printed up for Maddie on his own. She's not an officer yet, but he is trying to launch her.

For the evening events, Maddie changes into a sleeveless, V-neck midnight blue dress and matching heels. She sprays a little cologne and touches up her make-up, darkening her eyes with smoky shadow and liner. For good luck, a few more swipes of mascara.

Dennis is already mingling, feeling more energy and vigor than he has in ages. And confidence. He stands a little taller when Maddie enters, charm turned on full power. Never, in the two years she has worked for him, has he seen her like this. She was always so tired, counting the minutes until five when she could leave. Since Doug left, Maddie is coming into her own. Divorce empowerment.

He pulls out her chair at the table. She unfolds her big white napkin and sips the wine already poured. When Dennis sits, they clink their glasses. *To the conference. To the conference.*

Wine is refilled by waiters at the ready. During the keynote Dennis looks at the speaker, scribbles a few notes. He hasn't a clue what the investment banker is saying. Maddie leans into him, to get a better view of the dais. The combination of wine, the darkness of the room, Maddie leaning into him and the delicate fragrance surrounding her has him confused and delighted. If they could just stay like this for a long while, maybe it will be enough. When she squeezes his knee as she pulls to sit back, she sighs deeply.

They ride the elevator together. They have already compared room numbers. Madelyn's room is directly above his. He's 635, she's 735. When the door bings open at six, he makes his way from the back of the car, parting the other passengers, but not before Maddie's's fingers dance a few light steps on his, teasing a mingle.

Dennis fiddles with the remote, playing the channels, one after the other, not able to stop on anything. It's all noise; a poor distraction for his brain and revved up body.

A little after one, he jumps at a light tapping on his door. He's wearing only boxers; he opens the door with no hesitation. Maddie enters, her pink satin robe brushes his bare skin. Dennis pushes the power button on the TV. No words, no sound. The hair of his chest against her breasts, the width of his shoulders as she wraps herself around him, legs locked, tighter, tighter. Yes. Yes.

~~~~

When he wakes in the morning, his head is pounding. He is alone.

He wants to think he dreamt it. He had so much wine, but last night was no dream. That was flesh and blood and sweat. That was life seeking life, power seeking power until they exploded together, faces strained, eyes wide open. A silent assent. But an assent. He could have turned her away, he had, at least, that much power. He chose not to. When he swings his legs over the bed, one foot hits the rough carpet, the other, something smooth. Pink satin panties, bordered in ivory lace. He jerks his foot away from the evidence. Maybe there is such a thing as mere sex. They didn't speak, didn't caress, didn't linger and play. Sex. Primal, guttural, physical, earthy sex.

He prays to God there is such a thing.

He goes to the first lecture of the day. She waves him over. She has his coffee prepared, just the way he likes it.

Chapter Fifty-Six

Rose sleeps. Not at night. During the day.

At night the shadows on the wall from the street lamps take on weird forms, like Shakespeare's witches around the cauldron.

At night the memories come. The ones she tried to push aside. Of being alone. Alone with her mother who couldn't look at her without accusation that she just didn't take care of Cilla better. Alone in the church basement with Dunleavy and his pictures of girls in short plaid skirts and tight white blouses. And all those times he looked her over, head to foot, checking to see if anything was inappropriate in her dress or demeanor. "Don't laugh with boys, it only encourages their dirty little minds. Don't wear lipstick, they'll think you're open for business. Don't wear sleeveless shirts, that little curve here"— with his forefinger he pressed against the crescent through her uniform that would show if she wasn't wearing sleeves— "that's enough to drive the boys to impure thoughts. You don't want to be responsible for their sin, do you?"

She shudders at the images. Shudders at the grotesqueness of the man. Shudders at her weakness when she muttered "No, Monsignor" in response.

She's afraid of being alone with Jimmy, who, even before his divorce, took up ranting at all the social ills and what "they" were doing to the working man. The look in his eyes changed over the years, as his drinking progressed, as Kathy moved forward without him.

She wanted to feel safe with her father during those years. Like when she and Cilla played and he would be the friendly giant. But he disappeared along with Cilla's casket. Cilla took so much with her and left Rose to manage alone.

Chapter Fifty-Seven

For three weeks this is Rose's routine. She wills herself to get out of bed by noon after everyone leaves. Take a shower, put on some makeup, make herself smile. Then one day she needs to talk with Jimmy. She puts aside her reluctance to be alone with him. Her need to know what he knows is stronger.

"Jimmy, it's Rose. Call me back. I need to speak with you."

"Jimmy. It's Rose. Again. If you don't call me back I'll just come over and wait."

There's one spot on Jamaica Avenue a block from Jimmy's place. She fills up the meter with a couple of dimes. One hour. Hot dog buns and squares of waxed paper have settled in with damp leaves and cigarette butts in every cement step and gutter at every store and bar along the way. March is going out like a lion. She opens the door next to Mulvaney's. The tiny vestibule in front of the steep narrow staircase stinks. She doesn't want to know of what. That'll take too much picturing. She doesn't hold on to the cold metal pipe of a stair rail. No imagination needed to know she should avoid that.

Jimmy's apartment is to the right on the tiny landing, directly over the bar. Rose wonders how he gets any sleep. Maybe its quiet during the day.

"Jimmy. Jimmy!! C'mon, answer the door."

He opens the door when she's in the middle of her third set of knocking. She doesn't think he's shaved since their father's funeral, five weeks ago. He turns his face into his hands cupped around a flame and draws deeply. "Hey."

"Hey, yourself. God, Jimmy." But she stops. Not now. I'm not his mother. We don't have one of those.

He looks at her. Somewhere under there is the brother she knew years ago.

"C'mon. I could use some lunch. Or coffee. There's a place down the block, right? Let me take you to lunch, Jim."

"Sure, Rose." He picks his jacket off the floor.

They are pointed to a booth at the back of the diner. Rose brushes crumbs off the green plastic upholstery with her purse before sitting. Jimmy sits across from her.

Two large plastic menus are on the Formica table. They remain closed.

"Coffee. And an English muffin," Rose says to the woman in the short skirt and formerly white sneakers.

Jimmy doesn't answer.

"Make that two coffees."

"Sure thing, hon."

"Jimmy—at the funeral—we saw Jenny and her son—any thoughts?"

Jimmy looks at her sideways.

"Jimmy—come on I want to talk to you."

"Sure I did. It took a minute. Okay, a few minutes. Then I knew. He was who I was supposed to be. He was the son Dad wanted."

"So you know?"

"Know? I figured, like you did. Years ago, I figured Dad had a piece on the side. I didn't figure it was Jenny though. God, she was almost my age. I thought it was one of those dames who were always hanging around the club, volunteering to make calls and stuff envelopes—maybe that redhead with the cleavage—and those Barbie doll shoes- Mrs. Oh, what's her name? She was all over Dad at those stupid dinners. I figured Mom had gone out of the wife business."

"So you knew, or figured, Dad had someone else? Did you ever say anything?"

She knew that was stupid as the words were coming out. No one confronted their father. They learned that before they could talk.

"I almost spit it out when they'd rail on me about 'living in sin.' I caught Dad's eye during one of those yelling sessions and he couldn't look at me straight. He said "the hell with you" and walked away, leaving Mom to finish up the lecture."

He lights his next cigarette from the ember at his fingertips. It wasn't the kind of diner where anyone cared.

"I just left. I thought they were assholes. Phonies. I just left."

"Wish you'd taken me with you."

"Nah, you don't. Ya think when I got back to Kathy after that scene that things were all happy? Then they wouldn't come to see us after we got married 'cause they would be saying it was all okay, when it wasn't, so they couldn't look like they approved. Hell, no. And Kevin. What kind of grandparents were they to him? They did a number on me. What the fuck, I can't talk about this shit."

He turns away, holding the coffee cup with two hands. Rose reaches her hand out to him, but he doesn't take it.

"Whaddja want to see me about, Rose? You finally figured out who your parents were? What are you, 45 now? Jesus, it's about time. How'd you do it all these years? How'd you fool yourself that they were some models of middle class virtue? Didn't you see how fucked up they were?"

They sit a few more minutes like this. Holding on. Holding down. Rose lost Jimmy years ago. Blamed him for being weak. Giving in. Not living up to his potential. All that shit. It was all shit.

"Gotta go, Rose. Sorry your world was shattered. Why didn't you know? Why'd you leave me out there all alone, Rose? You with your perfect life. Perfect job. You didn't have any room for me all these years. Now you wanna blame me for not tellin' you?"

He tosses his cigarette in the cold coffee and slides out of the booth. He won't look at her.

She leaves a ten on the table. The meter is running out.

Chapter Fifty-Eight

"I LIKE BEER WITH POT roast."

"I know, Dennis. So does Jimmy. He likes beer with everything." After their failed meeting on Jamaica Avenue Rose called her brother and asked him to come for Saturday supper.

"You're asking for it either way. If we don't have beer or wine, you might as well tell him this is an intervention. He'll get all defensive and belligerent. If we do have it, he'll get all offensive and belligerent. No matter what, you end up with belligerent."

"Not always", Rose offers weakly.

Dennis gives her that look. "What can I help with?"

"I guess you should get some beer. But not too much. One six pack is too little, two is too much."

"Pick a number and we can put the rest in the cellar."

"Eight? Get some Cokes too."

He grabs his keys off the hook at the back door.

"Oh, and some Danish."

"Will do."

Rose is standing at the sink, a vegetable peeler in one hand, a carrot in the other. It's raining and the drops hitting the side of the house beat out a rhythm that pulls her under. The silver rain shifts her vision to a near blur.

Kieran bangs down the attic stairs two floors above. Reality. There are onions to slice and carrots to peel and garlic to crush.

When did this seem like a good idea? Jimmy hasn't been here in ages. He seems to think that Dad and Uncle John gave me the house. They weren't the kind of people who gave anything. Fair market value. Why did we buy this house? A comfort and a scorn. All the ghosts. How stupid am I? We shoulda moved out to the Island like everyone else.

"Mom. Mom, you okay?"

"Onions." Half true.

Marie smiles at her mother. "China or kitchen?"

"Kitchen. Pot roast on a Saturday sounds like kitchen dishes to me, don't ya think?"

"Yup." She gives Rose a quick hug and gets the dishes out. "Paper napkins, too, I suppose?"

I want to tell her to be kind to her uncle Jimmy. I want to tell her that he wasn't always like this. I want to tell her everything, just let go. But no. I won't do that to her. She's fifteen. Jimmy is not hers to take care of. He's mine.

The roast is simmering in the big pot. Carrots, onions, garlic, bay leaf. Needs a little salt and pepper. Red wine would kick the gravy up a notch. She pulls a bottle of supermarket red from the little rack on the sideboard in the dining room.

A cup for the pot, a cup for the cook. Not bad. Two cups for the cook. I toast the roast. Dribble a little more in the pot. Mmmm. Smells good.

Dennis comes in the back door carrying a case of Coke. "Look who I met climbing up from the avenue."

Jimmy is right behind Dennis, a six-pack in each hand.

"Jimmy, you're all wet."

Not enough sense to carry an umbrella. Probably never thought to buy one. God, wet dog has nothing on him. Old cigarettes and body odor. When was the last time he washed his clothes?

"Kieran, bring down a pair of thick socks for your uncle. And a towel. Jimmy leave those shoes right there."

He pushes down on the heel of one cracked sneaker with the toe of the other. Black socks, holes at the toes. Nails are long and ragged and thick.

"Here's some socks, Uncle Jimmy."

Jimmy pulls his chin up toward Kieran. The universal guy move that covers thanks, how-ya-doing, good bye, and yeah, that's something to think about.

"Hang your jacket on that hook, Jimmy." *I can close the vestibule door. Don't want his jacket wrecking the aroma of the roast.* He hangs the wet towel on the back of a kitchen chair. Rose bites her tongue.

I'll throw it down the cellar stairs as soon as he leaves the room.

Dennis grabs a couple of Cokes and hands one to Jimmy.

"St. John's is playing Villanova, Jim. Let's see how we're doin."

They head out to the TV in the living room. Rose wonders if there is even a trace of school pride buried in her brother. She always figured Kieran and Marie will go to St. John's, just like they all did. *Generation after generation.* And then: *the sins of the father will be visited upon the children. No shit, Sherlock.*

When Jimmy leaves the kitchen Rose swallows the rest of her wine. She wonders how long she can stay there. The roast probably needs another forty-five minutes. She pours a bag of pretzels into a large plastic bowl. She wants to send Marie out with them, but she makes herself go.

"How we doin?"

"Behind by four. But there's time. Ohh!! Make that six."

Jimmy's face is pointed toward the television. No reaction to the shot. He holds the Coke can in his hand. He's not watching the game. He can't. They're way beyond basketball games in search of common ground. His right hand is getting jittery; the left is tucked under his thigh.

"Need a smoke."

Jimmy goes through the kitchen to smoke on the back porch. First stop is the refrigerator to grab a beer. The long cold drink rushes down his throat, wave after wonderful wave. It hits his belly in a splash, immediately releasing its magic. There's his old friend. Now he can relax, get his hands steady. Tosses the bottle cap toward the metal can. It pings and misses. Leaves it in the mud.

It's dark. He turns right, to the aurora of street lamps along Forest Park Drive, to the diluted light pushing its way through the trees that have arbored this area for generations. Wind whips up under his shirt and slaps his back. Jimmy steps out from the awning. A smoldering cigarette in one hand, an empty beer bottle in the other, he raises his arms over his head breathing in the cold, clean, wet dirt smell. His upturned face receives the sharp needles of rain. A baptism.

The wind and rain pick up. A crackle of light breaks blue deep into Forest Park. Thunder reverberates his thin frame, tolling out the bell of him. *Somewhere in there, somewhere in here, I still am. I am.*

Rose spies her brother from the kitchen window. *He's standing in the rain!* She holds her wine glass in her left hand, fingers cupping the bowl, stem resting against her palm. Her nerves are barely contained under her skin. Any little thing and they will burst. She pictures herself popped like a balloon filled with confetti and way too much air.

This dinner was Rose's idea. Panic rises in her gut, grabs her center, weighs on her lungs. What if there's a fight? What if Jimmy says something really stupid to her kids?

He was so angry, so distant, so pissed off and drenched with misery last week at the diner. She is surprised he agreed to come. He hasn't been here in years. Was it Marie's First Communion party? Kathy and Kevin had moved out of Jimmy's life by then. Both their parents were still alive. Dad couldn't help the scorn in his voice when Jimmy came in. Their mother just sat on the couch wagging her head at her oldest child. It hurt Rose to see her parents be so cruel. So disappointed. They didn't seem to get that disappointment runs both ways.

When she hears the back door slam, she jumps.

Rose calls to Dennis.

"What, Rose?"

"Help me get dinner on the table."

"Okay, gimme a minute."

Rose stands there, waiting. Dennis gets up, keeping his eye on the television.

"Kieran, Marie!! Come down for dinner."

Jimmy is standing in the vestibule at the kitchen door, dripping. The thick white socks that Kieran gave him are squishy with mud, hair drips in his eyes, flannel shirt pulled tight around his thin chest.

Brother and sister look at each other. Rose almost says in a disapproving tone, Oh Jimmy, but OH JIMMY! rolls from her throat propelled by a roar of laughter. He has a goofy look on his face. Years ago, in the backyard, they were supposed to be watering the lawn. Jimmy turned the hose on Rose, then drenched himself. He dropped the hose on the ground and they roared as the rubber snake thrashed on the thin grass. Rose grabbed the hose and chased Jimmy around the yard. Here, in her kitchen they look at each other, certain they are sharing that ancient scene.

They laugh so long and loud that the kids come down the back stairway while Dennis dangles the pierced roast over the pot on the end of a long fork. Rose doubles over, rubbing her eyes. A smudge of mascara mars the back of her hand, and this, too, is hilarious. Her arms are wrapped around her belly as she steps toward Jimmy. Wet, muddy Jimmy with a silly grin on his stubbly face. They hold each other until their breathing steadies.

Kieran, meanwhile, has dashed upstairs to get his uncle another pair of socks, a sweatshirt and sweat pants.

"Pot roast and potatoes, anyone?"

During coffee and Danish the storm crescendos, interrupting conversation at the table with claps and then waves of hard rain against the shingles, testing the capacity of the aluminum gutters. If you listen you can hear the small river running down the driveway, under the dining room windows. Rose, distracted, pictures that river joining in the street with all the other driveway rivers on the block, moving faster than the sewer holes can pull them in, washing down Forest Parkway, taking oil and dirt and tar, away, away.

The situation decides that Jimmy will stay the night. No discussion, just arrangements. An extra quilt is offered for the bed in the guest room. Rose tops the clean, folded towels with a new toothbrush, still wrapped, waiting for this very thing: a guest. *Good nights*, all around.

Jimmy hasn't slept in this house since he was a kid. A daybed is pushed against the wall, across from the window. Years ago, this was his grandfather's office. His desk is still here. Jimmy thinks the filing cabinets are in the basement. For as long as he can remember this bed was for him to sleep on when he stayed overnight. Rose would sleep in the room that is now Marie's. She has added some feminine touches to soften the space, but the wallpaper is still a muted plaid, yellowed now.

There is a melancholy in here. The blinds are open; he leaves them that way. He doesn't want to shut out this night with its flashes and growlings. He feels safer in this storm, in his grandmother's house, under a thick quilt and clean clothes, than he has since before he can remember. He closes his heavy eyes to the strange comfort of the flashing bones of an old oak. The darkness follows like a wool blanket tucked around him by capable hands.

As he settles in he wonders why he feels safer in a storm than in the peace of a calm day. Is it a primal knowing that there are forces larger than us, stronger and more responsible? Are we cleansed in the roar of wind that blows away the debris, the flimsy protections we invent? Are we swept down to our essential selves, shivering and vulnerable with little choice but to trust that this terrible force is benevolent and big enough to absorb our pitiful weakness?

In this room of ancient memory, Jimmy smiles. The house itself is a reminder, a *remember me* moment. He turns on his side, pulling the quilt against his chest and belly, and falls asleep to the lullaby of beating rain.

Chapter Fifty-Nine

S UNDAY MORNING SUNLIGHT FILLS Jimmy's room, waking him naturally, gratefully. He doesn't hear anyone else awake. He tiptoes down the back staircase to the kitchen, then to the basement and gets his clothes from the dryer. His sister washed and dried them last night. First time they've been washed since he bought them. They smell like someone else's clothes with the body odor and smoke washed out of them.

Jimmy still has the socks that Kieran gave him. There is a pair of sneakers on top of the dryer, a post-it note with *Jimmy* sitting in the heel. No one has taken this kind of care of him in years.

He leaves quietly out the back door. Last night was too good to ruin with morning regrets and awkwardness.

The air is fresh and crisp after the rain that lasted through the night. Branches are down and trees have been stripped of their blossoms and fresh green leaves.

Kieran's sneakers are just a little wide on Jimmy's feet. But they have a thick bottom, giving him a bounce in his step. Feels like a kid again. He thinks of running down the hill, in a race with some make believe friend. He reaches for a cigarette, takes a deep breath first, the cool clear air something new for his lungs. Breathing in ends in a cough. Too fresh for his cloudy lungs. He lights up.

There's very little traffic this Sunday morning. When he reaches Jamaica Avenue, he turns left. Doesn't want to climb the stairs to wait for the next train. He'll decide at the next stop if he wants to go up and wait. He keeps walking. Some of the little stores are getting ready to open. The smell from the bakery is wonderful, but he doesn't want to take a chance on this mood and stop for a donut. He'll get coffee when he's closer to home.

Home. That word. Rose's house is the closest he's been to a home in who knows how long. His grandmother's house. He always felt safe there. He weakly pushes away a slap of resentment that Rose managed to buy the house and raise a family there. She has a home. *I used to belong there. I used to belong somewhere. Now I go up to that hovel. That stinking trash filled dark room. Home.*

For so long, so many years, Jimmy has covered himself over in a blanket of decay that one time caused him pain, but that decay has become thick, dulling the nerves and the consciousness it once rubbed raw.

He stops at a corner to let a line of cars pass. A wave of panic hits him in the gut. He reaches out to the street lamp pole to steady himself. Bits and pieces of memories flash like a deck of cards flipped fast to create a scene. Kevin as a little boy, Kathy as a pretty young college student; Rose as a little girl. Himself as a kid, running, running so fast he feels close to flight, every muscle pumping, breathing in, breathing out, easily, freely. Don't stop, keep running. Feel the wind at your back and the sun kissing your shoulders. *That's all gone. It's over. Keep walking. Pick up the pace so you don't stop before you get to the curb.*

With each step phrases tap on his brain. *I can't do it. It's too late. It's all gone. I have lost it all.* Tap, tap, tap, tap. With each tap the last fourteen hours seem a mirage. A cruel vision into what might have been. Might have, but wasn't. Couldn't. Because. Because of them. Because of his mother and father. No. An argument tries to slip between the cracks in his brain. *Because of me. I threw my chance away. Kathy, Kevin. They were my chance. I drank them away years ago. No! No! No! SHUT UP!!!*

Jimmy walks more slowly now. The peace he bought from last night is coming to collect its price. Another debt. Another rebuke.

Rose had me over to salve her own conscience. Selfish bitch. She's still trying to find her make believe family. It doesn't exist! Stop the fairy tale. Give it up!! He yells at her in his mind knowing he will never say this to her. She's all he has left. She's the only connection, however weak and self-serving, that he has left. This new sheet of resentment lays itself neatly over the pain of peace that he flirted with last night and this morning.

He keeps walking, block after block, no thought now of catching a train to finish the journey. With each step he gets closer to his dingy street shadowed by the scaffolding of the el train. Garbage is picked up by the breeze as if it were dandelion fluffs dancing on a spring meadow. He laughs at this mockery: a cracked sidewalk with bits of waxed paper and coffee cups squashed by countless feet sprayed with pigeon shit is his "lawn". The American dream. He hadn't noticed before. Now, he sees in stark relief his own life and what he has become. This new vision doesn't inspire him to change; it reminds him of how far he has fallen. He is given to despair rather than action. A mortal sin. He knows his catechism.

That glimpse of what could be was cruel. Somewhere, beneath the layers of resentment, of blame, somewhere he knows what he should have wanted out of life, but never wanted enough to make happen. He couldn't summon the energy to build a home for his family, a life beyond the next drink or the next outrage to satisfy his righteous anger.

He didn't know that Kathy wanted it in more than a vague way until Kevin was about two. Then, she figured, she assumed, that having a regular life, a life with a yard and a regular paycheck were what happened when you had a child.

But Jimmy never knew how to make that happen. He'd get a job, things would go along for a while. Whenever there was a possibility of a promotion or more responsibility, he would get nervous. He would make his boss nervous. He'd drink too much at lunch. He'd show up late several mornings each week. Eventually he'd be asked to leave.

He'd tell Kathy they were all jerks. It's all political. He just couldn't kiss enough ass. He couldn't play that game.

The rent would be late. The phone shut off. When Kevin was old enough for school, Kathy got a job at an insurance agency. They liked her. She did some traveling, had some important clients. Since Jimmy was usually "at liberty" he'd be home. He was supposed to make sure Kevin got to and from school safely, got his homework done, had a proper dinner.

Kathy started traveling more. Promotions, raises, a sense of accomplishment. When people asked what her husband did, she'd say he was a writer, he worked from home. Wasn't that good? That way Kevin had a parent around. What a great set-up. She never did say that he had no intention of writing anything but angry letters to the editor that never made it beyond his mouth and ever escalating voice. Kathy was glad he wasn't effective enough to have any of those rants printed in the NY Times or The Daily News with his name attached. She was glad he was all talk and no action. After a while she was glad he was making it easier for her to picture a life without him in it. A life where Kevin didn't have to be afraid that his father would embarrass him, and she wouldn't have to make excuses for his behavior.

Jimmy wonders if he stops drinking, if he gets a regular job, will he have to reach out to Kathy and Kevin? Its part of the twelve steps, make amends. But *they* walked out on him when he was down. They turned their backs on *him*. Kathy married some corporate asshole. She lives in the suburbs near Chicago. When was the last time Kevin thought to contact his old man? *They should make amends to me. They're the ones who left.*

What if they reject him if he calls? Would that kill him? He thinks it would. He wanders.

At night. He walks the streets of crumbling neighborhoods. Places where families once moved east out of Manhattan and Brooklyn, had a few square feet of green where their children could play. Now those children have moved out further east to Nassau and Suffolk, trying to stay ahead of the decay. Now those little homes with their few square feet of lawn are filled with broken bicycles and car parts, ratty couches and lawn chairs.

He walks past them during the night when more respectable people are sleeping, getting ready to work the next day, when children should have had their dinner and done their homework and now sleep safely under their parent's care. But few of these children have such lullabies of safety and satiety. These children drop to sleep to the sound of mothers fighting with an ever changing cast of men. The girls who should be doing algebra homework are on the streets in platform shoes and halter-tops and skirts impossibly short. The boys run errands for men in flash cars. Young entrepreneurs setting up their futures.

Jimmy wanders like Marley's ghost, dragging his chains of resentment and anger as his only companion. He drinks to suppress the pain but it creeps up on him, grabs his gut with hands of ice and heat. He doesn't belong in these neighborhoods. He was raised in a comfortable home, with gilt-edged china and crisp linens and sterling silver flatware. He is educated. Privileged. His skin the right shade of pale. His bone structure and vocabulary tell a contrary story to the life he leads now. He is not welcome in these neighborhood bars. He has to keep walking to find a place he belongs, with other sons and daughters who should have known better.

One of those nights, two weeks? three weeks? after dinner with Rose, he swallows his last and steps out into the street, having spoken to no one for the hours he claimed a seat. Between two cars he steps one, two, on the third he is clipped and thrown up and over. Up: confusion and clarity melded. Over: he smiles, quizzically. Down: his young and loving mother holds her arms out to him, her only child, her heart's delight, running with a dandelion in his rounded fist, to present this wondrous gift to her.

At that moment between life and death, between here and then, between flight and thud, Rose awakens. Energy leaves her body. She reaches from her sleep to grab it with her hands, but it is gone.

She lies still, next to her sleeping husband, waiting for the phone to ring. *And when you have no words, the Spirit of the Lord will plead for you before the throne of God.* An echo from the epistles whispers to her. *Hail Mary, full of grace...*

That's all I have, God. You will have to do the rest.

Chapter Sixty

Rose gave the funeral director the suit Jimmy wore to their father's funeral just three months ago, a castoff from his closet. She found it heaped in a corner of his room over Mulvaney's; socks stuck in the shoes, tie pulled wide like a noose, still knotted. She thinks about taking the shirt and suit in to the cleaners, but the casket is going to be closed, so it really doesn't matter.

She takes them in anyway.

So Jimmy is laid out, in a closed casket, in his dead father's suit, cleaned and pressed just yesterday. They don't need the shoes. She gives them a clean pair of socks, needed or not.

Rose sits in the front row, in the chief mourner chair. She is alone. Dennis took Kieran and Marie to eat about an hour ago. Rose took her own car and left them at the diner to have dessert. She told them not to rush.

They don't.

She called Newsday yesterday to put the obituary in the paper. Curt, no picture, no names of survivors, just the funeral home and church. She didn't have a number to reach Kathy or Kevin. She called a few relatives who said they would spread the word.

Only two elderly aunts came this afternoon. Rose doesn't expect much of a showing tonight.

So she sits here. Alone. With her brother. Her mind is simultaneously empty and filled with memories, pictures, really. There is enough space in her mind to pull away and wonder how this can be. What's that? Three minds? What would Jimmy think of that? He'd chew on it a while and then bring it up out of the blue days later. She likes to think he would. But did they ever have that relationship or did their lives diverge so much that this is just a wish, a false memory of familiarity? The absence of this possibility, of this assuredly useless conversation, makes her nose leak. She snuffles it back in.

Rose turns, mildly startled, when she feels a warm hand on her shoulder.

"Hello, Rose. I'm so sorry about your brother."

It's Jenny. Jenny and Paul. Paul takes her hand before she can manage to pull it back. It's what you do at wakes. You shake hands and allow people you hardly know to hug you and say things you will not remember. You will be covered in the rituals of sympathy. Covered in cologne and after shave and germs and body odor not always disguised by the ubiquitous floral smell of funeral parlors.

As Paul holds her hand between his, Rose thinks they mist that floral scent through the vents as a nerve agent that makes every smile a simper and all words sound as though they are coming at you through a long megaphone.

Mother and son go over to the casket and kneel on the prie dieu. They bless themselves. Rose imagines them running through a quick Hail Mary. But they take a little longer. Maybe an Our Father and Glory Be thrown in for good measure.

Jenny wipes a tear from her eye. Something in Rose rises up in disgust and anger. She wonders what Paul knows of his brother. As they stand Paul puts his arm around his mother. They take the few steps back to Rose and sit beside her.

After a few minutes, Paul leaves the room. Jenny takes a deep breath, squares her shoulders and turns to her son's half-sister.

"I'm so sorry Rose. So sorry."

What are you sorry about, Jenny? Of all the things you should be sorry about, what in particular are you sorry about now? Taking my father away from his family when we needed him? When I needed him? Having his baby and keeping his secret all these years? Having the only child of my father's that he was proud of? Are you sorry that he preferred your company to ours? Rose doesn't say any of these things. She fixes her eyes on the crucifix over Jimmy's casket. Her nostrils flare and her eyebrows rise in derision, in anger, in *how dare you?*

Jenny doesn't pick up on the nasty energy Rose is emitting. She has a purpose and she wants to get through this. "Rose, I don't know if this is the time or the place, but I have wanted to contact you for weeks now, since Phil's... since your father's funeral."

Rose turns to Jenny.

"Rose, you know, don't you? I could see it in your face. In Jimmy's face. You know that Paul is your brother."

"My brother is lying there in a closed casket, dead at 53. Too damaged for viewing. My brother is James Thomas Banfry, son of Maureen and Phil Banfry. Paul might be my father's son, but Jimmy is, was, my brother."

"You're right, Rose. Jimmy is your brother. I know. Now is not the time." She gets up to leave.

Dennis and the kids enter the room just as Paul returns. Rose glances back and sees Paul extend a hand in greeting to Kieran and Jenny to Marie.

A few of Rose's neighbors are coming in as Jenny and Paul leave. Sheila and Frank brought them. Sheila takes on the role of greeter; she sees that Rose is in no condition to do that.

They are in the same funeral home as just three months before, same church in the morning, same cemetery where the ground will still be rounded, she thinks. Soft anyway, not having had time to be hardened by time and long memory. Easier work for the gravediggers.

Chapter Sixty-One

Rose processes down the aisle behind Jimmy's casket. This is the place where every major event, celebration or mourning, occurred in her life. This place marked the beginnings and ends of countless people.

The ancient rituals since men gathered and looked at the stars for guidance in the driving need to find order out of chaos and hope there is something bigger than the accidents that direct our lives. Some benevolent, powerful force that gives meaning to all the suffering and the joy; that it is not random but that somehow, it all works together to bring us where we need to be. The economy of salvation.

Here she is back in the same church, same aisle, same altar for Baptism, First Communion, Confirmation. Cilla's funeral, her wedding, mother's funeral, father's funeral, now this. She takes Dennis' arm. Kieran and Marie follow. Sheila and Frank are here. But, the few aunts who attended the wake last night had no one to drive them this morning.

A lonely life. A lonely farewell.

No crowd like the one in January. A few elderly people are in the church; she wonders if they show up at these things as their regular works of mercy, or as a preview for when they are the main attraction.

The church is cast in cool shadows from the marble pillars and the trees that have grown tall and old outside the stained glass.

The red glow of the lit sanctuary lamp is a welcome comfort that Jesus is home, right here in the tabernacle. *God. I need you Jesus. Deeply. I can only stand so much. You overwhelm me; your presence crushes me.*

The cool stillness and the undercurrent of awe and reverence in this place is bound tightly with foreboding: if you take in the holy, you are a target to the unholy. Is that what happened to her? She wonders if the imagination that saved her, protected her from "reality" was connected to this vulnerability of taking in the holy, and because of that, left the door to the unholy nudged open.

With each step down the aisle, up to the altar, she mixes up phrases from psalms and prayers *my refuge and my hope to thee do we cry mourning and weeping in this valley of tears...* No, that's not right. She substitutes *my life my sweetness and my hope* to *my life my refuge and my hope* playing out the words like she has to recite the alphabet in order to find where the letters lie, or the pledge of allegiance for the order of words.

Hail holy queen mother of mercy

Our life our sweetness and our hope

to thee do we cry poor banished children of Eve

Banished? Why are we banished? Banished before we are even born?

To thee do we send up our sighs

mourning and weeping in this valley of tears

Did you create us to mourn and weep? Everything that's wrong is because of sin? Whose sin? Did I do this, did I make my brother's life so miserable that he ended up smashed into a dirty street? Why do you send us to live in a valley of tears? What kind of parents are you?

Turn then most gracious advocate thine eyes of mercy toward us and after this our exile, show unto us the blessed fruit of your womb Jesus

O clement o loving O sweet virgin Mary Pray for us o holy mother of God

That we may be made worthy of the promises of Christ.

All in a rush, as armor against the dread. *This prayer of pathos, of weak, helpless, victims, and this is my armor!!*

Protect us from your holiness, O Lord. Protect us from the evil one who creeps in on the tail of the holy.

Poor banished children of Eve—after this our exile. Banished and exiled. What a plan.

Rose hasn't been in church since her father's funeral. Every Sunday morning she's been ill, well, fragile, vulnerable, open to attack, anxious. So, ill. Every Saturday the dread would build: she'd have to come up with another excuse for not going to Mass with the family the next day.

How many Sunday mornings could she have a headache or upset stomach? One Sunday she couldn't stand because her back hurt so much. And it really did. And she really did get terrible headaches and stomach upset. By the end of the day, after it was too late to go to Mass, the troubles would subside. Not all at once, but like the air being slowly let out of a balloon, or a sigh released in a long relaxing *hwooh* through her nose. The foreboding receded until the next week.

As rage builds on the ruins of her exhaustion, some pieces move into place. This rage has been seeping out in ugly ooze for two years now; two years since the scandals broke in Boston; two years since the cover-ups and deceit laid bare. Dam after dam burst, parishes all over the country, the world, could no longer hide the secret sin, the ugliness behind the mask. All the talk of chastity and purity drummed into her head by the same priest who looked on her with salaciousness and convicted her of the crime of being a young girl round and soft and therefore irresistible and the "occasion of sin".

Two years of stoking the flames, chipping at the hard shell of her denial of her family and her church until she saw them parallel. Her father's deceit and secret life. He was her hero, her pride. And the secret lives of priests, men called by God, consecrated to celibacy and purity, festering in lust toward the weakest, toward her.

Her faith was in her family, in her church. She believed in heroic and saintly virtues. She believed her father embodied these virtues. She believed her priest was supposed to embody these virtues. Somehow the two were inseparable. She was mistaken. She was naïve. They were all too pleased to let her believe the lie. And they, or her foolishness, had betrayed her.

How could she pass this legacy on to her children? What could they inherit from her? Someone who kept her eyes shut against things she preferred not to see? Was she a coward or an idiot?

Was she part of the lie? Yes, she had to admit she was part of the lie. A mute and blind part. A fool. Where did she begin and end in relation to the church, to her family—they are of the same tree—her identity, her DNA, the lives of all who came before her whispered in her veins, directed her course.

Look back and confront. Find good, avoid evil. Right now she can only try to avoid evil. It surrounded her, shadowing the sacraments, a curtain over grace. Laughing at her, calling her fool, leaving her to see herself trampled and used like dirt under the heavy foot of cavalry.

Her knees buckle, Dennis braces her. She takes her seat in the pew.

She had gone to Mass every week of her life. She was a good girl, did what she was told. A conscientious mother, bringing her children up in the faith.

For years they had a routine, a tradition. Go to early Mass then stop at Schultz's bakery. Sunday morning in the McGuire house smelled like sesame rolls with butter; fried egg sandwiches with bacon; coffee percolating. That is what safety smelled like, what home smelled like.

They would linger and talk and laugh. Eventually the kids would go and finish their weekend homework or the doorbell would ring and they'd be out with friends. She'd put a roast in the oven and they knew to come home for dinner at four. The Sabbath.

Dennis has been taking the kids without Rose and they still bring in the usual bakery fare. But there's been a shadow over the meal with Rose staying upstairs, reluctant to join in breakfast while the question of attending a later Mass hangs in the air unspoken. She wouldn't let her kids get away with that when they wanted to sleep in. How can they let her get away with it?

Once upon a time. They are collateral damage in her own private war. But there is no such thing as a private war. There are always casualties.

Something broke when her father died. Like a spell lifted or a vessel smashed. All that held her identity, her life, destroyed furiously at her father's wake. No more hiding. The truth came out old and moldy and rotted and twisted. The whole façade gone and she was naked and cold.

She cannot hear a word of the homily or the consecration. She pictures her mother at Cilla's funeral. Sitting straight and rigid, a space between her and her father. She would not touch, she would not cry.

Rose now sees that her mother in her terrible grief could not stand to be touched. The pain was too much. She would shatter and be destroyed never to be re-gathered if her armor was breached. So she withdrew, further and further inside herself until she was a tight little ball of being lost in her own heart.

Rose sits, stands, kneels from years of habit. The sacrifice on the altar, the holy unbloody sacrifice of the Mass.

But there is blood.

Those who hid behind the holy to tell their lies and their judgments and rules that were a millstone around the necks of the innocent drew blood.

Jimmy, who disappointed his parents with his sin of living with Kathy, his sin of not following in his father's footsteps, his sin of disappointing in every thing he touched or avoided, turned to alcohol and despair because he could not meet their expectations, his blood is there.

After the quick Mass, the incensing and the folding of the baptismal garment on the casket, they walk out to the somber tunes of the organ playing *May the Angels Lead You Into Paradise*. Rose hopes her brother has an escort of angels. She wonders where they've been for the last fifty-three years.

Jenny and Paul are standing just inside the aisle several rows back. Jenny meets Rose's eye steadily. Rose stops. She takes Jenny's elbow and pulls her into the procession. Paul follows his mother.

Chapter Sixty-Two

Rose takes the arm that Dennis offers as they exit the church. It snowed overnight and this morning Rose feels she is standing inside a pewter bowl; the image of Don Quixote with the shaving basin on his head makes her smile in a quizzical way. *The thoughts we have, at the oddest times,* she thinks.

She takes her seat in the limousine next to Kieran and Marie. Dennis drives their car. The heavy clouds have snuck into her brain somehow, causing her to feel muffled. Every thought she has is dull and impotent, a soft mess of tragedy and comedy.

The hearse drives slowly through the stately iron gates that separate this bit of earth from the homes across the street on one side and the cars zipping by on Metropolitan Avenue on the other. Angels and saints and large stone crosses rise up alongside ancient trees that stand sentinel over the occupants covered in dirt and memory. This is a place of reverence, there is no rushing here, no need to rush ever again.

There is no direct route to the patch of ground this dark procession is heading toward. This is some kind of metaphor, Rose thinks, designed to symbolize the winding roads of life that bring us ultimately, here. The earth is blessed, words echoing baptism are proclaimed by the deacon whose job it is to minister to the dead, to sprinkle holy water and make the sign of the cross that bought our eternal life, so she has been taught since infancy.

The ground is still soft at the Banfry family plot, still rounded from when their father was buried just weeks ago. The big square hole next to Phil Banfry's mound is deep. The casket is suspended on straps so it can be lowered gracefully into the damp dark earth, to rest above the bones of their sister. Rose wonders what is left of Cilla, thirty years here. Surely the flesh is gone. In movies they open caskets to expose naked bone, hollows where eyes and nose once lived. Lips and face evaporated, teeth large and bold in a mockery of the once living person.

Ashes to ashes.

Her dress is probably still there, Rose thinks, covered in the dust that was once Cilla, that white dress she wore so proudly on her First Communion, holding a small bouquet, twirling the skirt out, tapping her white patent leather shoes on the tiles in church. The white is probably gray, maybe yellow. Empty dress. You've done your job. What was she spared, Rose thinks, for the first time, what was she spared being taken so young?

She turns back to her brother. In that box, such a lovely box, with brass handles, polished to a high degree. He slept on the floor in a room he never cleaned, now his broken body lies on satin, wearing his father's suit. *Our father*. His dead face was not fit for viewing, smashed and torn on the rough asphalt. She had to identify him hours after he died. *Yes, that's my brother, that's Jimmy*. Though she only nodded and turned into her husband's chest.

We had that one night, that last dinner of pot roast and beer. *Do this in remembrance of me.* He stood in the backyard, arms open to the rain, to the lightning. A second baptism; his last rites. Rose asked for the chaplain who served the morgue, asked for the anointing of the dead, though Jimmy may have scoffed at that, she asked for him because she needed to see her brother prayed over, signed with blessed oil. The ancient rites that join us generation to generation. Words of consolation and hope. Words of promise that this life was not in vain. This life mattered.

And, sudden as a gust of wind, a terrible possibility indicts her.

Did I do this? I wanted to save my brother, didn't I? I wanted to have him in my life, I wanted him to be whole. I wanted him to be someone other than who he was. Someone clean and happy and successful.

But more, I wanted him to know my wounds! See, you were not the only one hurt by them. I wanted to let him know that all the years I was alone had taken their toll on me. I wanted him to take some responsibility for this. He was my big brother!! Why didn't he protect me? Protect me from that soul disfigured priest. Protect me from our mother who lashed out because I was the only one there. Protect me from the pain of the absence of our father.

Did I do this? Did I kill my brother? The questions echo in Rose's head. *Did I ask too much of him?*

This wildness in her! Standing here while the deacon reads from the gospels and they make the sign of the cross, even now, she makes the sign of the cross in unison with everyone while beneath these gestures, the real Rose is accused, tried and condemned because of her selfishness.

Pay attention! Here these men, strangers, in their dull black suits and black ties. Their uniform. Professional pall bearers. Professional mourners. We have to hire people to show us how to do this, this act that is just as much a part of life as birth. They go home to their lives and tomorrow there will be another family to escort to the grave.

They are so careful with his remains. Would they have noticed him just last week? Would they have crossed the street if they saw him coming toward them? Disheveled, dirty. His anger contagious. His illness a disease to guard against. *I would have crossed the street. Hell, I wouldn't have even been in the same street with him to begin with.*

What did he need from me? Need from me? I only thought of what I needed, wanted. I wanted him to go back in time and save me from that priest, save me from my aloneness. I wanted him to be the son my parents wanted so there would be peace in the family. Was that too much to ask? Why did you have to make trouble, Jimmy? Why did you have to move in with Kathy? Why couldn't you just be good, like they wanted?

This is just a nightmare, right? A nightmare and now I've learned the lesson. Now I can awaken from this terrible dream and know not to have expectations of Jimmy that he cannot handle.

What's the use of learning if the price paid for my mistake is his death?!!

There is no coming back from death, no chance, no second chance, no third. I've learned my lesson, God. I've learned. Oh please, let me wake up!! Let me wake up and see my brother, alive, whole, happy. Let Me!!

Who am I yelling at? A God who will not hear. A silent God, a God whose only answer is that Jimmy will remain dead and I will have to live knowing that I killed him. Knowing that I killed Cilla because I was tired of her being sick all the time?

It's time to go. Dennis steers her with her elbow back to the car.

Chapter Sixty-Three

SHE GATHERS HERSELF IN the short ride to the restaurant. She points her cannon of anger at the only two left of her father's arrogance.

Rose insists that Jenny and Paul join them at the luncheon after the burial. At Haufbrau's in Middle Village they settle in to a round table that seats eight. Since Sheila and Frank made the trip to the cemetery she invites them to lunch.

The waitress is a woman wearing what is supposed to be a traditional German countryside dress, complete with frilly apron and a tight peasant blouse for which she is thirty years too old. Glasses of ice water are placed at each setting and menus handed out. Rose spends a long time holding the menu at arms length. Without consulting anyone, she orders the family lunch special of sauerbraten, schnitzel and beer, for everyone. No one objects.

When the pitcher of beer arrives, she takes all eight glasses and fills them, even for Kieran and Marie. Rose raises her glass and toasts Jimmy. A murmur of *To Jimmy* passes among them.

"Dennis, Marie, Kieran, I don't think you have been introduced to my brother, Paul. And Frank and Sheila, you are practically family, you should know everyone, too. Paul, this is what's left of your father's family." Paul nods to each of them.

"I see it is not a surprise to you Paul, to hear that I am your sister. Your half sister, anyway."

Dennis turns full bodied toward Rose. He reaches for her hand but she pulls it away. Kieran lets out a long *sheeesh* while Marie turns to Paul and Jenny.

Rose begins. "Well, here's my understanding of the situation. Jenny worked for my father, your grandfather, a long time ago. Around the time my sister Cilla died, when I was 13.

"Dad, Granddad, had always spoken so highly of Jenny, how smart you were, how you should get your degree and all that. I didn't pay much attention to that then.

"Now I don't know about the timing exactly, but near as I can figure, after Cilla died, your grandmother wasn't able to cope very well, Jimmy wasn't able to cope very well, but, apparently my father found a way to cope while I was left alone with a mother who swallowed vodka in her afternoon tea and I was on my own. Did I mention I was 13?

"I learned to cook my own meals. I learned how to be alone and since no one was there to help with homework questions,I learned how to study. Isn't that good? My father was always at some meeting or a political dinner. Silly me. It turns out that I invented my father, in my imagination. I told myself he was doing important work, making the world a better place. He was only trying to make his world a better place with his pretty secretary. The rest of us be damned."

Here she trembles.

"So, as you can all see, he had found a way to ease his loneliness and grief and it had little to do with me. And that is where Jenny comes in. Such a good worker, so smart, she anticipated my father's every need and desire.

"So, here we are. My brother has died, alone, broken. Here is Jenny. And her son. My half brother. Your uncle."

No one has spoken, so Rose continues.

"He looks a lot like Jimmy don't you think? Same eyes, same chin and nose. But so much healthier—Jenny you must have been a good mother—I remember you got married—not long after Cilla died—around October wasn't it?"

Jenny answers her question with a steady look.

"I do wonder when your husband found out. That must have been tricky. But you were so pretty and clever I'm sure he believed whatever you told him."

Dennis interrupts, "Rose, that's enough."

Rose ignores him. "Eat everybody. This is delicious. They always do such a nice job here, don't you think?"

No one has touched the food.

Rose continues, "I have been wondering, since I met you two at my father's funeral, what exactly is it that you want, Jenny? There's no money—that all went to the nursing home—so it can't be that."

"Rose, I don't want anything."

"Just a little family re-union?"

285

"Just a little honesty, Rose. It's about time."

"About time for honesty? Well, you didn't take in all the lessons Phil Banfry could teach you, did you Jenny? Good for you."

Here Rose takes a long drink of beer.

"Hiding the truth, pretending, that's the Banfry way. Wonder if it's trained or inherited. Maybe Paul could tell us. I don't imagine dear old dad showed up much in your life, did he Paul?"

Paul just shakes his head somewhere between a yes and no, a nod and a nay—he certainly doesn't want Rose to know how Phil was helpful to him in getting into law school, setting up practice and recommending clients.

"So Paul, when did you learn about honesty? What about your mother's husband? Did he think he was your father?"

"He was my father, Rose."

Sheila and Frank reach for each other's hands. Sheila instinctively turns toward Jenny and Paul, and as she is about to speak, Rose begins:

"Well, of course he is. In that Lifetime movie of the week kind of way. But Jenny you're not wearing a wedding ring. Marriage couldn't take the burden of truth I'm guessing."

"Rose, don't." Sheila tries to interject some restraint on Rose's cruelty.

Jenny is holding back tears. Folding her napkin on her plate, food untouched, she stands. "Paul, its time to go."

Chapter Sixty-Four

"Dad! Its red!"

Dennis glances up at his rearview mirror as he hits the brakes. "Shit!"

They sit at the intersection, half way through the pedestrian lane. "Goddammit, Rose."

Rose is silently looking out her window beyond the iron fence into Forest Park.

"What—did you use up all your words for the day at lunch?"

Kieran and Marie exchange a look in the back seat.

"All these months you've kept your mouth shut. What the hell else haven't you told me?"

The car behind him honks. Dennis makes a right turn into the park. They're going to take the scenic route the rest of the way.

With her face to the window, Rose says, "Oh, Dennis, did I tell you I quit my job?

He turns his head, brow wrinkled, WHAT! is contorted on his face.

She turns, just a bit, to her left, concentrating on the strip that separates windshield from side window.

He is trying to form a question when she says in a degree above a whisper, "Did I tell you I had a breakdown on the J train? Hey, that could be a song—Breakdown on the J Train—la-di-da-la-di-da."

She tries to pull her knees up to her chest, but the seatbelt limits her movement.

"Yeah, I was spilling my guts to a man who wasn't there. Isn't that funny, dear?"

"Ah, Rose." Dennis glances back at the kids. They shrug, just as confused as he is.

"For three days I talked to a priest who wasn't really there? Isn't that hilarious, everybody?" Her head falls toward her chest. "That's me— hilarious Rose!"

As she pulls her head back up "that's better than second hand Rose, right?"

Now she sits facing forward. "I recently realized, guys, my whole life has been a lie. I've been making believe for the last thirty years" She speaks in an ascending whisper, then faces right, releasing a sigh into her window. She runs her finger through the condensation her sigh has formed.

They pull into the driveway. Kieran and Marie scramble out the back seat and disappear into the house.

Dennis stays in the car, clutching the wheel. Rose is still looking out her window.

"Jesus."

She turns to him. Her face is set. There is a coldness there that he doesn't recognize.

"When were you going to let me in on any of this? Who the fuck am I to you? Just a goddam roommate?"

Rose descends deeper into her silence. Then, finally, "What do you want me to say, Dennis? Couldn't you see I was a mess? Didn't you notice?"

"Your father died."

"My father was eighty-friggin'- four years old. I knew he was dying. He's been dying for years. I just didn't know he was going to leave all his goddam lies to me! What was I supposed to say, Dennis? Everything I believed in, set my course by, was a lie! And oh, by the way, I have another brother?"

"Yes! You should have told me."

"Why the hell didn't you notice?"

"Notice what? You put on a damn good act."

"Tune in, Dennis. Nothing occurred to you last night at the wake? You couldn't see how much Paul looked like Jimmy, like my father?"

"No. He could have been a cousin I never met. Why would I be looking for a resemblance? Your father was full of righteousness, he acted like he was better than everyone."

"Exactly."

"Oh, so it's my fault for not assuming that your father had a bastard son out in the world because he was a self-righteous prick?"

Rose shakes her head. Something like a laugh escapes from her throat. Then she shakes her head, left to right, left to right.

Dennis unbuckles and goes over to Rose's door. He reaches across her and releases the seat belt. With his left arm around her shoulder and his right hand at her elbow, he leads her into the house.

After he unbuttons her coat and folds it across a chair, he puts on a pot of coffee.

Dennis sits across from her, takes her hand. "We have to move. Get out of here. Start over."

"What? What does moving have to do with any of this?"

"You're living in the past, Rose. Here we are in your grandparent's house. There's no room for me or the kids. We're crowded in here with all your family shit. I want to move out of this fucking mausoleum."

"Mausoleum? This place was my refuge. My safe place when things were ugly at home."

"Well, now it's your prison. And my prison and Kieran and Marie's prison. We have to go—I'm trying to save you, to save us."

"I can't think about that now. I just buried my brother."

"Maybe he buried you. He and your father and mother and sister—they buried you years ago. You just never noticed."

"I never noticed? What about you? You don't notice anything until its just about too late, until you are about to lose everything, then you wake up. Now, your grand solution is we have to move?"

"Can't you see it? You're supposed to bury your dead not carry them around and pet them."

"Pet them? Pet them! I'm raging at them. And some of my ghosts saved me—my grandmother saved me."

"Don't you think she might want to tell you to give it up? Don't you think she might want to tell you to get on with things? She might tell you to live and let us, your family, live?"

"You want me to just abandon them all? Leave this place and move out to some new development?" as she was saying this she worries that Dennis knows about her seeing her grandmother and her sister right here in this house. *How could he? I never told him about that. I never told anyone about Cilla in the attic and Grandma in the living room.*

"New development? That's rich. You'll probably carry all the damned ghosts with you even if we move to a new country—a new planet. You love those ghosts and you love the pain and anger more than you love your living family."

"I just lost my brother. He died alone. Tragically."

"Don't change the subject. Jimmy lived alone. He lived tragically. Maybe he's better off."

"Better off? Better off dead? Is that what you're saying? That all the pain that was his life doesn't matter, that he couldn't achieve some kind of happiness? What do you think I am? A robot like you?"

Dennis slams his fist on the table. She's gone too far. Her expression is almost vicious. He realizes she wants him to hurt.

He stands across the room in the doorway. Very steadily, he says, "you're right, Rose. You have been living a lie. You really are a cold, self-centered, manipulative bitch. I don't know you at all."

Dennis walks out through the front door. He backs his car out of the driveway. He has to go.

He gets on the Long Island Expressway heading east. After forty-five minutes he pulls off at a hotel and checks in. He didn't pack, but he knows that if he needs anything there is a mall close by. There's always a mall close by on Long Island.

After an hour of staring up at the ceiling from his polyester-quilted bedspread he reaches into his trouser pocket for his cell.

"Marie, it's Dad. I'm fine. Mom will be all right. Just give her some space. Yes, it will be okay. Listen, Marie, tell Kieran I'll be home tomorrow. Sure, you can tell your mother. Don't cry. I'll see you tomorrow."

He has the choice of Chili's, Red Lobster or Denny's in the adjoining parking lot. He holds his cell phone in his palm, looking at it as if it is an oracle. Maddie lives close by. He could call her. He wants to call her, he wants her to come and eat dinner with him, pour out his complaints about Rose. Tell this woman with the listening eyes, the receptive body, the needy heart, that his wife has been keeping secrets, big life-altering secrets. He wants Maddie to believe that Rose made the first move away from their marriage by hiding, pulling away and retreating into herself.

He puts his phone back in his pocket.

Dennis takes a booth at Chili's and orders a burger, fries and a beer. He can't remember the last time he sat alone in a booth at Chili's. He can't remember the last time he sat alone.

As he's squeezing ketchup on his burger he thinks of Maddie. Neither of them ever mentioned the middle of the night visit. There was no next morning awkwardness as they sat through hours of lectures, had lunch, networked. At the end of the conference, he revoked his reservation to stay another night. He arrived home around seven, just in time to order their Friday night pizza. Back to normal. Rose went to bed early. Dennis stayed up with the kids and watched Letterman.

When he takes his last sip of beer, he brings his plastic bag with toothbrush, paste, a disposable razor and shaving cream into his room. He makes a pot of the complimentary coffee, sits on the big bed and zips through channels with the black wand. He settles on a docu-history on the Hitler channel. All Hitler All the Time. When his cell rings he startles out of sleep.

"Yeah. Oh, Kieran. I'm in Smithtown. Calm down. She'll be okay. Yes, she will. Alright, I'll come home. You get some sleep, okay?"

He's on the edge of the bed in his t-shirt and boxers. His anger dissipated somewhere around a scene panning over a mass grave of skeletons covered in loose skin.

Out of the back of his brain he sees Rose and their college friends at Poor Richard's Pub on Union Turnpike. Randy has wormed his way into their circle of beer buddies after classes on Friday. Each time they gather Randy moves closer and closer to Rose.

One evening he's telling her about this place on the Island that's a lot of fun on Saturday nights. They have dancing and talent contests. Rose says something like 'it sounds like fun'. Randy looks across Rose to Dennis to catch his eye so Dennis can witness him closing the deal for the next night.

Dennis feels again the heat rising in him, his heart beating loudly in his ears. Someone crashed a couple of beers on the floor and table. For the first time he puts his arm around Rose in a proprietary way and jumps into Randy's move. "Sounds like fun, Rose. Wanna go tomorrow?" Rose looks between her two suitors, gives Randy a little smile, then turns to Dennis and says "I thought you'd never ask." That was the beginning. A last minute, 'gonna lose that girl' move.

Now what?

He dresses, leaves the plastic bag of toiletries and checks out.

Dennis comes in through the kitchen door. At the sound of his key, Marie leaves her watch over her mother to fill Dennis in.

"She hasn't moved since you left. She won't eat, she won't speak, we barely got her to sip some water."

"Okay, Marie. You and Kier go up to bed. I'll handle this."

"Dad, I'm really worried."

"Everything will be all right. Go to bed."

Dennis pours a cup from the pot he started hours ago and puts it in the microwave. Old and stale, but it's still coffee.

He fortifies himself with a few sips, then goes to be with his wife.

Chapter Sixty-Five

"They come at night, you know."

"What comes, Rose?"

"The thoughts. The memories and the what ifs. I haven't been able to sleep. I've been trying. I go to bed when you do. I tuck into my pillow, press it hard against the front of me, tight, tight. So stupid, I want it to suck up the panic like a big sponge. And a shield. Sometimes I pull the quilt over my head, curl up tight. But it still hurts. And I can't sleep. I look at that clock, sometimes 'til three, three-thirty. I sleep for a bit, then it's time to get up. Go to work. Pretend to go to work."

"You could wake me, you know. You could let me in, let me be a part of your life. Part of your pain. You've pushed me away, Rose. It's lonely out here by myself."

Rose looks at Dennis, sees the trace of pain in his face. His solid, dependable, always there face. She hadn't noticed his pain at all. Hadn't noticed he felt pushed aside. She only had room for her own troubles, they took up her whole heart. Now, though, there is the tiniest crack forming in her heart, just enough to think that Dennis might need to be let in.

"I know. But I've been hoping it would go away. It's been creeping up on me for a long time now. Long before my father died. Then when he died, it just got worse. I used to be able to keep myself busy at work, too busy to think about anything, you know? But I couldn't do it anymore. Not after his funeral when I figured out who Paul was. I couldn't hold it back anymore."

"Hold what back, Rose?" Dennis is holding her hand.

She looks at her husband, brow furrowed. She's shaking. Shrugs her shoulders. Shakes her head.

"It. All of it."

Dennis puts his arm around her. "I'm so very tired, Dennis. So very tired."

"So am I, Rose, so am I."

Finally, she sleeps.

Dennis stays awake as long as he can. He lays on his back wondering how he could have missed all that Rose was going through since her father died. The street lamp just feet from their house and the glow of the clock are the only light in the room.

He looks at the still fan blades over their bed reviewing the last few months. She seemed her regular self. She'd been a little more quiet, he guessed, but she was usually quiet. They had a routine of dinner then settling in a for a night of sit-coms or cop shows, and if they hadn't yet fallen asleep, the monologue on The Tonight Show. Jay Leno was usually their its-time-for-bed alarm.

When Dennis wakes in the morning, Rose stays in bed, her eyes closed. He tiptoes out of the room. Rose holds a pillow to her chest and belly, her mind full of scenes, nearly forty-five years telescoped, open and close, while she lay in her warm bed.

Some things come into focus: Jimmy laughing, pushing Rose and Cilla on the swings in the park, giving them piggy back rides, teaching Rose to ride a two wheeler. Then, other images of her brother: a portrait of loneliness and sorrow, shrugging his shoulders and walking down the block, away, to where? She couldn't follow. Now she wondered if anyone could have followed. What if their father got in the car and caught up with his son, took him out for a meal, a chat. Let Jimmy know he was interested in his life, in what was bothering him. But that had to remain a fantasy. He never did that, it wasn't in his bag of tricks. He wouldn't risk a conversation with his son that might reveal some fault on his part, or their mother's part. The only talk he could have had with his son would have been telling Jimmy to buck up, take responsibility for his life, get a regular job, cut his hair, fit in the box.

When Rose was twelve, thirteen, fourteen she wanted Jimmy to do that too. Fit in, don't fight. Please, Jimmy, please. Maybe then they could have something that resembled a normal family, a happy family, a family that wasn't defined by pain and loneliness and blame.

Before that desire died in her, she wanted to shake him. She wanted him to be like her friends older brothers who looked like they found their way into adulthood. She wanted him to pull himself through, just do it, it can't be so hard, other people do it.

Now she knows that he couldn't. He didn't have that power. It was bigger than he was; it had more gravity than he could fight against.

Lying here in her bed, the bed she's shared with her husband for more than twenty years, she is drowning in the loneliness that has been pulling her down since Cilla's death. She cannot be victorious against it, it always wins. All the years she struggled against it, all the times others thought she seemed okay, like she could cope, she'd smile and go to school, go to work, be a wife, a mother, all that time it was tugging at her, heart and soul. And now she can no longer pretend. All her protection is gone, crumbled, less than the dust in Cilla's casket.

Now it is coming to her that her need was so great, the depth of her loneliness created a vortex that pulled Jimmy in. She wanted Jimmy to witness her pain, to pull her out of it. But he couldn't. His own pain was killing him, and finally it did.

There were albums full of photos, though. Albums full of happy little Jimmy and his proud parents. The look on her mother's face, beaming at her beautiful boy. Rose had only seen her look at her that way occasionally. *How soft and lovely Mom was. Once upon a time. Before I was born. Before Cilla.*

Jimmy's life before Rose and Cilla was privileged. He had a happy mother. Rose never knew that mother. Her mother was exhausted, unpredictable, dark. Jimmy's mother smiled in pictures. She looked like the television mothers, like Donna Reed or June Cleaver. Rose's mother was hard around the mouth and eyes, tired, worn out, angry. There were few pictures with her mother and the three children. She didn't want her picture taken anymore. She said she didn't recognize herself.

So, Rose thought, Jimmy's idyll ended when Rose was born. And then Cilla. Cilla needed it all: all the energy, all the oxygen, all the patience, all the time, all the love.

All of it. He was the darling of his mother and then he had to babysit his sisters. Never again to have that connection with his mother who had changed so drastically once the girls came along.

Rose was dizzy. This was the first time she realized what it was that Jimmy lost when she and Cilla came along and eclipsed his world. She had spent her life fending off the desperation of her own pain, and now that Jimmy was dead, she was beginning to understand his pain.

As much as Rose carried her wounds of abandonment like a family heirloom she had Dennis and the kids. They bridged the gap. Soothed the terrible pain that could become as raw as a fresh cut wound without notice or warning. It could strike at any time, so she became wary. Always on guard against its attack. As much as she hurt, Jimmy hurt worse because he could not keep his wife and son. His abandonment left him too broken for healing.

The first need he had was his mother. Their father stood by as a necessary player but not intimately involved. Maybe they were props in the production of his life. He was part of the economy of the family,but Jimmy and Mom were their own center. And then Jimmy wasn't enough. There were more children. His mother became someone else. It was all too much for her. Later, it was too much for Jimmy. Life, that is, was too much. They had that in common, but it was a canyon, not a bridge.

But, now, there's more death. All of her original family was dead. Jimmy's death following so closely on her father's death decimated the fragments of the wall she built, that kept her enthralled, all these years.

Even now, her primary thought is that they should have protected her. That was their job, their duty. As men. As father and brother.

But they didn't. So she protected them from the knowledge that neither of them was man enough to protect her.

Her silence protected their shame. Her silence protected her shame of their failure. Of their devastating weakness.

She did not press her claim on them. Her claim to protection. She knew they were too weak to do their duty. They kept their illusion.

And she let them.

Chapter Sixty-Six

Since everyone knows she's not going to work, Rose can sleep in. She sleeps for long hours. Sometimes most of the day. For the first time in her life she has the freedom to fall apart. *Humpty-dumpty sat on the wall; Humpty-Dumpty had a great fall; all the king's horses and all the king's men couldn't put Humpty together again.*

She prefers not to leave the house. Gets as far as the little vestibule with the linoleum that has been there as long as she can remember— a small brick pattern held down with black carpet tacks. The mail is still delivered through the iron flap, bigger things are left on the porch. Sometimes she leaves the mail there until someone stumbles upon it later in the day.

I prefer not to. She repeats this to herself, or rather it repeats in a rat-tat-rat-tat-rat in her mind. Good ole' Bartelby the Scrivener. She smiles as she realizes that this strange man from a Melville short story has become her role model. From way back in a high school English class where she first met him, he shows up once in a while in her mind. Funny what sticks. A man who preferred not to. And no one could make him budge. Good for him.

But prefer is not really the right word. She cannot leave the house. Since the day of Jimmy's funeral, the day she finally broke open enough to let Dennis in, she has not been able to leave the house. She doesn't go grocery shopping. Dennis and the kids have to do that.

She cannot leave. There is a force keeping her in. She feels too vulnerable, too exposed, at the thought of going outside. Once upon a time, a short time ago, she would make herself go out, vulnerable or not. But that was when her armor had not completely cracked. She is raw now. Every nerve exposed and electrified.

Rose eats. Cookies, frozen pizzas, lasagna, ice cream. She is so hungry. She doesn't remember ever being this hungry in her entire life. There's not enough food. How can there be enough to fill the gaping ache in her gut? All the fatty, salty, creamy, starchy food she didn't allow herself to eat before. Bags of chips, of cookies, pretzels and dip. She can't eat fast enough.

She takes to wearing sweat pants and some of Dennis' big shirts. Never in her life has she put on so much weight. Even when she was pregnant she was a disciplined eater. She walked off that baby fat with diligence and speed, pushing a stroller through Forest Park and up and down Woodhaven Boulevard and back again.

She flips through the channels on the television. All those real life murder shows on cable. All the histories of war and ancient times. Trying to explain how we, people that is, how we ever got to be who we are. Wars and invasions and deceptions and murders. The human condition. *No wonder I'm so fucked up.*

There is a strange comfort in all this ugliness reenacted in living color right here in her own home. The history of civilization, or lack thereof. She takes it all in, hardly processing, just soaking it up. One terrible action after another. *That's what makes us human?*

The shows that she takes a special interest in are the ghost shows. The ones where a team of amateur ghost busters take their night vision cameras and try to capture blurry images on video are mildly amusing. But she has begun to record the mediums speaking to loved ones from beyond the beyond shows. That's where she has some experience.

She plays with the idea of going to see the host. He has a studio right here in the city. He grew up in Queens. He's not much different from me, she thinks. But she is not ready to go out, much less get on a train and wait in line to get a seat in his audience on the off chance he will pick her out of the crowd. It's always someone else who is picked.

Besides, Dennis still thinks her 'ghosts' are a metaphor for the past bothering her. She thought he guessed about Cilla and Grandma. But he didn't. She is worried that Jimmy will start showing up and blame her for his death. As vulnerable as she is in here, there's some safety. Cilla and Grandma have been good ghosts and they have been here for years. Jimmy's anger worries her. She doesn't want to be out of range of Grandma if he does decide to visit her.

She has to figure out how to tell Dennis about the ghosts. She tried to tell him a little bit that night he left, but she could hardly speak. *Will he think I'm crazy? Maybe he'll try to explain them away— a figment of my active imagination, a protection, a coping mechanism. Could I ever tell him about the promises that Jesus made to me when I was little? How I was special, chosen for something? I still don't know what it is, but something.*

That promise that came with the light was the pebble she wrapped the yarn of her life around. The touchstone that helped keep herself together as much as she was able. She might not believe it anymore, but she is grateful for it. Delusion or not, it was a light in the darkness. It was hope.

Chapter Sixty-Seven

After that night at the conference, it was over. The flirting, the little laughs, stopping by her desk to chit-chat.

If she hadn't come to his room, if they hadn't had sex, then, maybe, then, he could talk to her about Rose. Then, maybe, again, always, maybe, they could talk about marriage and relationships and enduring the tests. But he had failed the test completely. Since they had achieved that primal level of intimacy, there could no longer be the conversational intimacy, the heart sharing intimacy, the human, soul baring intimacy. They lost whatever tentative friendship they had in that one middle of the night joining. It separated them more than it united them.

Now, he had to find a position for her in another department. In a department where he wouldn't see her everyday, where she could be in training for a promotion. A place she could think was better. A place better enough that she would keep their secret, pack it away in her arsenal if she had to, but pack it away.

Dennis knows who he is now. He is fallen. He is alive. He is ashamed. He is. And now he has to deal with it.

Chapter Sixty-Eight

"Dennis, do you have a minute?" Sheila is placing a plastic bag in the big trash barrel.

"Sure."

"You look defeated. How's Rose? I haven't seen her about lately."

He is grateful that Sheila asks. He won't give her the 'she's fine' answer. He's way past social niceties, lies, that is. Anyway, Sheila and Frank were witness to Rose cutting in to Jenny after Jimmy's funeral.

"She's a mess. I thought maybe a little time would help. But, instead of getting better, she seems to be falling deeper into someplace I can't go. I come home from work and the TV is on, some dumb medium show she's replaying from the afternoon. She mentioned something about ghosts and I thought she was thinking of some family stuff she hadn't gotten over."

He shifts his weight from right to left foot, assesses Sheila's receptivity and proceeds.

"I think she sits all day, eating and watching television. She's not taking care of herself. Doesn't even run the laundry or do dishes. I mean I know she's upset, but I don't know how to handle her. Now that he has this chance to talk, he can't seem to hold back.

"Marie tries to help out with laundry and cleaning up and cooking some frozen dinners. Kieran's never home. I want my Rosie back. How long should I let this go on?"

The look on Dennis' face moves Sheila. The poor man is miserable.

"Would you like me to try and talk with her?"

"She won't leave the house."

"Well, then I'll knock on the door."

Dennis gives Sheila a hug for the first time in all the years they have been neighbors.

Chapter Sixty-Nine

Maureen Banfry always gave a haughty sniff and said "oh, that one" on the few occasions Sheila was referred to. "Your grandmother had no sense when it came to taking in strays. Women with loose morals should not be treated the same as decent people."

In all her years of knowing Sheila, Rose had never seen her be anything but kind and loving, especially toward her grandmother. Grams told her they were some kind of cousins.

Maybe Mom resented that Sheila had such a warm relationship with Grams. Mom couldn't seem to figure why she and Grams had such a coldness when she tried to do everything right. It never occurred to her that everything right was not the ticket to her mother-in-law's heart.

The remote falls to the floor when Rose's fingers open in her state of almost sleep on the living room couch. She rolls in toward the back of the couch, letting the television murmur in the background.

Jenny at Haufbrau's pops into Rose's sleepy brain. She looks so stricken at the cruel words thrown at her.

A familiar voice whispers: *maybe she was thinking of what a scandal would do to your father and the whole family, you included.*

Maybe Jenny thought, hoped anyway, that she could come to fall in love with the man she married. That a marriage would protect her child and her family's face. Cover over the shame. Maybe, Rose, maybe that's possible.

Rose is in that stage of sleep where she is unable to move. Held paralyzed so she cannot awaken, so she has to hear the whispers.

Rose, let go. Give it up.

No! Jenny was wrong! That's all there is to it.

But Paul, what about Paul— he's my grandson, Rose and he is your brother.

Half-

Okay half, but he's fully my grandson.

Bells are ringing in Rose's brain. Church bells? No, it's different. She rolls over and nearly falls. The doorbell.

Rose stands, runs her fingers through her hair, shakes the sleep out of her brain.

Sheila is at the front door, holding something.

Rose doesn't have the energy to be friendly.

Sheila rings again.

Rose opens the door and before she is able to word an excuse Sheila is inside the vestibule, the presence of her backing Rose into the living room.

"I've brought the same teapot that your Gran'ma used when I was feeling poorly. I expect you have a kettle."

Rose nods.

"Well, good, then."

Sheila takes herself back to the kitchen, pushing through the swinging door and turning the faucet on with the kettle beneath it.

Rose realizes she hasn't had a chance to say a word.

"There, these are nice cups. Have a seat, Rose. These cookies, they were your grandmother's favorites. I'll put them on a little plate for us. Sit, sit."

There's no use protesting. Sheila is clearly in charge.

"Rose, did I ever tell you how your grandmother saved me?"

"No,."

"Well, she did.

"As you might know I came over here when I was 21, all full of nonsense in my head about New York and having romances and smoking cigarettes and looking irresistible, you know, all the stuff that fills a young girl's empty head when she lives in a two cow village in Ireland."

The kettles whistles. Sheila gets up in one deft movement, pours the tea, settles the cups on the table and pours some milk into a tiny pitcher and places all this on the table.

"So, my mother sent me off with all kinds of advice on what not to do and a letter with the name, address and telephone number of a cousin of hers. The only thing I kept was the letter. The rest of her advice I discarded when I traded in my old sturdy brogues for a lovely pair of heels. By the way, the heels gave me blisters."

"Okay, so where does my grandmother come into all this?"

"Wait, I'm getting there. So I move in with four other girls who have their heads filled with the same sort of Hollywood nonsense that I did. They got me a job waiting tables in Times Square where actors from the local shows would turn up for a beer or a burger. Sounds exciting, doesn't it? Well, I was so green, so fresh off the boat that you could smell the kelp on me. I cut my hair and dyed it black to look like Leslie Caron, wore uncomfortable shoes and lost my peasant pounds.

"And what do I do? I take up with the first bloke who smiled at me. I was foolish enough to think that this is what I've been waiting for my whole life. A bit of romance, a bit of real American living. Did I tell you I was a fool of a girl?

"Mmm, these cookies are as good as I remember them. I'll have to get them more often."

Rose has barely uttered more than an uh-huh and a yeah while Sheila goes on with her tale.

"Well, the long and the short of it, I ended up in a jam. And, as I told you, the only thing sensible I saved of my mother's advice was the piece of paper with her cousin's name and number on it. Her cousin, you know, was your Grandmother.

"Well, now, she took me in. Remember, this was 1955 and we were all Irish Catholics. I know many children began life on the wrong side of the blanket, but the fella, the actor with the malarkey,

I never saw him again after he got what he was after.

"So, what options did I have? I was here on a visa and can you imagine me going back home big as life to my mother and father and younger sisters to be a cautionary tale for all the foolish girls who wanted to get out of the two cow town? I would've died of shame.

"Drink your tea, it's getting cold." Rose lifts her cup to her mouth and takes a sip. The warmth of it going down her pipes melts some of her tension.

"My friend Colleen was the one who actually called your grandmother. I was that frozen with shame to do it myself. I thought I'd be sent away to one of those homes for wayward girls and how would I have stood that?

"But Aunt Meg, your grandmother, opened her door to me and Colleen, fed us a meal and made a fine pot of tea and took me in hand. I lived right up stairs where your Marie has her room. And some years later she gave me this very pot that I've brought over to you."

Sheila looks away, at the wall, seeing that long ago scene re-play.

"Now where was I? Oh, yes, God was watching over me, despite my sins, or maybe because of my sins, hmm, maybe that's it."

She sips her tea and takes a bite of the cookie.

"Anyway, he sent me here. And not only did God send me here, he sent me my Frank. Right next door, where I live now with him all these many years. That was his parents house and somehow or other he loved me, and I loved him back and he never thought of our Margaret as anything other than his very own daughter."

Rose shifts a bit in her chair.

"A few years later we had the twins. And for all my fussing about not living the kind of life my own mother had tending to husband and children, that's exactly what I got and I couldn't be more grateful that God didn't listen one bit to what I wanted, but instead gave me what I needed."

"Okay, Sheila, that's a great story. But am I supposed to get something from this?"

"Now Rose, maybe you don't think my story has anything to do with you, but give it a minute, I think it does.

"What have you got right now? You have a strong and kind husband, two beautiful children and you live in the home of your wonderful grandmother, not bad."

"But,"

"But, nothing. So you had parents who didn't know their ass from their elbows about raising kids. Forgive me for saying this, but your poor mother didn't know how to let up and let go. Everything and everybody had to be perfect, what ever that meant in her mind.

"So your father was a wanderer. What man could stand your mother with all her rules? I'm not saying that he should've taken up with Jenny. No, he shouldn't have. But he did. That's the fact of the matter."

Rose returns Sheila's observation with a stony face.

"And I'm sorry poor Jimmy had such a hard time. Now, your little sister died, your parents died, your brother died. So now you have nothing? Well, of course you don't. You have another brother."

"Hmmf." Rose starts to turn away from Sheila, but the table is up against the wall and there's no place for her to turn.

"Rose, none of what happened is his fault. And wasn't Jenny a young foolish girl when she found herself in a difficult situation? I suppose she could have made a big fuss and exposed your father. But she didn't. I don't know anything about the man she married but she did find a father for her son and now, I don't know why, but now she is reaching out to you."

Sheila reaches her hand out to Rose.

"You can't live angry the rest of your life Rose, you'll lose Dennis and the children as surely as your mother lost her family."

Rose is looking into her cup of tea.

"We are some kind of cousins, but really, you were dear to Aunt Meg, and that's enough to make you dear to me. Your real family legacy is one of kindness and generosity not judgment and anger. You can choose your inheritance and you can choose your graces. Before it's too late, Rose, you need to pick a direction and I hope and pray that you reach out to that woman and her son."

"Why do I have to do all the forgiving?"

"Because you're the one who's wrapped up tight in anger."

"She destroyed my family."

"Rose, haven't you heard a word I said? She didn't destroy your family. Your sister's death sent your mother over her edge. Your father was a lonesome man. Jimmy, well, who knows how Jimmy could have had a happier life.

"But you, Rose, don't you see you played your part in all this? You wanted to pretend your family was something they weren't. Maybe something they could have been, even should have been, but they weren't."

Rose wipes some tears from her cheek.

"We don't get it all. But we have to make the best of what we do have. And now you have another brother out in the world. Maybe he needs you, needs your family. And Jenny, poor Jenny, think of what she must have been living with all these years."

Sheila takes a breath, then squeezes Rose's hand.

"I've chewed your ear enough for one afternoon Rose. If you ever want to talk again, I'm right next door."

Sheila leaves the remainder of the cookies, the ceramic tea pot and the tin of loose tea leaves on the counter, then goes home through the kitchen door.

Chapter Seventy

Dennis has a client coming in from Atlanta for several days this week. The plan includes meetings and the hammering out of a deal that will probably go long hours into the evenings. Dennis has arranged for this client to stay at a local suite, complete with kitchenette and a little sitting room. Contemplating driving from Smithtown to Woodhaven after a couple of long nights, Dennis books himself into the same hotel. It's not like there's anything to rush home to, so why break his neck?

After the incident with Maddie, Dennis expected to be covered in shame, guilt, regret, worry. He is surprised at the anger that fills each breath, the anger, not at Maddie for coming into his room and leading him astray so easily, but at Rose, and at himself. This anger is almost new to him. He has always tried to maintain balance, always tried to correct course when emotion threatened to overrule his brain.

He is also more attuned to the signals in the air. He notices the smiles, the pleasing lines, the wave of hair, the fragrance, of the women around him. He wasn't aware that he had turned those receptors off in the last decade or more. He's a married man, a husband, a father, a bank executive, not some dude on the make. He had tidied those messy distractions away so he could get on with life in an orderly and predictable fashion.

Now, instead of the expected guilt and shame, he if full of angry regret. All this life going on around him and he felt none of it! Did his sin awaken him to the life he was neglecting? Was it a lure to the possibilities, the tastes, sounds, touch, color, of the life he had turned off? A flash of revelation: it is sin, not anemic virtue, that lets us be human. Sin, the fall from complacence, that awakens the need for redemption, the need to be engaged in the struggle, the wrestling, the aliveness that can lead to redemption.

While he is away, he calls at night to check in with his family. Kieran tells him that Rose has gone to bed. He pictures his wife, lying in bed, hearing the ring of the phone, just looking at the thing, willing it to stop making noise.

She'll try to listen, though, to hear her son speak to his father: "Not much. You?"

"'kay."

"see ya soon."

The Morse code of father/son communication.

Dennis is glad Rose doesn't get on the phone. A feeble exchange would be too sad; a lot of nothing after twenty years of marriage.

When the deal has been worked out and the need for staying at the hotel is gone, Dennis has to go home. He pulls off the LIE ten exits from work.

"What kind of trade in deal can I get?"

"This the car you want to trade? A little tired of the dad van? Don't I know it. You fellas are our best customers."

"Yeah. I want a stick shift. Tired of automatic." *Every damn day is automatic. Every goddamn day.*

"You want something powerful, but smooth. Good sound system, a little rev in the engine."

The dealer, Dave, his name tag says, has already taken Dennis by the back of the elbow, directing him to the lot. There's a line of Eclipses, shades of red, green, blue, black metallics shimmering in the setting sun. "This baby here", he walks Dennis over to the dark blue metallic with purple hues teasing through where the rays of the late afternoon sun hit it, "was traded in by a fella who gets himself a new model every two years. Takes good care, he does. This car here was treated with lots of love."

Dennis is circling the car, low to the ground, sleek lines, powerful. His heart beats a little faster; he breathes in the possibility. *Why the hell not?* He runs his hand along the hood, pulls on the handle. Dave is walking back from the office, remote in hand. He clicks it open just as Dennis pulls the latch.

Dennis slides into his seat, his legs spread out in front, under the steering wheel. The seat holds him in its soft embrace. Leather wheel cover, shifting gear, fit perfectly under his palm.

"Let's take'r out for a spin." Dave slips in the passenger seat. It's been some time since Dennis drove a standard. Shifting gears comes back to him like an old friend.

When Dennis pulls into his driveway, Sheila is the first to witness Dennis, the sports car owner. A couple of years of payments, but close enough to an owner.

"Well, look at you. Won't the kids be excited."

"Oh, no, this is mine. They get to ride in Rose's sedan."

Sheila smiles at him, "good for you, Dennis, you deserve a little something for yourself."

Dennis goes in the back door. "Anyone home?" he hears some footsteps overhead. "Kieran! Marie! Rose! I want to show you something."

Rose pulls herself off the couch, the kids bang down the stairs. "Whaddja do? Get a dog?" Marie asks.

"Come on out, it's in the driveway."

Kieran is quicker than everyone else. When they join him, he's squatted in front, looking at its great body. "Pop the hood, Dad."

Marie sits in the passenger seat while her brother looks at the engine block. Dennis stands by, smiling at the kids excitement.

"So, what do you think, Rose?" He looks at her, wondering what kind of response she might grace him with.

"It's very pretty. I didn't know you were interested in that kind of thing."

He mutters, half out loud, half to himself, "there's a lot you don't know I'm interested in."

~~~

"Change your clothes."

"What?"

"Put on something" he gestures at her searching for words, "I don't know, put on something better."

"What are you talking about Dennis? I'm tired."

"Too bad. Okay, then, just put on some shoes."

"Why, what's going on?"

"I'm taking you out."

"Out? What about the kids?"

"They can heat up a frozen pizza. Can't you, guys?"

They eagerly nod yes.

"Come on."

So Rose gets some shoes, and leaves with Dennis, still dressed in her sweats, no makeup, hair unwashed.

He backs out of the driveway and takes the route through Forest Park, winding their way to the Interboro, from there to the Grand Central.

Neither of them speak for the ride. The Grand Central turns into Northern State. The trees are in full bloom, the further east they go, the more green surrounds them.

"We're moving, Rose. And we're moving this summer."

"What? What are you talking about?"

"I'm not living like this any longer. I'm not tip toeing around you for the rest of my life. I'm not going to watch you become your mother."

He takes a breath, keeps his eyes on the road, not chancing a glance at his wife, a glance that can weaken his resolve.

"So, we're moving. We shoulda' moved two years ago after 9/11 when everything went to hell."

Rose has folded her arms over her chest, trying to summon the energy to fight with Dennis. He continues his speech.

"But no. We stayed in that house, that ghost house of yours, we stayed. Always excuses, not even reasons."

Rose tries to interrupt, but gives up before she can start.

"So, we're moving." Each time he says this he convinces himself a little more. Rose is silent.

"Goddammit, Rose. Talk to me!" Dennis has pulled off into the parking lot of a strip mall.

"Talk to me." He turns to her, asking now, not demanding. "So you're father had another kid. So your brother lived a miserable life, so so so. Everyone has shit. Everyone."

Rose is still stone faced. Not even a tear to fill up the hard look in her eyes. He keeps trying.

"Why do we think we're entitled to unmitigated happiness? What a crock of shit! Get over yourself! Just get over it."

Now she turns to him, pouring energy into her effort to remain in control of herself.

"There's more stuff I haven't told you about."

"So, what is this more stuff? You're pissed off. You're angry.

Okay then, be angry. Don't be this, this" again he gestures to her, head to toe. "Don't be this," he cannot say the words, cannot hurt her that much. "Fight back, Rose. Fight back, for us, the kids, our family. Fight back."

Some token of anger in Rose tries to break through. "Fight back? I hardly have the strength to have this conversation. I'm exhausted. Can't you see that I'm exhausted?"

"Well, I'm pretty exhausted too." His voice is softer now. "You never talk to me. You hardly look at me. You know I get lonesome too." He turns his head when he says this, turns and looks out his window, ashamed of his secret, ashamed at his anger at Rose for leaving him so vulnerable. So damn lonesome. "You know we're in real trouble here, Rose."

He holds back. He's not going to tell her the sin that is eating at him. He is fighting for his family now. He has scared himself, seen what he is capable of. It scares him. It empowers him. He doesn't know which it does more.

His world is shattered by Rose's breakdown. "I could just stand by and let this play out. But I know what your mother turned into, all her anger and grief turned her into some thing, something hard and cruel."

Rose has relented a bit. She reaches into the soft pocket of her sweatshirt for a tissue.

"What a waste. For her, your father, Jimmy, you, the grandkids. A colossal waste."

Rose blows her nose, wipes at her eyes with the back of her hand.

Dennis changes course. "Come on. I'm hungry."

Rose looks down at herself. "Look what I'm wearing. I'm a mess." He smiles at this first sign of self-consciousness in months. He reaches over to the glove box, "here, comb your hair. No one knows you here." To himself he thinks, *this is the last time you'll look like this.*

Rose hadn't thought of Dennis in this light before. Dennis, agreeable Dennis, went along with whatever she suggested. For the first time in, well, maybe, ever, she sees her husband as an attractive man with red blood, strength. Willing to fight for her. The first, real, man willing to fight for her.

Now, she knows, she has to let go of her fantasy of Father Joseph. It shocks her that she conjured the heroic actions of this priest, once so young, once so beautiful, like the Jesus on holy cards; more mother than father.

He moves the car closer to the restaurant. The happy kitschy noisy trendy place is so far removed from their moods that its perfect.

For dessert, Dennis orders an ice cream/cake concoction and two spoons. Dennis scoops some ice cream, leans over and feeds it to Rose. She takes it, grateful for this touch of gallantry.

When they get outside Rose slips her hand into Dennis'. When he opens her door she hugs him.

"I didn't know how much I missed you."

Chapter Seventy-One

I *DANCED WITH THE GIRL with the strawberry curls and the band played on.*

Round and round the bit of old fashioned waltz turns in Jenny's head as she walks home from school. She times the words to a play of orange and red leaves as they make their way to the ground, one two three, up, a little down, to the side and then a bow, a little breeze, then down, a graceful curtsy. *And the band played on.*

Today was a good day. Her students paid attention, a little distracted by the cool fresh breeze that came in through the four-inch opening of the window. But, they managed to cover the Pilgrims making it over on their little ship and setting up camp on the rocky New England coast. Quiet distraction is fine, and what can one expect with those waltzing leaves?

It is a perfect October day for walking. So that is what she will do. Go home, leave her book bag, change into jeans, a cozy soft jacket and sneakers and her afternoon is planned.

The colors, the cool breeze, the way the sun sits a little lower in the sky, just there, over the rooftop, in the late afternoon. Red and yellow leaves are mixed with browning ones on her lawn and under the bushes in the garden. They have gathered at the triangles at either side of the garage doors. She is in no hurry to rake and bag them.

She cuts across her lawn, noting the crunch as she heads right, around the bend to Webster then south to Hewlett Avenue toward Sunrise Highway and the Long Island Rail Road. Woodbine is her favorite block. The colonial and Tudor houses, the trees and the gardens, are an advertisement for autumn in the suburbs of New York.

There are big lush oaks and elms with patches of bark chipped away and birds calling, *still here, awk, still here.* This is nature at its showiest, Jenny thinks. Some argue for spring and summer but for her this is the time when earth is at its fullest, its wisest, so to speak. It is the atmosphere for contemplation, for gathering wisdom, for quiet time to put some order on the chaos of the eruptions of spring and summer.

She thinks of the old trees as wise, but smiles as she wonders why wise and old are so often paired. Surely she has known enough old fools in her life, people who managed to tick out the seconds of their clock without softening, without deepening into their wrinkles and soft bellies. Isn't the trade off for some frailty a dose of wisdom? Is it a choice, she wonders, or a disposition?

These thoughts stroll through her as she breathes in the sweet air of decaying leaves, delighted at the bit of red, blown and dancing on October's breath. *Thank you, God, for letting me walk, for letting me see again this beautiful garment of autumn, the colors and the sun splitting its rays through these branches that have survived season after season. Most older than me, older than my mother and grandmother.*

Jenny sees this showing of colors as a message from God to get our attention before we waste any more time. *You can still understand, grieve, and allow pain to take root and grow compassion in your soul.*

The sun falling lower in the sky and that breeze, just a bit chill, not yet cold, reminds us, grounds us. A yearly ticking, the bass sound of it gathering depth through the blanket of leaves. Forgiveness and generosity and abundance need to be our first things, not our last.

She winds her way back to her house, goes in and sets the kettle to boil. When it whistles she fills a cup and lets a tea bag steep. The back porch that needs cement work and some new wood around the screens is one of her favorite parts of this house. It is far from perfect and for this she is glad. Jenny sits back in a patio chair and enjoys the view.

When she was a child, eleven, twelve years old—old enough to be wandering, not old enough to be burdened yet by high school and all the disruption that brings, she wandered the streets of Rosedale from the time she changed out of her uniform and into corduroys, a sweater and Keds.

She'd go up past P. S. 38 where the boys would be playing handball or basketball on the cement courts then down the steep hill that was 241st Street that fed into Merrick Road. It was just a few blocks down Merrick Road to Anna's Italian deli, the same smells that were the perfume of her life with her mother and grandmother always cooking, getting ready to cook or cleaning up from cooking. Anna's deli reminded her it was time to go home and set the table.

With no effort at all Jenny can smell those delicious meats and cheeses, can see the jug of chianti at her father's place and the short glasses he would use for his wine. Every one had a little in a glass. Jenny loved the rich dark color and the way the wine rose through her nose to hit the back of her throat, then down, warming her lungs. Breathing it in was enough, only on occasion did she take a sip.

When her mother would say, "Jenny, you need to learn how to make this", her grandmother would take her mother's arm. "Enough time for that. Let her walk." Then she'd wink at Jenny, partners in a small conspiracy.

The tomatoes and the basil were from their own backyard. Long flat sticks were planted upright in the ground inches apart and the growing vines would be secured by strips of old clothes too worn for the St. Vincent's bin.

In spring and summer Grandma would get on her knees, the dark rich soil between her fingers, tenderly planting. Jenny would see her bless herself, a prayer for a good harvest, a benediction for the food provided by the abundant earth.

Her grandfather sat in a kitchen chair he took with him when they moved here from Brooklyn. He straddled the chair, its back to his front, a place to put his hands and rest his cane. He had a special pair of shoes for gardening: sturdy thick brown leather cracked in places, with thick rubber soles. Even though his back prevented him form getting in the dirt, he always gardened with his wife. He was well practiced at supervising. She was well practiced at ignoring him. They worked together; it didn't matter who was kneeling in the earth.

Pink and red roses lined the back fence. Even in October one or two might still bloom, because Grandpa always left a few branches to grow after he had cut the others down for next season. For his bride. Every year for more than sixty years.

If her early years were spring, she continues her analogy, then all the banking of love, goodwill and strength she received from her parents and grandparents was what she drew on to get through the summer of her life.

That summer of 1972, she was twenty-three years old. She didn't mean to fall in love with Mr. B, but she didn't try very hard not to. She knows now, thirty-two years later, that it was not love, but something quite different. He was tall, handsome, powerful. He was a presence.

Jenny attended Adelphi College when Paul was little. She took a course in anthropology that gave her some insight into why she was so reckless. It was a call of the wild, a call of her reproductive brain to mate with a powerful and attractive alpha male. That's one way of putting it. That's one way to excuse her lack of willpower, go against all her religious and ethical training.

But then there is Paul. Beautiful Paul. A child born of deception and compromise. A child received in great joy by a man who was thankful for the blessing of a strong and healthy and beautiful child.

And he was David's child. It was David who Paul looked to for protection when they neared a big dog or went to a museum and the dinosaurs growled. It was David whose hand the child held. It was David who picked him up and presented him for all the world to see. My son. My son.

And Jenny knew she needed to keep her secret from him, from this good man she had tricked. From this gentle man she could not fall in love with. But she could love and care for.

Some gifts come disguised as pain, as trouble, as a problem that needs a solution.

There are two large evergreens in the back of the yard standing together like a married couple. Paul used to play there when he was young, the trees providing just the right amount of coverage for the space to be a fort or a hiding place or a place for him to take his toys and make for himself an outdoor playroom.

Paul is 31 now. Playing in the trees was so very long ago, but no, it was yesterday, just yesterday. She can still hear him play with the children on the block and the small voiced yells and whoops of children that should be put to music. *I'm sure someone else has done that. That is not my gift.*

What is my gift? To take it in. To absorb and reflect and grieve? Live a widowhood of sorrow, sorrow for the lies I lived. Sorrow for the man I hurt.

The tea grows cold in the mug; her hands wrapped around the ceramic are not enough to keep it warm.

There is just a bit of orange sunlight behind the pines and the cotton fleece of her jacket is too thin to keep the chill from her. But that's okay, it's a good chill. A reminder.

As Jenny watches two squirrels chase each other through the yard and over the fence, she talks to her companion, Melancholy: *Do we only get this one chance to make things right? This one lifetime? No, that cannot be right. That's not enough.*

We don't start to understand until it's too late. We don't really foresee the consequences, even though we should. Even if we were taught the words or rules of morality that should keep us on the straight and narrow.

We have to have more time. We are stupid for so many years.

We don't know. All the words written in books, in catechisms, in all the warnings throughout time.

Passions blind us; make us see only what we want to see. And this passion has its own logic, its own morality.

And then the deed is done.

And then another to correct that first wrong deed. And it continues. And we pile up the pain, pile up the bodies of those we have hurt. Those we have destroyed.

Even when we try. Really try. We are still blinded by love or resentment or anger. So many get hurt.

And the pain lingers. It keeps us awake. Won't let us sleep. It is the echo of the old ache that stays.

And when we try to sleep it pokes at us. Haunts us. Its that knot in the pit of stomachs that won't go away no matter how much food or drink we shove in to shut it up.

It won't shut up. It shuts us up.

Forgive yourself? Forgive yourself? How crazy is that?

Such easy words. Such meaningless words. Those words cannot reach back in time and stop us from saying the ugly thing or prod us to do the kind act that could have changed history. That could let us sleep now.

They are all just words. Words written in self help books. Words we dare to hope to believe. But we know we cannot. Not really. Not truly.

So we wait. Hope there is a heaven. Or a purgatory where we can purge the pains with the people we were supposed to love better. Be kinder to. The people we were given to care for.

This lifetime is not enough. There has to be more time after we are gone. To heal. To forgive. To love.

She goes in to the kitchen to heat up some leftovers for her solitary supper.

Chapter Seventy-Two

"Dennis."

He looks up from the paper, "Yeah?"

"Do you think your father and brother's success had any bearing on your success?"

Dennis twists his face into question mode.

It's Sunday afternoon in late October. The sun is getting low in the sky and the old grey sweater that Rose found in the attic feels just right pulled around her.

"Well, I don't know if I ever thought about it that way, but sure, I guess. I guess they showed me what was possible, they were an example to me. I'd like to think that I had something to do with it, but a good example is a bonus"

"Well, of course you had something to do with your success. You made choices and worked hard and all that, but you had a guide, I guess you could call it, in them, that they did well, so you could do well. Permission, I suppose."

"All right, that's one way of looking at it."

"I've been wondering about how Jimmy and I turned out. Our father was successful. But, he was never there much.

"Your father and mother did things with you guys, didn't they?"

"Uh-huh."

"You were all healthy and intelligent, right?"

"Yeah."

"Hmm. How do you think things would have been if, say, your brother was slow, or sickly, or autistic, or something else that would be a real burden?"

"I don't know Rose. I don't think about that kind of stuff much."

"Yeah, but indulge me a bit."

He nods his head at her to continue.

"You know when you have a pie, say an apple pie, for dessert?"

"Uh-huh."

"Well, if one person takes a skinny slice and someone else takes a bigger, but not really big slice, then there is a whole bunch left over for someone else to have a giant slice. And then if the others decide they want more, it's too late, the greedy one ate the rest of the pie."

"Well, then, get another pie."

"What if there isn't another pie?"

"Then, I guess there'd be a fight, or resentment, or some name calling."

"Yeah, but, here's something a little different. What if the pie was sliced by someone else who gave one person a medium slice, one person a small slice and the other person a giant slice. Would there still be resentment and anger?"

"Probably—the others would think 'who is he that he gets the biggest slice?' Then there's none left for us to have more later."

"Exactly."

"Exactly what?"

"Just a minute."

Rose is on a roll now, becoming more animated the more she goes on with her theory.

"How do you think the one who got the biggest slice would feel? Oh, I forgot to say that they weren't allowed to give away their slice or any part of it, they had to eat the slice they were given. So how would the one with the biggest slice feel?"

"That depends.

Dennis puts up one finger at a time to count the ways.

"He might be grateful for the bigger slice. He might feel guilty about the bigger slice. He might have to live for a while being considered greedy and selfish even though someone else gave him the bigger slice."

He couldn't think of anything for his fourth finger.

"See what I mean?"

"No. See what you mean about what?"

"Oh I was just thinking out loud."

"Care to share?"

"All right, I've been thinking about the economy of the family."

"Okay."

"Well, I think in some families, among the brothers and sisters, anyway, there is a jockeying for equality. You don't let someone get too puffed up, but, you try to pull one up when he or she is too low. Even keel.

"But what if there are too many problems in a family? What if someone is sickly or a poor student or has some other kinds of things that put them outside the norm, but some kids are healthy and alright?

"And the ones or one who is healthy and smart wants more than what the family will allow, wants still more of a piece of pie. Even thinks maybe there are more pies out there and instead of sharing one pie there are plenty of pies for everyone.

"But the less healthy ones keep saying 'no. There's only the one pie and if you are happy then that makes me miserable because, there's only so much pie we can have and you took it all.'"

"Does this make sense?" Dennis asks.

"Not really, but when has sense had anything to do with family dynamics?"

"You're talking about your family, right?"

"Yeah."

"So, you got the biggest slice of pie, Cilla got a little slice, Jimmy got a medium slice and you feel guilty."

"Yeah, that's about right."

"But you know there's more pie. Pies are always being made."

"What if the giant guarding the door doesn't let the other pies in?"

"Well, then the giant needs to be toppled."

"What if you can't topple the giant because the giant provides the food and the shelter and even the one who gets the bigger slice is always told she she should just shut up and not complain because she got the biggest piece and it's not fair and all that kind of stuff."

"Then that one with the bigger piece of pie needs to escape from the giant's castle and build her own castle."

"How?"

"With the help of a valiant prince. At your service, m'lady."

With this he flourishes the kitchen towel he is holding, falls to one knee, offers his hand and pulls her out of her seat.

"Shall we dance?"

"We shall, valiant prince, we shall."

"And then we shall go to the bakery and purchase many pies and everyone in the kingdom can have all they want and grow fat and jolly and laugh all the day long."

They bow and curtsy to one another. Then waltz around the living room.

~~~

Rose is making her bed, the Miraculous Medal still hangs around the bedpost. These late October mornings are breathtaking—in another week the leaves will be swept off the trees as November settles in. Late October in New York is the height of autumn, nature's magnificence on bright display as something to take forward into the darker days to come.

She takes the small gold medal from its resting place and runs her fingers over Mary's face and hands. Months ago Rose asked for a miracle. She got a breakdown. Jimmy died. She went into a tailspin. Her marriage was in crisis.

Her faith shattered into shards revealing what? Seed planted on good soil, like she thought when she was young and untested—*I'm the good soil that hears the word of God and keeps it*—such arrogance in a child, such childishness in faith, yes, childishness: she was a child.

She discovered that she was more like the seed planted on rocky ground: roots shallow, pulled away at the first strong wind leaving only bare pebble and sand. What could be planted on that kind of heart? Something cold and stony, hard and unyielding.

But no, the rocks have been shattered. Under the rock the soil is soft and rich, tender. New faith stepping out. God, it's hard. *I cannot see, I'm battered, broken.* Questions replaced answers. Questions still don't have answers, and maybe they never will. And maybe that's just the way it is: open ended, messy, ambiguous.

No one with any sense would seek out a broken heart. We try to protect ourselves from broken hearts but at some point the protection is more expensive than the truth and then it all must crumble under its own weight.

We just can't do any more and we breakdown. Can't hold back crying. Can't hold onto what passes for dignity and if we ever cared about such things, we just don't anymore.

We see how stupid it all was. Broken hearts hurt down to the core of us. They rend us alone in the dark, unconnected, cut off. All the ways to describe isolation, severance: birth. We do what we can, desperately if need be, to be connected, encumbered even, with lies.

Its better than being alone. Abandonment as our most basic fear, not falling but exile. If I tell the truth I will be exiled. I will have to connect with other exiles. The island of misfit toys. All the children's stories were written to warn us, weren't they?

Is this the theology? The theology of the broken hearted, the crushed, the humbled.

The road to perdition is broad, but isn't the road to salvation broad, also? The narrow way is just that: narrow.

I asked for a miracle. What I got was a breakdown. Just what I needed. Don't mind if I fall apart, there's more room in a broken heart. Carly Simon's line now the undertone of her thoughts. *Miracle of the broken heart.*

Rose undoes the clasp of the gold chain and fastens the medal around her neck.

Chapter Seventy-Three

Rose has the radio on in the kitchen. The DJ is playing hits of the seventies.

She's dancing around preparing dinner, chopping onions and celery and carrots, making a beef stew. It's finally cool enough to have autumn food. She smiles as she realizes that this is the first time in who knows when that she has danced to the radio. Well, yesterday, she and Dennis did waltz in the living room. And the bedroom. Been a long time for that, too.

The voice of the disc jockey breaks into her thoughts… *Time in a Bottle and Bad Bad Le Roy Brown topped the charts in the summer of 1973 just months before Jim Croce was killed in a plane crash…*

The summer of 1973. She and everyone her age listened to Cousin Brucie and Wolfman Jack on AM radio, their distinctive voices as much a part of the hit songs as the bands who played them.

1973. A lot happened. Rose left her job at the rectory, she graduated from elementary school.

Jenny had her baby that spring. Paul. *My brother, Paul.*

Rose spent a lot of time at her grandmother's that summer.

Far away from her silent and angry mother and her never there father. Not to mention the good monsignor checking out her summer wardrobe.

Rose had to deal with a creepy priest and a broken family.

Jenny had to deal with a rushed marriage, pregnancy and a baby.

Rose wonders if her father was of any help at all to Jenny. He wasn't much help to her and Jimmy.

Standing in her kitchen, as *Time in a Bottle* plays its melancholy air, Rose cries for Jenny. For the first time, she cries for Jenny. She thinks of Marie. What if her daughter was in that situation? Nowadays it wouldn't be as bad, but it would still be very difficult.

Now they would expose the man involved and after a few months another scandal would take its place and no one's career would come to a halt. A wife might leave him, but that's status quo these days.

But back then. Here parents gave Jimmy such grief for living with Kathy. Then when they did get married they said too bad, too late, you've already sinned too much for us.

All the while their father had put a young woman in a terrible situation. That didn't stop him from joining in the harangue with Maureen on Jimmy for breaking the rules of the church.

Something bold rises up in Rose. Right from the floor, like electricity through her legs, her guts and then through her throat. *If any man did that to Marie I would kill him!*

But Phil Banfry got away with it. Jenny paid the price, as did Jenny's husband and Paul.

What slice of pie did Paul get, she wondered. *Or Jenny?*

Probably not very big.

Chapter Seventy-Four

Rose had overheard Jenny say that she is a teacher at Calhoun High in Merrick. She went online, got the dismissal time, looked up Jenny Cellio in Merrick, found her house number and did a Mapsco search.

About twenty miles east of here. She'll have to leave early to avoid traffic on the Belt Parkway and Southern State. First, she stops at Schmidt's bakery and purchases two pies: apple and blueberry.

She gets to Jenny's neighborhood, parks down the block a bit and waits for her to come home. About 4:15 Jenny comes walking down Garfield, a book bag over her shoulder. She looks tired, Rose thinks.

After a few minutes, giving her time to settle in a bit, Rose pulls up to the front of the house.

She is nervous. *After how I treated her, how will this look, me showing up with a couple of pies six months after Jimmy's funeral?*

She's come this far. It's now or never.

Rose walks up to Jenny's door. There is a doorbell and a brass knocker. She chooses the knocker.

Jenny opens the door, some cash in hand. Must have been expecting the newspaper boy.

"Oh... Rose. What a surprise."

She hasn't slammed the door in Rose's face, so that's something.

"Hi, Jenny. I've brought you something. For you and Paul."

"Paul doesn't live here Rose. But come in."

Rose takes note of the house, even though she is worried about how this encounter will go. There is a living room to the right, a dining room and kitchen to the left and straight in front of the door, a set of stairs. Jenny leads her to the couch in the living room.

Rose places the pies, in their Schmidt's bakery bag, on the coffee table.

There's a bit of uncomfortable hemming and hawing, when Jenny says, "I usually have a cup of coffee when I come in from work, would you care for one?"

"Yes, please, that would be great."

So Jenny busies herself in the kitchen, giving Rose a moment to catch her breath.

It is a comfortable home. In the back of the room there's a French door that leads to a porch and a yard with a few tall pines near the back fence.

Jenny returns with two mugs of coffee, some milk and sugar.

"I know this is a surprise, Jenny. First of all I want to apologize for how I acted at Jimmy's funeral. That was unfair of me. I, well, I was in a difficult state from the time my father died— when I first realized who Paul was, and of course, who you were to Paul and my father. That was a big shock. A really big shock. And when Jimmy died, that just threw me." Rose starts to cry.

Jenny starts, "I'm so sorry Rose, I didn't mean…

"Let me finish, Jenny, or I might never get through this."

Jenny nods.

"Anyway, I had kind of a meltdown, maybe even a breakdown, though that sounds so dramatic and men in white coats wrapping someone in a straight jacket— not that bad, of course. But, but, I crumbled.

Rose wipes away some tears with a napkin Jenny had put out with the coffee.

"Anyway, the pies. Those are pies. Apple and blueberry. I don't even know if you like pies, but they're kind of a stage prop.

"So, I've been feeling all kinds of sorry for myself, angry at my parents, angry at Jimmy, angry at you." Here she looks at Jenny who nods a bit and sniffles. "But then I thought about pies."

"Okay, pies. Yes, what about pies?"

"I thought of families and who gets what and sometimes one person gets a bigger slice or a really skimpy slice and then there is all sorts of resentment and family nonsense. That was on Sunday. Yesterday I was making supper and it occurred to me, what kind of a slice of the family pie did Paul get?

"You see, it's just recently that I've counted him as my brother. And then, of course, that lead to, what kind of slice did Jenny get?

So I thought, I better not wait too long, so I looked you up and brought you pies."

Rose explained her theory to Jenny, and they both laughed and cried. Then for a little while the two women sat in silence. A companionable silence.

"Rose, I'm going to get some plates and forks and a knife and we are going to have pie together. As much pie as we want."

"Sounds good to me."

Chapter Seventy-Five

It is the middle of November. Summer came and went with no offers on the house, but at the end of October they got a buyer. A young couple with a baby.

Rose sits with her second coffee in an old soft chair by the window in her room. It is mid-morning, the house is quiet, the cup warm between both hands. The oak in front of her house is old, its roots have invaded the little lawn and cracked the sidewalk. Its branches reach out over the street and back, at the house, right up to the window. The upper branches lay on the roof. Some leaves cling to the tree, more on the ground. Orange fading into yellow, some red, and brown, fluttering to the sidewalk to join the others in this lovely dance of death.

Beautiful in their youth of soft and lively green; beautiful in their dying, going out with brilliance and brittleness as they dance the breeze to break into bits and feed the earth with their life, with their death, quietly continuing their work under winter snow for the next generation.

Which is more beautiful, their youth or their maturity? Their youth is soft and green and filled with birdsong and blossoms, but it is their dying days that are brilliant. It is their dying colors that make Rose pause, a quiet, a peace, descends on her and invites, what?

Wisdom? Perhaps. It is their dying days when they are most beautiful, most true to themselves, Rose decides.

Her coffee is cold now. She continues to hold it, thinking about the past months. This time last year her father was in the nursing home, winding down his days. They invited Jimmy for Thanksgiving; he showed up late, drunk and belligerent, then he melted into maudlin as the day wore on.

Rose turns her attention to Dennis. Since their showdown last Spring he often seems on the verge of telling her something, then shakes his head. Turns away. She has not pressed him. There's been enough revelation, enough rawness. She decided months ago to respect his silence, respect his secret. There aren't many options to account for this change in him. She will not open that door.

He's taken the lead more than he used to, making appointments with Real Estate Agents, scoping out neighborhoods for a possible new house, eager to share the benefits of a new setting, a new home. A fresh start. His recent uptake in energy and decisiveness has seeped into her, a buoy to her sinking into darkness.

She is grateful.

Time to make the bed. She pulls up the sheets, taut. The quilt she gathers at the foot of the bed, a bunch in each hand, pulls up to a tent. As it rises and falls she sees little Priscilla and little Rose playing with dolls and teacups; just a visit. She smoothes the quilt, folds down the top and tucks the pillows into the fold, like her mother taught her so long ago.

Smoothing the quilt over the pillows, she is again smoothing a cardigan around her old mother's bony shoulders, slipping her frail arms in the sleeves, drawing out her hand. Her hand is cold. Where once it was smooth and firm, veins show through the skin, thin with tiny folds. She is always cold these days, always needs another sweater, another blanket.

In those last years her mother relaxed into dementia, almost like a relief, Rose thinks now. What a terrible thing, to lose ones' memories, people say. It's worse than cancer because you lose who you are, is the usual protest.

But what if you become more of who you are? If your authentic self can finally emerge from years of cowering behind rules and judgments and perfections that were impossible to attain, that became their own prison? What if the softening of the mind is a blessing? Yes, a blessing which takes over the space formerly filled with her need for perfection, for hard lines and cold looks? The dementia melted the barriers, the constructed barriers, against the anarchy she feared would rule her life if she let down her guard, lowered her standards, accepted weakness.

In her dementia, Rose felt, she was meeting her authentic mother, the mother she never was allowed to know, the mother with a heart big enough to hold her, Rose hoped.

Rose smoothes the pillow again and remembers, the months before her mother died, she was tucking a blanket across her lap. Marie stood in the doorway, Maureen calls out.

"Priscilla! Priscilla! Come away from the door. You'll catch a breeze on your back. Put your sweater on, you don't want another cold."

Marie looked at her grandmother, then her mother. Rose gave a lopsided questioning smiling to Marie and beckoned her over to her grandmother's chair; Marie hesitates.

"You're a nice woman." she pats Rose's hand, "What did you say your name was?"

Without waiting for an answer Maureen looks to Marie "What did I say, Priscilla? Step away from the doorway, you'll get a chill."

At ten years old Marie was taller and fuller than little Priscilla ever got to be. Marie knew she resembled her aunt who died as a child, with her curly dark hair and blue eyes.

"There was another little girl. What happened to her? She's a nice little girl, too. She plays with Priscilla. They play right over there on the stairs with their dolls. Where did she go? What is her name?"

"That was Rose, Mom, Rose." She looks right into her mothers face, holding it. Her eyes fill, water and confusion. "Rose? Where is my Rose? Where has she gone? I've lost her, my little Rose."

"She's right here, Mom. She's waiting for you to come home."

Made in the USA
Charleston, SC
29 November 2015